Metaphorosis
2024

Also from Metaphorosis

Metaphorosis Magazine
Metaphorosis: Best of 20xx
Metaphorosis 20xx: The Complete Stories
annual issues, from 2016

Monthly issues

Plant Based Press
Best Vegan Science Fiction & Fantasy
annual issues, 2016-2020

from B. Morris Allen:
Chambers of the Heart: speculative stories
Susurrus
Allenthology: Volume I
Tocsin: and other stories
Start with Stones: collected stories
Metaphorosis: a collection of stories

Verdage
Reading 5X5 x3: Changes
Reading 5X5 x2: Duets
Score – an SFF symphony
Reading 5X5: Readers' Edition
Reading 5X5: Writers' Edition

Vestige
The Nocturnals, by Mariah Montoya

Joyful Heave
Museum Piece: an unusual collection

Metaphorosis
2024

The Complete Stories

edited by
B. Morris Allen

ISBN: 978-1-64076-286-2 (e-book)
ISBN: 978-1-64076-287-9 (paperback)
ISBN: 978-1-64076-288-6 (hardcover)

from
Metaphorosis Publishing

Neskowin

Contents

From the Editor

... 97, 98, 99, 100!

Metaphorosis published continuously since 1 January 2016: with a new story every Friday, without fail. The end of 2023, our eighth year, brought us to issue #96. Sometime in 2022, it occurred to me to mark that milestone by doing something special for issues 97-100.

What better to do than to bring back my favorite writers and artists? These are the folks whose work I've been most impressed by, who've been the most fun to work with, and who I think represent what we've tried to achieve with Metaphorosis.

So, in 2024, we published just one story a month, but you're in for a treat, in these dozen stories. Sit back and enjoy!

B. Morris Allen
Editor

Winter

A word about Candra Hope

Candra Hope is a marvelous artist whose characters are lived in, maybe weary — they've seen something of the world, and it hasn't always been happy. But I've been very happy with her work for *Metaphorosis*.

We were first in contact in mid-2016, but it took me until 2017 to commission a *Metaphorosis* cover from her. From then, she (also a member of Meta4osis) produced covers for the April and August 2017, May 2018 (a phenomenal image of an octopus), June 2018 (gryphons!), and August 2019 covers. The latter (with gauzy elephant, bear, and spider) is one of my favorite *Metaphorisis* covers ever.

I'm very happy to have her back providing the cover art for this issue, illustrating Vanessa Fog's "The Cold Inside". I urge you to look up her work!

About Candra Hope

My name is Candra Hope and I've been doing some sort of art since I was old enough to hold a pencil. I've always loved fantasy, horror and science fiction stories so thats mostly what inspires me, along with movies and nature and history and, well, whatever catches my soul at any given time. I work traditionally or digitally but refuse to use ai image generators because its non copyrightable and uses non consensually scraped art for training.

www.candrahopeart.com

A word about L. Chan

We've been lucky enough to to have worked with L. Chan since *Metaphorosis*' very first year. His story "Whalesong" appeared in one of our earliest issues – 15 April 2016, to be precise. It's a seriously sad story about a forlorn and lonely whale and about pollution and responsibility and consequences. I still think about it frequently; it's one of my favorites of the stories we've published.

Happily, that wasn't the end of the relationship. In fact, L. Chan is one of the rare members of the Meta4osis club — authors we've published four or more times.

He next appeared in *Metaphorosis* with "Heartwood" on 05 May 2017, another beautiful story about change and wisdom. In 2018, his story, "The Fourth Pillar Says No" appeared in our anthology, *Reading 5X5*, an unusual and intriguing anthology in which several authors wrote stories from the same prompt, giving insight into how different authors approach the same material.

In 2020, *Metaphorosis* started experimenting with serialized stories, and L. Chan's was the very first we published, with the three part Sonata appearing in January, February, and March of the year, followed quickly by "Seven Scraps Unwritten" in April — an unrelated story, but set in the same universe.

I've enjoyed L. Chan's stories all the way through, and I'm very pleased to be able to present another one now, in these special 2024 issues. Here's the latest, "This is How We Stay Alive".

This is How We Stay Alive

L. Chan

It was the six hundred and thirtieth day after Jeff became a ghost, and things were not going well. Jeff had a routine, as did all the other ghosts. He made coffee, as he liked it, black and without sugar, but the liquid sloshed over the edge of the cup and spilled onto the floor below. Wisps of steam disappeared into the muggy morning air, and lazy sunlight glinted off the crystalline leaves of the plants the Preservation Society had left behind, throwing little rainbows onto the walls of the government flats they crept up.

The mornings were when Pris' absence bit the hardest. Pris had already given Jeff some of the best years of his life, and then after the Preservation Society came and stole one hundredth of the world's population, they'd still had each other. They'd woken up, disembodied and confused, amidst the crystalline alien blossoms that had sprouted in their bed, ghosts in every sense of the word. Finding themselves prisoners, first, of their condition, as they learned to engage the world anew without flesh. Second, of the strange alien garden that now flourished in their bedroom. It anchored them to world, tethering them to their home. They found their ghostly forms fading into incoherence the further they got from their garden. Leaving their home was near unbearable. They fumbled their way through their new existence, while the rest of the world came to terms with the ghosts and discovered how to live with them.

Jeff and Pris had learned. They had adapted, discovered that ghosts could still interact with electrical devices. They had reconnected with the world, finding others like them. Of course, this had been before the Government finally came in with their cleanup crews and their neat little pamphlets in four languages telling ghosts about their new rights (few), their responsibilities (many) and a short catechism on prolonging their newfound existence, helpfully titled 'This is how we stay alive'.

But now Pris was gone, her laptop silent where it had lain for years. Space was scarce in Singapore and there was no room for flats solely occupied by ghosts. Eventually, hastily passed laws allowed the government to seize the flats by eminent domain for reallocation. So Jeff was getting a new roommate.

This is how we stay alive: We acknowledge the Preservation Society has taken our bodies, and we will not get them back.

Hao Ming sat amidst the ruins of someone else's life. He knew what to expect from a haunted apartment, what the ghosts were capable of. Ghosts were nearly impossible to perceive. They had almost no power to manipulate the physical medium, but anything electronic was fair game. And they needed to be near one of those alien plants. In some jurisdictions, panic had set in the first morning after the alien Preservation Society did their work — the populace had set upon the plants with firearms and tools, blows and bullets shattering the plant's crystalline stems and glass leaves. As the gardens died, the tinkling of the fragments produced an uncanny resonance; an unnatural timbre that reminded people of screams. It was only later that the symbiosis between plant and ghost was elucidated and the lament set in.

A triptych of portraits went up on a display cabinet, a nascent mirror of the ancestral shrine. Hao Ming had not yet brought a pot to burn joss sticks for the dead, and the abduction of one percent of the world's population by the Preservation Society had robbed them even of the dignity of a physical farewell. There were no bodies to be burned or buried, only the strange creeping of the alien plants. That, and the ghosts.

The government had allocated this flat to him with scant information about the previous occupants. The garden in the bedroom was intact, so the ghosts had not been evicted by violence. Not every garden had ghosts, although evidence suggested that gardens all started with them. Some ghosts, for reasons still not fully understood, just faded. Not for the first time, Hao Ming wondered if that was what had happened to his family.

But Hao Ming was certain there was a ghost still in this flat; there was always a steaming cup of coffee under the coffee machine, the overflow spilling onto the counter and dripping onto the floor, dried coffee staining the tile in a creeping Rorschach pattern. Netflix would channel surf when he wasn't looking and the lights would go on and off to match a stranger's circadian rhythm.

Even after a week, Hao Ming had not spent much time in the bedroom, but now he wandered back in, where the flower patch sang as it slowly grew its crystalline leaves and petals. Years after the occupants had been taken, he could still make out the outlines on the bed where the plants had first taken root. The plants were the most obvious signs of the cataclysm that had befallen the world. The Preservation Society had executed the heist in a matter of hours, an alien force of such technological advancement that governments had still been puzzling over sensor data when the crisis struck, and the Society was gone again before the scale of the damage was known, leaving nothing but tears and a single message in their wake.

Everybody had heard the message at least once in the chaotic days and weeks after the event. A data packet of strangely dense encoding, the artistry of which still puzzled scientists. For a few hours, the message had been broadcast on repeat across all channels, from old analogue radio to air-gapped networks. On it, the Preservation Society said they would take, without permission, without forgiveness, a sample of every sentient species they came across, but would leave a gift to soften the parting. People remembered the message in fragments, like a half-lost dream. No one could say for certain what the aliens looked like or sounded like, any impressions were vague and contradictory. The only thing the recipients agreed on was the message. The substance of it defied scientists, stills only captured static, analysis of the audio only output white noise.

Whatever the Preservation Society was, their values were vastly different from those of humankind. There was no pattern in the selected abductions. Rich and poor alike were taken, with no discernible pattern. The bed in his new home reminded Hao Ming of returning to his silent apartment the night the Preservation Society struck, looking at beds bearing strange silicaceous growths whose beauty could not outweigh the panic rising in his throat.

The news had eventually said that the plants produced a sustained bioelectric field that allowed for the long-term existence of self-propagating signals of untold complexity. Commentators stripped the jargon from the science and added a little conspiratorial seasoning — the alien gardens were haunted by those that had been taken. It might have surprised the aliens to know that their gift of functional immortality was first greeted with fear, confusion, and in short order, violence. Then, the ghosts began to talk. Haltingly, at first, as they relearned how to interact with the world. Each ghost had their own journey back to the world of the living. Some never made it. Hao Ming's original home remained frustratingly silent, more like a tomb than a home. He had laid out funereal offerings to his family, hoping to lure them towards the material world. But doubt had set in, and more than once he thought to smash the plants sprouting from where his family had lain in slumber. Instead, he left, though the only opportunity for housing was another abandoned flat, another modern sepulchre.

Hao Ming stood now over someone else's bed, again tempted to violence. Instead, he shifted over to the bedside table and placed the wedding portrait face down before leaving the room.

This is how we stay alive: If we are not anchored, we will drift free.

Panic was a physiological response, a flood of neurochemicals provoking changes in body chemistry: the muscles tightened, the breathing quickened, the stomach contracted. A ghost did not have the benefit of these, only a disembodied feeling of doom as a stranger approached their garden with violence in his hands and murder in his eyes. This stranger turned away at the last minute, shifting Jeff's wedding photograph on the table. Even sighing in relief was a pleasure denied to ghosts, but Jeff felt tension ease all the same.

He followed the new tenant to the living room and paused with him at the small memorial to the other man's family. A plaque at the bottom of each portrait marked out a year familiar to Jeff. At least he had one thing in common with his new roommate.

It was not possible for Jeff to right his wedding picture, even if he felt his existence solidify the nearer he was to the garden. Once, he could have traced where he and Pris had lain on their last night from the outline of the leaves, in the curl of stems over the bedsheets. Now, the plants were rampant, with their strange hum, and that last physical reminder of Pris was gone. All he had was the memory of her and her quiet smile, saying that she had to go first and that he could follow when the time was right. There was little he could have done to stop her as she stepped out of their flat, away from the nourishing field of the growing garden and into dissolution.

They'd argued about it before, while watching the news about ghosts disappearing. They frequented forums populated by the recently disembodied, even held down some gig work doing speech to text transcription until those opportunities dried up. Three fates awaited the ghosts. The gardens could be, and had been, destroyed. They were hardy but not invulnerable. They did not burn well, but like all things made of glass, they shattered on impact. Not only did assailants report the plants screaming, but even faraway gardens keened and scintillated in distress when one of their own was murdered. There were no documented observations of what happened to ghosts during the violence, save that they did not survive it.

Second, the gift of the gardens was not permanent. Like all living things, they needed nourishment. Laborious observation distinguished the gardens that thrived and those that withered along with their ghosts. Governments, organisations, and religions all over the world had boiled the mysteries down into insipid catechisms like the one Jeff and Pris had gotten, because what fed the gardens was a ghost's attachment to the world. Stories abounded about ghosts who, despite proximity to their gardens, faded all the same, and their gardens withered not long after.

A third way out was whispered about in internet forums frequented by ghosts. A ghost could just leave their garden. Nearby gardens could still sustain them, but eventually the ghosts would find the edge of the gardens' succour, whether it be at their doorstep or miles from home. Beyond that lay dissolution. Speculation was rampant amongst the ghosts that escaping the gardens was not a death sentence. Pris had bought into these theories unequivocally, that the Preservation Society had left humanity the gardens, but the gift was only a stepping stone. Debates between Jeff and Pris grew heated, blossoming into shouting matches. Perhaps they would have fought, but ghosts could no more touch each other than they could the physical world. Words alone hadn't been enough to stop Pris, and his last memory of her was of her fading as she left the flat that imprisoned them, disappearing like motes of dust on the morning breeze.

With Pris gone, Jeff struggled to maintain his connection to the garden, throwing himself into the banal rituals of daily life to cling onto existence. Grief, too, had a physiological component and Jeff felt guilty that his own mourning lacked the tightening of his throat and the unbidden leakage of tears.

Now, he found himself staring at the sleeping form of the intrusive tenant. He could not be perceived by the other man, but there were ways of making his presence felt, at least on anything electronic his tenant used. Some ghosts became malicious digital tricksters, getting into social media accounts, banks and worse. They were impossible to evict and rendered their homes near uninhabitable.

Jeff could have done any of those things to the interloper, but he didn't want to go down that route. Instead he just left Pris' photograph on the man's computer, with the dates of her birth and death inscribed below, save that the latter was the date of her second death, the day she had walked out the door to the sound of the garden trilling in the background.

Some days, Hao Ming couldn't even tell that his new home was haunted. There were terms of the shared rental, fixtures he couldn't move, rooms he couldn't change. He respected the ritual of morning coffee, even emptying and washing the cups after the coffee had grown cold. Industrial bleach returned the kitchen tiles to their previous insipid off-white.

Hao Ming found the picture of one of the flat's previous occupants on his computer one morning. The date stuck out. The previous occupants were ghosts, but the date of passing was much more recent.

Pricked by his conscience, Hao Ming slunk into the bedroom with the gait of a dog returning to the scene of a stolen treat or mangled cushion. He set the picture by the bedside upright again. The plants seemed to tinkle in appreciation.

Hao Ming knew there were ways to reach out to the ghosts, but his family had never gained the facility to communicate through the electronic ether. To be fair, his mother couldn't even use WhatsApp when she was alive. His wife and son, on the other hand, had been digital natives. It made their silence all the more frustrating. Not so in his new flat; the ghosts here made their presence known with the constantly refreshing picture on his computer screen.

The fittings in the flat were slowly in the process of being overwritten, a palimpsest of two lives overlapping. The bedroom was untouched. Hao Ming replaced the living room couch with a pullout and kept the study as his office. The date of the woman's passing was odd, past the date of the Preservation Society's visit. He remembered the verdant garden on the queen bed. Somehow the wife had died later. Hao Ming's hands hovered over the keyboard and then he reached out to the ghost.

Your wife, how did she go? Did she fade?
No, she left.
Ghosts can't leave their gardens.
That's right. She believed the gardens were just a stepping stone.
What do you believe?
I'm still here, aren't I? What happened to your family?
I don't know. They never reached out to me. They could be there, they could be gone.
But you left.
Yes, I did.
Then we have something in common, Hao Ming.

The first leaf fell one stormy morning before Jeff had completed his daily ritual. The garden's leaves were arranged in fibonacci spirals, their translucence shot through with veins that networked into aperiodic motifs. When the leaf bounced off the bed sheet, it shattered into identically shaped shards.

Jeff could not touch the shattered leaf, but when his finger approached the pieces, a residual charge almost made him tingle. The other leaves sighed. He'd read about the signs of a garden withering before, he'd just never thought it'd happen to him. The nearby gardens seemed to know; they'd emit a low hum, undetectable to human ears, that discomforted pets and grated on ghosts like fingers on chalkboards, crying in anticipation of death.

Pris' research had grown increasingly esoteric before she left. She had said the gardens were only the first step in the gift the Preservation Society had left behind, that the instructions were in the message. It sparked another row between them, Pris insisting that the single most consumed piece of media in the world had layers that the best scientists and worst conspiracy theorists had not yet deciphered.

"Everybody in the world has heard the message," he'd said to her.

"Only the message they've chosen to hear," she answered.

How long was the message for you, Hao Ming?
Two minutes and fifty-four seconds.
Mine was three minutes and fifteen.
Did Pris ever ask you about the difference?
She would have said I was not ready.
What does it say? The rest of the message?
That the gardens weren't the true gift. That we have to take the first step.
No ghost has ever come back from leaving a garden.
Pris once told me that the largest living organism on Earth wasn't a whale, or a tree. It was a fungus, growing under a forest, a massive network of mycelial cells, big as a city.
Like the —
Each garden knows what's happening to the other gardens. All other gardens. Not just here. Everywhere.
Even the ones back in my home?
Even those. The garden is still there, isn't it? There's a chance that your family is there.
They were quiet for years, Jeff.
Maybe your home has the same thing Pris was looking for beyond the gardens, what the Preservation Society left in their message.
What's that?
Faith.

This is how we stay alive: We never leave our gardens.

Hao Ming had left in the morning, at Jeff's insistence. He had a family to get back to, if they were still there. Jeff's assurances didn't help. He couldn't have explained how he knew people he'd never seen before were still waiting next to their garden, or how their garden had told him this. The refractions in his bedroom were particularly vibrant that morning, as though his own garden already knew. Broken rainbows danced on the walls and followed him into the living room. Hao Ming had left the front door open. Jeff wanted to see, and the sunlight beyond the threshold looked very bright indeed.

There was no way of knowing what lay beyond the sanctuaries of the gardens. In the first half of the message, the world had come away with the knowledge of the Preservation

Society's gift — that the gardens gave life beyond flesh. But the second half, the part that only the few heard and even fewer acted on, that part was a reason. A reason, and a promise.

The Preservation Society did just that — they Preserved. The first precious few became ghosts, and even fewer of the ghosts could take a step beyond. Perhaps the message was more than a collection of data that bypassed comprehension. Pris had believed that the second part of the message was a test of faith. Jeff thought different, that perhaps the message itself was choosing those that were ready to hear it in its entirety. Those that were ready take that step. Jeff felt the familiar tug of his garden, anchoring him to the only existence he'd known for years. The nearer he got to the threshold, the more he felt himself stretching out, pulled taut like a sheet nailed down to his garden. It was an old fear, that the garden was the only thing keeping him alive. Not this time, only the promise of something more.

So he went forward and out and took the first step into the rest of his life.

See L. Chan's story "This is How We Stay Alive" online at Metaphorosis.
If you liked it, leave a comment. Authors love that!
Remember to subscribe to our e-mail updates so you'll know when new stories are posted.

About the story

There seem to be two types of post-apocalyptic stories — the more popular one being the ones where a majority of the population has been wiped out. Or turned into vampires. Or zombies. I do like the other one — where everything on the planet has fundamentally changed in the near future. I liked the idea of ghosts in a science fiction setting — disembodied spirits but with clear rules. The resolution of the story had very much to do with Dan Simmon's *Hyperion Cantos*, it's resolved in a very similar way! The story was originally written from a single point of view, but I went for the split point of view in the end, trying to show that the resolutions for each character were equally valid. At the end, the story is very much about connections and letting go — the characters have to do both through the course of the story.

A question for the author

Q: Where do you write?
A: I used to write everywhere I could lug my tablet, but since I downgraded it, it's all been writing at home on the PC.

About the author

L. Chan hails from Singapore. He spends most of his time wrangling a team of two dogs, Mr Luka and Mr Telly. His work has appeared in places like *Clarkesworld, Translunar Travellers Lounge, Podcastle, the Dark,* and he was a finalist for the 2020 Eugie Foster Memorial Award. He tweets inordinately @lchanwrites and can be found on the web at lchanwrites.wordpress.com

A word about Evan Marcroft

Evan Marcroft first came to our attention in 2018, and we published his story, "The Little G-d of Łódź" on 02 November of that year. It's a story of Nazis and war and golems and sacrifice that's dark but still uplifting.

He appeared again in *Metaphorosis* not long after, with "The Color of My Home is Red Like an Apple" on 29 March 2019, pondering just what it means to have faith, and how that intersects with choice. Things took a distinct turn toward funny with "Devilish Calliope and the Ungrooviest Apocalypse" on 14 August 2020.

Just before that, Evan had participated in of our most demanding anthologies to date, *Reading 5X5 x2: Duets*. While the first *5X5* anthology asked 25 authors to write from just five prompts, the *x2* anthology asked five authors to write with *each other* — four collaborative and one solo story, all in a short period. Evan's stories, "Lambs Fight to Die" (solo), "Boro Boro" (with J. Tynan Burke), "Snakeheart" (with Douglas Anstruther), "Titanotheosis" (with David Gallay), and "The Blood Dance of Ape and Mouse") with L'Erin Ogle, were among the most inventive, with wild and memorable worlds that I'd love to see more of — particularly the weird and wonderful world of "Lambs Fight to Die", with its furniture of zombie body parts, and the bizarre and majestic "Titanotheosis" with its constructed gods fighting for dominance.

Here's his latest for *Metaphorosis*, "The Bloodless Cut".

The Bloodless Cut

Evan Marcroft

I glance at the bracelet on my left wrist. *Nineteen minutes and fifty-eight seconds,* it reports. *Fifty-seven now. Fifty-six.* Meanwhile the door is dilating shut behind me until it disappears entirely, rendering the seven-by-seven-meter cell as airtight as something meant to hold monsters must be.

The room is almost entirely featureless, the bed just a pillow-less slab of the same impervious substance as the floor. No faucets or drains either; I wonder idly where water comes from, where waste goes. Light emanates directly through the walls and with no shadow in which to hide, the room's ghost haunts in plain sight. She sits upon a backless stool in the geometrical center of the room facing a vertical blue stripe on the wall that creates the illusion of a window-slit. The pale arc of her back resembles that of a flesh-tearing fang with a ratty black tuft skewered on the tip. Her gossamer shift conceals nothing, not her rippling alabaster ribs nor their dermatitic rosettes.

Fifty-three, fifty-two...

This dwindling time is the last we'll ever spend together.

"Doctor Nichirei."

Her voice is a dungeon hinge shedding four months of rust.

"It's good to see you. I'm so happy my teacher came to visit."

Teacher. I want suddenly to bite my fingers, but I've had years to master the urge.

"I wish I could say the same," I reply. "On both accounts."

"Is it done then? Has the Peacock finally scratched the Fox's eyes out?"

"It was inevitable, once the Fox lost its teeth." I adjust my spectacles. "The word is unconditional surrender, as of two weeks ago. The rebel princes are all in custody or dead. This madness is done."

"And yet an Emperor still sits the Sapphire'd Chair," the prisoner muses. "But then, I long suspected that would be so. You were always so stubborn, Doctor."

The shadow of an accusation chills me.

"Just before you arrived, a guard gave me this to drink." Her hand swings out, holding a paper cup too small to choke on. "Was it poison? It tasted sweet."

The empty phial in my pocket smolders against my thigh.

"No. But you are to be executed today." A choice made above even my lofty reach. Were it my call, this woman would fall into a gap in history from which she could never climb out.

Water on white canvas. The news soaks spotlessly into her. "That's good. I can almost hear them now — the public that is, out there baying for my death. Seeing it is the most important thing. The spectacle *always* is. The spectacle is all."

How did she know? I tell myself that anyone could have guessed a crowd of thousands surrounded the Citadel of Scales, all jostling to witness the moment the guillotine falls, but nothing is certain with this woman. Even these walls can't guarantee they'll hold her even when all logic says they should.

I turn over my palm. A silver tablet, pillowed in callused pink corduroy. A gentle toss. Halfway to the prisoner it unfurls propeller arms that lift it into a stable orbit. Her ear twitches towards its fey hum.

"What's this? An autoquill?"

"His Perpetual Will has commanded your final words be documented for historical and scientific purposes."

I can't help but flinch as she swivels to face me with a motion so smooth and unsignaled it is almost mechanical. Four months of solitary confinement are etched invisibly into this woman. Her bun is solidly black where my curls run with autumn colors. She seems too young for this aftermath-era, also unlike me, my lines deep as grief.

"That's not the Emperor I know," frowns Vasani Stirio. "What combination of words is he hoping to hear, pray tell?"

"Everything," I say simply.

Our wars lousy with criminals who would rather not be infamous.

Some of the best worked for me.

You'll find them hardly the cackling villains that popular conception make of men like them. They're the ones in the backgrounds of the declassified photographs, the little ones with the shiny spectacles and soft, nervous faces. *I was only following orders*, they invariably plead until the guillotine cuts them off. History remembers them with a kind of smirking scorn, as if their real sin was a dearth of pride. That is not Vasani Stirio now and it wasn't her then.

No student of mine ever made excuses.

She arrived at the Quintelzean Empire Military Defense Institute a serious, almost solemn scientist, deferential to her superiors, a reliable volunteer for undesirable chores — the same as all the bland brains I employed. My subordinates all came from the top academies and I assumed her story was formulaic. I scarcely noticed her then. Just another set of hands to help screw together my grand designs.

For years that was the way of things. It wasn't until our hands met within the innards of the same town-flattening rocket that I noticed how quickly Vasani had climbed to where I was. As we scrubbed our greasy hands at the same sink, I saw that her fingertips were chewed to rubbery coarseness. And the following month, when word reached us that our rocket had transmuted an entire enemy battalion into radioactive bauxite sculptures, she spoke only to suggest how the effect-radius could be expanded, tugging at her gloved fingers all the while.

It was then I knew I needn't ask her story.

Your reflection remembers where you've been.

"Care to sit? There's plenty of floor."

"I don't have long," I say. *And it's easier to run from a standing position.* I'm only realizing now that I really am in here with Vasani, sharing her air, her proximity. There is a circle of red paint in a three-foot radius around her stool. While she remains within the circle my safety is guaranteed outside of it, but that assumes anything is guaranteed near Vasani Stirio.

"Suit yourself," she shrugs. "How *have* you been, Mirchelle? Is your littlest well? I understand young Vasri endured an aerocopter accident some months ago."

My breath catches at the sound of my son's name between her teeth. How does she know about that? How, after everything I did to keep my son invisible throughout the war. My hand tightens involuntary around the phial in my pocket, almost crushing it. I force myself to let go. What's done is done, what's known is known, and I have eighteen minutes left to work with.

"I'm not here to reminisce."

"If you won't answer my questions, why should I answer yours?"

"I've been authorized to administer force."

She once described my stare as surgical. *You take people apart with a scalpel and forceps.* Now I wish I could swat away her gaze as it probes with implements beyond my imagining. "That's not you," she says disapprovingly. "Don't tell me you're still the Emperor's little do-anything device after everything that's transpired? Did that war we fought teach you nothing?"

The autoquill whirs needily in every small silence. What I say next I say as quietly as truth must sometimes be.

"His Perpetuity the Emperor is a lion and a sun. I speak only with his voice."

It's where I place the stresses that makes Vasani's eyes sparkle with convincing mirth. I have also watched soldiers cackle as they die. I have difficulty interpreting expressions, but I have rarely missed the knack. Why would I? The face speaks a language that means nothing.

"Your master will get what he wants, but it will be of no use to him."

"Why?" I demand, suddenly suspicious.

That smile. That awful, scalpel-cut smile. I've given her the tool to slice me open and do with me as she pleases. I catch my fingers creeping towards my lips and force them into a fist. I don't like that she knows this, but if I am to ever understand what killed Vasani Stirio and came to live inside her skin, I must endure her, as all her victims did before me.

"Because what I do is no method that can be taught," she purrs. "Rather, it is a height of craft reachable only through a supremacy of will far beyond your Emperor. But you, Doctor Nichirei... I suppose you may understand."

A finger stands up on her hand, translucent around the edges where the light perforates its meatless skin and blurs the shadow of her bone. My foreboding doubles and redoubles again when two more join it. "The perfect torture requires the mastery of three impossible cuts," she says.

"Let us discuss the first."

The Unhealing Cut

Vasani Stirio vanished a week after the Schism that split the Empire in two. A month before the war began in-earnest. *Abducted by the enemy,* was what I first suspected.

I would only learn the truth once the Screaming Ships came home.

The first few clashes were a series of successes for the Emperor's Peacocks. We smashed the Foxes at Thoracic Ridge, at the Glass Plains, drove that cabal of rebel princes across the River Quyle, all within the first few weeks. The Foxes fought cleverly, but my brain was itself a military asset. The state-phasing ghostrounds I provided made a joke of enemy body armor, while my magma-mortars flooded emplacements with fire. The campaign proved taxing even so, but if we could just push through and end the war fast, we could spare those soldiers yet outside our firing range. Then came the so-called Just Offensive, our chance to liberate the rebel-held Chelenon and unseat the Foxes from the region. The town, however, sat beneath a fearsome gunfort, and it threatened a grueling siege.

A siege that never came to be.

The night before our assault began, soldiers began complaining of ants infesting their bedrolls. They went to their medics reporting insect bites and were given standard-issue salves, which did not work. Within the hour, itching progressed to burning. Within two hours, that burning worsened to a pain so unbearable that men begged for fewer limbs. Dawn broke over a siege-camp in chaos. Six in ten had been stung, and no combination of painkillers, styptics, or sedatives could ease their agony.

The true horror, however, lay dormant for weeks, waiting for those soldiers to be packaged home aboard what came to be called the Screaming Ships, where our best military scientists could only scratch their heads. I examined the victims myself, ears muffled against a wailing that only a hacksaw could quiet, and reached the same conclusion which the following years would prove true. The pain was permanent.

Those bitten would howl forever.

The Emperor's war-ministers were in a fury, partly of fear, partly envy. *How,* they demanded. *How was it done? How could we do the same?* Specimens recovered from Chelenon offered few answers. Magnifying only a few degrees beyond their chitin revealed a labyrinth of manipulated genetics impenetrable even to me. But that mystery was, itself, an answer.

Biofabrication was never *my* specialty.

Some passengers of the Screaming Ships still live. In hospitals they reside now, kept in medical comas from which they are woken for mere minutes of the year to plead for sleep or death — confirmation that what they suffered not be forgotten or escaped. A man stung on the finger could lose a finger. A man stung on the leg could lose the leg. A man stung on the breast? That man was damned alive. Our armies never returned to Chelenon; the ground there was cursed, and the only shots fired there were suicides. While I toiled in my laboratory devising weapons that could terminate life ever more efficiently, Vasani Stirio had already determined not to fight a war at all.

"Would you prefer I had bombed them, Doctor Nichirei?"

Her expression betrays only infinite patience. She will die waiting for the answer she covets.

Sixteen minutes forty.

"Yes," I admit under time's duress. "I would have preferred that you bombed them."

"Would you have done it?"

Monster that she is, of course she craves more. "I've never once made a tactical decision," I begin, "but... you know I try and speak with soldiers returning from the front. I listen to their stories, what they tap out on my hand with the fingers they have left. A life you cannot live is worse than hell, Vasani. You replaced everything those soldiers might have felt with fire. I don't see why you couldn't make it quick."

The corner of her mouth twitches up and her eyelids droop. *I'm sorry, that must have been difficult,* is what I'd normally trust that face to say. "That would have been a waste," Vasani says, almost tenderly. "A body can be written off in a ledger. Numbers never persuaded anyone. Is that not why you meet with soldiers? Because their words say more than the official report ever could? You can chew if you like, by the way."

It's a very her thing to say. Both mocking, caring, neither, and both. I dig nails into my palms in a substitute stimulus. "Life is the best teacher."

"And life taught you to fear pain before death, but remember: pain is the *younger* monster of the two, born only when death for the first time ever *failed.* You taught me so much but you never appreciated suffering for the resource it is. Tanks and artillery are only vehicles for the delivery of pain, and less — the threat of it, the execution of it, proving our stockpiles are full... that is how castles fall and monuments rise. Before there were words, there were rocks and sharp sticks. Knuckles across the eyes. *Do what I say or else.* Speech is a useful abstraction, but torture is and always will be humanity's first language. Do you disagree?"

Sixteen minutes, thirty-eight seconds.

"War too is an abstraction," she continued. "It is the democratization of torture, but the objective remains the same. We're always looking for ways to extract consequence without dirtying our things, even understanding that the cost will always be brutality. I simply did away with these unnecessary abstractions and returned to our species' roots."

There's a sickness percolating through my guts. I am nineteen again, watching my professor spread a fetal piglet's numbles to show how they work. *Here is the liver. Here is the spleen. Here is the heart. Remember to take careful notes.* "You can't honestly believe what you did was preferable to death."

"Only when death manifests as warfare. The weapons you and I designed reaped soldiers by the thousands yet took only a moment's hurt from each. How was our foe to fear that? A flash of agony, then peace? Do you take a sip of wine and toss the bottle? That young dumb men still strapped on boots and rush against your inventions should tell you something Doctor Nichirei. War is wasteful." She shakes her head. "Were one to transmute the body's total potential suffering instantly into energy it would wipe the Emperor's palace off the map."

I hope she's speaking colorfully, not theoretically. I've seen too much of Vasani's technology not to be wary. "You and I both sought to extract the greatest consequence from the smallest bloodshed," she says, "but only I dared approach it. Only I dared touch the sublime."

My fingertips are itching furiously.

"What you fear more than pain and death alike is perpetuity. A body can endure unimaginable suffering but the mind dreads forever so badly that it chooses instead to age. Only once you accept the infinite suffering within can you take the first step towards where I stand now."

Sixteen minutes, eleven seconds.

"The First Cut is the Unhealing Cut. The wound that does not close. Pain is the power source you turn to when all others are exhausted, and when released it must be explosion of consequence enough to lay armies flat on the ground. This you saw for yourself at Chelenon.”

“And in the survivors who begged for death in my arms,” I counter. “A simple smartfiber nanomesh added to our soldier’s fatigues gave our soldiers no reason to dread a bug-bite ever again. I finished the design in a night. The next month we pushed into Fox territory from further north and seized the Kruholidon Mountain Manufactory Complex. This ‘cut’ of yours came to nothing.”

Vasani’s lips purse. “Maybe so. But remember, Doctor: I had only just begun my journey.”

In two motions, hip and spine, she ratchets upright, and I take an unthinking step back towards the door. *Fifteen minutes*, my bracelet assures me. *Fourteen now, and fifty-nine seconds.*

Vasani smiles. “Be at ease. You’re perfectly safe. But that reaction, yes, that is... illustrative. For fear must come before the cut, doctor. The flesh must know it is to split. That must be its dreaded destiny, and for that your cut must violate all boundaries. Physical, spatial, temporal. You must make an idiot stroke capable of slitting the impossible.”

The Untethered Cut

I would only learn exactly how the Foxes swayed Vasani to their side in the war’s aftermath, from documents recovered at one of her secret laboratories. The covert politics aren’t terribly relevant. Knowing my student, I spared little thought for the resources those rebel princes offered. I only ever stared at the white blanks between the lines. What she never asked for in words, but received nonetheless. Always were Vasani’s reasons her own, and never put to paper.

It wasn’t long after Chelenon that the Emperor ordered a new offensive, this time into the Valley of Ten Lakes. If successful, it would have brought our forces practically to the Fox’s stoop, but that basin between the mountains was a fungal forest riddled with swamps, sinkholes, and blinding miasmas. Worse, the Foxes had seeded the area with guerillas who knew secret trails and spider-holes from which they could nip bites off our lumbering platoons.

With the memory of the Screaming Ships still fresh, I designed respirators that adapted to the marshland’s infinite poisons, built exoskeletons that could weather envenomed bolts and parasitic larvae. Thus equipped, the Imperial 31st Scouting Brigade began to make headway again. By the third night of the third month, our forces had very nearly cleared the valley.

My mistake was thinking Vasani would repeat herself.

History is smashed in that godforsaken valley. There is no complete record left of what exactly happened to the twenty-seven soldiers of the 31st who vanished into that malarial hell. Progress halted as the fragmented unit dredged the bogs, finding nothing. Either the swamps had swallowed them, or something that digested bone and body armor.

Then, six days and sweltering nights later, the Imperial 31st leapt awake at a screaming amongst the trees. Not animal; too familiar. There came a frantic splashing, and hard, scarred soldiers fumbled for their guns. They waited tensely for the wailing shadows to tell them what was wrong. Then at last, a figure burst out of the reeds and into the firelight. A shambling corpse it seemed, green with algae and embarrassed with bug-bites, until suddenly it raised its hands and called for help.

They called it a miracle that all twenty-seven escaped. None could quite recall how exactly; even their time in captivity was a nauseating blur. What mattered was that they were alive, unharmed, and homesick. All twenty-seven were sent once to the capitol to receive a hero's welcome. I intercepted them before they got that far. For weeks I subjected them to every test possible, yet for the life of me found nothing amiss. The men remained in good spirits, eager to hold their children again.

It wasn't until they were safe amongst their families that Vasani's trap sprung.

There had to be some sort of hormonal trigger buried insidiously deep in their genes, primed to spring when the poor men were at their happiest. It caught some of them at dinner, some in congress, others as they dandled their daughters on their knee and promised they'd never leave home again.

It would have begun with an invasive squirming beneath the skin. I know now that was their circulatory system uprooting and moving into a new position. That squirming would have become a burning as every connective subdermal fiber in them began to creep like a million millipede feet. How they must have fought their twisting, knotting flesh, trying to push their drifting eyes back into place, to keep their ears from crawling into new positions, all uselessly. They could only watch as their skin blanched with a grave-shroud complexion, and as their eyes, noses, and mouths gravitated together into new configurations too petite for their skulls. If they kept their wits they thought of knives — that or hot irons to cauterize the creep of features — but nothing could stop it, much less reverse it, and when it was done, the children they'd longed to hold looked up into twenty-seven gibbering facsimiles of Vasani Stirio.

By morning, the Empire knew monsters were real.

What can some nanomesh do against that? What can any armor do? What can trenches and bunkers and miles of distance and sloshing seas do? What can they do against a knife that can descend anywhere, upon anyone?

Thirteen minutes, thirty seconds.

"You're chewing, doctor."

She's right. I spit my fingers out, jam them in my pockets. "And you're mad."

Vasani tilts her head, a quizzical look left incomplete— now that I think of it, I can't remember when she last blinked. "That's a funny thing to say. Had your forces cleared the valley it would have meant a bloody battle. Your soldiers ran home instead of into our bayonets. Most of them, at any rate."

"They ran into mental wards," I hiss through gritted teeth. "They ran from something they couldn't escape, that *you* set upon them."

"They ran off with their futures ahead of them, Doctor Nichirei. That's more than His Perpetuity offered when he ordered them into the meat-grinder."

My every fibril tenses when Vasani begins to pace. Her bare feet suck softly at the concrete, as close to the red circle as they can without touching it. Does she know she's frittering away my time, her time, our time? A wormier thought: is this a ploy? "You still had to capture all those soldiers you warped. You had to lay your hands upon them to ruin them." *Hands that once met in the guts of a rocket.* "How can you say you achieved this second Impossible Cut?"

"Turn it around, doctor. They were not my subjects; they were my *instruments*, and through them I reached the Empire's heart. That was where I made my incision." Her finger is upon her breast, an untrimmed nail digging into her flesh, making it blush. "The Untethered Cut is the cut that appears anywhere. On any flesh, on any continent, past any defense. Sons, daughters, fathers, sisters, lovers, enemies — when you can perform this cut you will have transcended the boundary of distance, and the world will never feel safe again."

"Is that what you call an efficient use of pain? What did you even achieve besides misery?"

She stops her pacing suddenly and so does my pulse. All the peaks in my biorhythm flatten into a silent line. The core of human fear is the unknown. That is what Vasani is now, quite deliberately I think. Some crimes decouple ability from the limitations of flesh. That is why I flush cold when she doesn't blink. Why I start at every small motion she makes.

There is no knowing what that motion might make of *me*.

"You know you're perfectly safe, Doctor Nichirei," she grins, her point eloquently made.

"No-one will be until your head rolls," I throw back, suppressing a shudder.

"You're right. I showed them their Emperor was neither a lion nor a sun. That he could not protect them nor save them from what lurks in the dark."

"But it wasn't enough," I'm quick to remind her. Not for the Emperor's honor — I retch at the notion — but for spite. "In spite of everything you did, the war continued."

Ten Minutes.

One second.

The Unique Cut

When I think back upon the Schisms I imagine a no-man's land overcast by two shadows, but that's the bias of first-person memory. All I did was pack men into tanks. The real war was between Vasani Stirio and His Perpetuity, the Emperor of All Quintelzéa.

That man did not feel what his body felt; that much I can't argue. Princes of the imperial family are born into a complex of nested seraglios known as the Tesseract Halls, at the center of which a developing child cannot possibly catch a whiff of the real world. Hence, his war-verve remained a straight line while public enthusiasm dropped at a sharp angle. It didn't seem to matter what new thing to fear she discovered — waves of dissent met riot shields and broke. Magtrams kept freighting fresh recruits towards the front and returning only empty seats. All of this meant that a war we should have lost continued, and Vasani's tactics continued to evolve.

Nevertheless, the two fed into one another. The Emperor's only response to the newest atrocity was rageful escalation, in turn prompting some of Vasani's worst, most ingenious inventions. In response to his encircling of Grivbaénk, she unveiled the Finger Eater and sent his men into a rout. At the Hydrokloric Falls, she presented a piece dubbed the Living Skeleton. Two in ten live witnesses took their own lives. Amidst the siege at Steampike Castle, Vasani somehow spirited away a senior officer and reinterpreted him as something papers called the Tear-Stained Puzzlebox, which remains tragically unsolved to this day. There were others examples I could recall — Vasani always was a restless tinkerer — but some memories go into you like shrapnel, and it's safer to leave them be.

Steampike Castle still fell, but the poor officer's fate was a tipping point back at the capital.

Vasani Stirio seemed impossible to capture. The woman was a ghost haunting abandoned labs full of half-baked horrors. She'd transformed herself into a magical evil that could snatch up anyone, anywhere, and do anything to them. When citizens no longer felt safe in their homes, they took to the streets. Soldiers stopped enlisting and began deserting in greater numbers. Curfews and public executions scaffolded everyday life in the same brutal military logic that held the war together.

Faced with domestic mayhem, the Sapphire'd Throne elected to ignore it. For all of the above, the Foxes were losing. Vasani's creations strangled public morale, but they couldn't make up for quantumflame rockets or my inversion mines, nor topple the implacably stomping trenchwalkers I devised to trample enemy emplacements. I built the Emperor all the excuse needed to continue as he always had, but only I seemed to notice that Vasani's methods were growing more meticulous, less bloody, though my warnings went unheard. All I could do with all my power was tighten the screws on the war-machine. Days and nights spun into a crepuscular blur as I worked myself to insomniac extremes devising new technologies, more powerful weapons.

I must have believed that by fine-tuning my craft I could eliminate all but that one miraculous invention that, with just the touch of a button, would instantly neutralize Vasani Stirio. Surely it was somewhere in my imagination.

That was my naivete: not realizing Vasani believed something similar.

"Originality," I say. "That's your third ideal."

I'm against the wall now. I have to sit and hold my knees. It's that or bite myself. "People always adapt to suffering. Souls scab over if not freed. Negative feedback loops. You know what I mean. Nerve boredom." I'm rambling as I do when overstimulated. It's better than chewing. "Keep calm carry on. Keep calm carry on. That's what we're coded to do. And to get around that, you issued yourself a challenge: never to make the same cut twice."

It's hard to look at her now. I don't know what I'm seeing. The mind I glimpse is vast and tentacular. Instead I look down.

Seven minutes, nineteen seconds.

"We live with the wounds that don't kill us," she says approvingly. "Even when they bleed and bleed and bleed. And wherever it might be made, one little scratch is just that. A scratch. And so I set off towards a third Impossible Cut. If the Untethered Cut is liberated from space, the Unique Cut transcends the past. It is the cut that never repeats and therefore cannot be anticipated."

She reaches so easily into my complexities. It's true. I was only ever reacting to Vasani. I built weapons to sink thundercruisers and turn hostiles to glass, but in retrospect I was repeating the same old stratagem. The only one I knew. "And meanwhile I was complacent."

"Yes. But luckily for you, I failed."

"What?"

Vasani spreads her hands. "No matter what I did, I couldn't reach the Emperor. I fell just short of infinite. And meanwhile that mind of yours trampled on like a town-leveling juggernaut. Now look at us. You are still my teacher, Doctor Nichirei. In the end, I could never best you."

With an oh well sort of shrug she turns her back. "Tell his Porcine Perpetuity whatever you please. It won't do him any good. In the end, it didn't help me either."

I wait, but her silence goes on and on. Is that it?

I glance at my bracelet.

No, we aren't done.

Five minutes.

"The war may not have stopped," I say, rising shakily to my feet. "But... neither did you. And you would never fight a battle you couldn't win. There must be something more at work. This third cut... It isn't really one cut, is it? It's every cut you make, an endless creative challenge, no — a very finite narrowing of both technique and possibility to the eventuality that no cut can be made at all. You could have re-used your ever-stinging ants or given everyone in the capital your face, but you didn't. Even when it would have saved your life. Instead you chose always to innovate no matter what, to push the boundaries of your craft past the borders of known science..."

The autoquill whirs closer as if hanging on my every word.

"And yet," I continue. "A certain theme runs through your methods. It was present from the beginning; I just didn't see it until now. For a handful of bug-bites you turned the tide of a siege. You lent your face to the nightmares of millions without a single death. But your victims were never actually your victims — you let that much slip yourself. It was all about making wives weep and children wake up screaming at the memories of their fathers, yes, but also about learning, no — elimination. The Unique Cut isn't a peak, it's a method hidden in a method, a hidden path to — to —"

Silence again, but for the subaudible dribbling of time out of the world.

"—There is a fourth Impossible Cut, isn't there?"

My question throbs out into her cell's white void. Bare feet shuffle on cold stone. Vasani's smile makes me remember when our bitten fingers first touched within the innards of a rocket. Hers are eyes that say, *I am feeling what you feel, remembering what you remember.*

What you see in me is what I see in you.

"After all this time," she murmurs. "You are still my teacher."

The last time we met was not the last time we spoke.

"Why do we aim shells at armies?"

My kitchen. The yellow table. The purpling evening through the window. The lime-green tiles above the countertop flecked red from my cutting board. *Klat.* My cleaver whacks the head off a plucked fieldfowl, and blood helpfully leaves the body. A pot simmers on the island stove behind me, salivating for meat. *She* sits over the counter beyond it, smeared by steam.

"Why not aim them at kings? Wouldn't that save everyone a lot of trouble?"

To this day I am not sure why she asked. From where I stand on the autistic spectrum, it is hard for me to read the currents that move individuals along. The face is beautiful beyond scrutiny. I understand people better in aggregate. When a population smiles, it is easier for me to understand why, but Vasani was always, in every regard, alone.

"Kings," I told her, "are hard to reach."

Klat klat klat. The bird spills open in fatty pages.

When I was seven, I tell her, my family was displaced from a kingdom that no longer exists. The old king died and his nephew came next to sit the throne, though ill he fit it, a sneering boy-tyrant who believed a boy's war would make him a man. *A king is his country's dignity.* When they drag him before a greater king and defile him with bayonets, what does that make us?

I reach for vegetables next, ripe and sweating.

Three years I spent barefoot on a mass resettlement march to a barren corner of the Empire. The harsh road took my younger brother first. A soldier's warning-shot killed my mother's leg, and when father's heart gave up on carrying her, she gave up herself and let the endless procession swallow her. Two sisters went on until the soldiers took the elder, never to be seen again. Only two blackened feet and a hard-won certainty reached my new home: that if on the first day of war we had been annihilated completely, we would have at least all gone together. For a time I dreamed of a magical bomb.

"A magical bomb," she murmurs thoughtfully. "One that kills only kings, hm?"

Done. I take my cutting board to the salivating pot. *Hiss.* The broth foams with relish.

The fact is this: the nation is a body. The king is the brain and the hands are his legions. Another fact: when threatened, the brain reflexively puts its hands in harm's way. You've seen it, that instinct manifest. For the sake of survival the brain will sacrifice everything but itself. The head is always the last to die.

"Tut. That's a broken metaphor. The 'hands' are their own beings. Should they not be spared?"

When possible, yes, but it rarely is so. I remind her that the enemy is a body too. They deserve everything that we do, but if we must fight them anyway for whatever stupid reason then let us make it as bloodless as possible. Bloodless, and brief for all involved."

"The mercy of overwhelming firepower," my student notes dryly.

The mercy of euthanasia, is what I say.

"Oh? When you called the enemy a body I didn't know you meant the four-legged sort."

Four-legged, four-legged. That is little Vasri sing-songing from the floor behind her as he stacks his blocks in coded columns. He loves to build things, my youngest son. I hope he turns out nothing like me. "The brain puts the hands before it," murmurs Vasani. "But... isn't hurt felt in the brain?"

As she said, it is a broken metaphor. In the coming years, I'll wish that I'd been more careful with it.

Broken, mama! Vasri's delighted cry heralds a *smack*, and a clatter of building blocks across the floor. I laugh and even Vasani almost chuckles as he gathers them up to begin again, and meanwhile the pot fills my kitchen with savory steam. The dish I am cooking is almost done, and it's time I laid the plates out side by side. Mine and hers, hers and mine.

There are memories that go on a shelf beside the heart.

"The Unhealing Cut extracts the fullness of pain but leaves an unsightly mark. The Untethered cut is free to strike anywhere, but still requires the analogue passage of edge through flesh. The Unique Cut hurts like the first you ever felt, every time, but some cannot be cut by knives alone. Some are too thick in hide *and* head. But there is a cut that does not parse flesh. A cut that leaves no wound at all."

The torturer's hands flower open, two lopsided albino stars. She takes one step, two, arms extending, starved tendons protracting. Her palms flatten perpendicular to the circle of red paint and mime a more solid wall into being, her fingertips all but indenting from pressure. My gaze lingers there.

Her hands. The few fingernails she has left are rusted chisels, but the pads beneath them are as immaculate as if she never once chewed them.

"Only when you have exhausted all other cuts will you find it," Vasani continues with a mounting grandiosity. "We must search for it amongst the vitals. Within the soul. Do you remember the Tear-stained Puzzlebox? Remember how two armies stopped to stare? That unlucky man was my instrument, and all who witnessed him my subjects. By the time the war entered its final stages I was pushing you back for a pittance of blood, while back home I was strangling your will to fight. Whatever form of torture we prefer, the goal is always to achieve maximal consequence through minimal violence. The acme of torture is simply success. It is a singularity of achievement where technique sublimates into will. When you can make a subject scream without a touch, you can do anything. Even stop a war – though in that I fell a *little* short."

Her cackle fills the room inescapably. "You told me it couldn't be done! But I did it. His hands whole, his belly-rolls unblemished, his very body *unbloodied!* Hah!" Suddenly she is shouting. "His Perpetuity will never understand! He is the sniveling, selfish monster-mind that throws its hands up before a knife, and I... I... I am the knife that loves the flesh and only cuts evil where it hurts. Where, doctor, where?"

"The brain," I finish hollowly.

"Nowhere," she corrects, and in a dizzying rush it all connects and I glimpse the sinews of logic conjoining the brilliant young woman I knew to this creature before me. I don't want it I don't want it I don't want it but her logic is so vivid in its twisted, mutilated symmetry and I am so attuned to patterns in the fabric of things visible and not that I cannot help but think as she thinks for a gut-wringing second, and I perceive the world emergent from its rampant fractalization.

"Name it, doctor. I know you can. *Name it!*"

"Name it!"

She almost seems to speak through me.

"The Bloodless Cut."

I have never known Vasani Stirio to laugh, but now she does. As with everything about her, it is a performance. Her eyelashes flutter and her cheeks pull back from her teeth like washed-out curtains revealing a display of mummified heads. Her mouth is a hole where a victim decomposed, the knife still in their back, and from it sounds a titter tinged with the sweet perfume of rot-riddled gums. All I can do is cower against the wall in absolute, electrifying dread. I was wrong to believe her immune to prison; it got into her like a cavity, rotting her from the inside. It is just too easy to forget that she is human when I shouldn't, for human is the most terrible thing that a monster can be.

Three minutes.

In the end, Vasani Stirio was not some intangible spirit of pain. There was a body there, however foxily it ran and hid. My understanding is that someone on the other side eventually grew disgusted with her and gave up her location. War can be ordinary like that.

I arrived by aerocopter at her secret compound high up in the frozen crags of Coldfire Mountain just a week after she was captured. The wind tried to rip my hair away as it fled, the sun just a neon rim along that shadow peak, almost gone. I reported to the camp commander, ate a tasteless ration in my habitat, and forged directly into Vasani's lab. While I'd advocated leveling the mountain with a bomb, the Emperor wanted it scrubbed of its every last secret, and in the end, I couldn't resist the lure either.

I was bundled against the lab's sterile chill and breathing out vaporous ghosts. A security detail went ahead of me into those dimly lit tunnels, clearing out booby-traps left for the unwary. I'd expected displays of inventive lethality, not simple explosives disarmed without casualties. They seemed almost... perfunctory. It was as if she knew she'd be found and couldn't resist giving her enemies a last tweak on the nose.

I won't relate what I found there. I can't. All I can say is this. If you twist and construe and deconstruct a living body long enough it will die, but at the point of balance between those two polarities it becomes something close to art. The soldiers found me retching in the snow outside. I might have stayed there forever had one not said, *ma'am, you should have a look at this*. They'd found a sealed room in the back of the complex, one that mysteriously unlocked at their approach.

I'll go, I said.

And... the rest?

Burn them.

I could smell it hovering around that steel door in the depths of the lab, a sweet-sour muddling of dung and disinfectant. It misted in the air as the identity beam scanned me and then turned green as it had for the guards. It was instantly plain to me that Vasani would have seen the Foxes losing, would have known she'd be captured, and would have formulated accordingly, and I knew that the wise thing to do was report that I'd found nothing. My chest was colder than the mountain air. Sometimes you can hear the future screaming the answer at you.

I'm not sure why I chose to ignore it; I couldn't have known what I'd find inside. It was like a moment I'd already lived repeating itself in the nightmare of a Mirchelle Nichirei who'd already made this mistake. My thumb brushed the door and it opened like a giftbox.

A living stink gusted from the dark within.

Vasani always knew more than she should. We both knew the Emperor wouldn't relent no matter the cost, but inexplicably she knew one other thing that I did not.

More than big meals and bloodshed, she knew the Emperor loved his wife.

Two minutes, three seconds.

"You didn't achieve a fucking thing," I manage, lest Vasani's madness swallow me whole.

Her hyenoid mirth subsides. "Oh?"

"The Emperor still bled in the end."

"That was his choice. He made the right one. Not that this brother of his is any better..."

There is an image that throbs inside my head. Sometimes softly enough that I can present a façade of normality, sometimes so loudly that it is all I can see and I must scream and scream until it subsides. It is a wound unlike any made before or after it, a cut made without puncturing the skull, a cut that will never close because it never bled to begin with.

"You didn't give him a choice," I say. "Vasani, you did the worst thing anyone has ever done."

I utter this as plainly as the fact deserves.

"Someone had to," she replies, just as matter-of-factly.

"And the Empress?"

Her expression is beatific. "Ah, you see, that is how you touch the sublime. *Even she did not bleed.*"

Vasani's head tilts slowly back and her open palms lift heavenward. "Something for nothing." She seems to shower in an imaginary light from an imaginary firmament. "The impossible, from my hands. Are you not awed? Consequence without pain; pain without a cut; a cut without blood; *blood without consequence!* This is the better way, doctor! The end of war itself! It is like a miracle! The miracle of the *Bloodless Cut!*"

Finally, the moment for the words I carried to her all these years.

"You're a monster."

The torturer's hands descend, a certain light leaving her.

"That's rich."

I look up and watch two tears make trails down her cheeks. I try to tell myself that I know better, that true or false these tears are just another act. But that's the thing about Vasani. She's human; all humans contain truths; anything she shows me *could* be real.

"Sometimes I have nightmares about the millions we might have killed together," she says. "All those children you made orphans will grow up broken, yes, but they *will grow up.* I took their pain without a knife and left them their lives!"

"Pieces of lives," I spit back at her. "Fucking stumps of lives! Stumps I gave them to try and fix what you did!"

A miserable giggle spills out of her. "And here I thought you only saw humans in deep-enough burn-pits. *I* see them for what they are. Beautiful vessels of possibility, and consequence, and love and brilliance and pain! Years you pelted me with Peacock soldiers, wasting all they could have been. How could I hurt my fellow man with such great care unless I loved them more than you?"

Then before my eyes her face warps like nightmare-stuff. Suddenly she is shrieking, spittle flecking from black gums, her eyes leaking liquid hate. "You're the monster! You, Mirchelle Nichirei! Everything I did could have come to something if not for you, who damned the world rather than stop butchering children, you barren-hearted unstoppable *steel creature!*"

On and on her frothing rage strobes over me, more than I can process, a leveling bombardment that drives me cringing into the corner. Are these emotions real? Are they fake? I cannot tell. This could all be another performance, but if not, then the worst has come to pass. Empathic overload drives my fingers to my teeth and there is pain, mine, something I can clasp to keep from being swept away.

My bracelet rattles warning against my varicose wrist.

One minute, three seconds.

One minute, two seconds.

One minute, one second.

One

The last time we spoke was not the last time we met.

Vasani reached the strike-site three hours before me, my aerocopter being delayed by malfunction. From the air the enemy warcamp seemed untouched, but this wasn't the kind of devastation you saw with a bomb. On descent I was given a rebreather to wear in case traces of our weapon still lingered on that salt-plain's paralyzed winds.

This was nothing to do with Peacocks and Foxes, I should say. This was another war, another foe.

The Schism was still weeks away.

The invading Vridic technomads were warned what would happen if they kept pushing into Empire domains. Now, they were a successful test of our newest microbial weapon. A sleepy sort of autopilot setting seemed to move our soldiers about their business, which was gathering the dead and laying them out in a flat clearing. This was common soldier work, but these bodies were difficult. They didn't drag right. They had to be carried. They were hard to look at.

Current estimate has it close to seven thousand, the supervising commissar informed me.

I thanked him for the report and asked him where Vasani was.

I lingered there to direct the organization of incoming cadavers according to my preferences, then found an empty tent where I could weep in the dark. Afterwards, I went looking for Vasani.

Tents billowed on endlessly like the sails of a fleet sunk hopelessly in the sand. Their snapping was the only sound. The first rows were empty. The latter would be soon. I found my student squatting before an open tent. I asked what she'd found. She said nothing. Venturing closer, I saw why.

Torquedust is a synthetic bacterium meant to be dispersed in cloud-form by an aerocopter. Once inhaled, it attacks the vertebral ligaments and hyper-inflames them until they cause the body to break its own neck. Instantly lethal in ninety-nine out of a hundred cases. These two were unexceptional. Comrades? Lovers? I couldn't tell; the windblown infection had caught them both in nude embrace, slipped in on the breaths they filled with one another's scent, took root, and then contorted their skulls one hundred and eighty degrees so that they last thing they saw was nothing.

I told Vasani we'd found no survivors. Every respiring thing in a miles-long tract was fatally rotated, down to the twisted lizards and the little wrenched mice.

Vasani said nothing.

I said that the enemy commander just transmitted terms of surrender. It's over.

Nothing.

It was instant for them, I said.

Then she said, *for ninety-nine in a hundred.*

A sweetly sulfurous stink reached my nose. A yellow pool was growing slowly beneath the leftmost body, a girl. My gaze traveled up a body that sagged as abandoned flesh should, going first by mistake to where her face should be — just a skirt of ringlets there — then over to the other side, where it was now.

Blue eyes shot with blood flicked to mine. A purpled lip twitched.

In the girl's piss-puddle I glimpsed Vasani staring. Not at the bodies but at me. My wavering reflection. Waiting, it felt, for what her teacher had to say.

I take my fingers from my mouth. The taste of iron remains.

You steel creature.

And yet I bleed. Red wells plentifully from the impressions of my teeth.

This cut is not so bloodless.

Vasani is not the all-seeing demon she presents as. Infinite compassion is not something I ever thought I had. No one does, and that is right. I do not understand people very well, and those I do often disappoint me, but I can love people in their sometimes sad, sometimes beautiful mosaics. I can trust that in aggregate they suffer as I suffer, laugh as I laugh, and love as I love. Even now I wish I could trust Vasani that way. But that's what a lie does. A lie is a cut. Your world, my world — that mark there, between them. If everything that Vasani did really was to outmode me then I would be released.

It would mean that I hadn't loved a monster.

Only made one.

But...

But in me...

Unextractable by science...

The fear that this creature the government caught...

Or thinks it caught...

Is a fake and she's free right now and sharpening her knives her tools

And that fear will always be there, and that is her fault.

Fifty seconds.

"What if I told you that autoquill isn't recording?" I ask.

"What?" Her eyes pinch, then flick to the bee-buzzing machine.

"I never turned it on." I reach for it as I stand.

"Why not?" she demands hotly.

The autoquill nestles into my palm and retracts its rotos, goes still. "Emperor be damned," I say. "I wasn't going to lose this chance to speak to you one last time. But I still don't know whether I created you, or you created yourself. I don't think I ever will. What I do know is that I'll never get the truth from *you.*"

I raise a finger. "Except for one thing."

"And what is that?"

"That this was never about right and wrong with you. It was about *you.* When you were about to lose, you decided to die famously. You'll go to the gallows tall and proud, where the world will see you smile as you drop and think that you were right. Battle fought with machines will become a thing of the past. There will be no peace through fear, but instead a new and crueler kind of war where battles rage across bodies instead of battlefields, all in honor of your genius. But you don't deserve that. I'm glad I killed you, Vasani."

I lift the phial from my pocket and show it to her.

Her tears have all dried up. The performance is over. Vasani confirms nothing, only stares.

"What is that?"

Many sleepless nights I guessed futilely at what had made Vasani put on fox ears. The Emperor's cruelty seems likely. His belligerence, his excesses, his pointless wars. If not, perhaps those nestled lovers lie forever in her eyes. Maybe it was what I said over dinner. Maybe it was all of that or nothing I can possibly imagine. Whatever it was, it doesn't matter now. There is a point between their most innocent and their most monstrous where nothing you know of a friend can undo what they become.

I really believed there was one invention that would defeat Vasani Stirio instantaneously. A magic bomb. I'd failed to find it; our forces took her anticlimactically with weeks of fighting left to go. I was too late to stop her. Instead, I discovered a different kind of miracle.

"This is a ferrolipid solution with a modicum of intelligence. I call it the Mnemophage."

Her eyes follow its spellbinding silver swirl.

"Once it enters the bloodstream, it is designed to seek out and kill those regions of the brain that house certain memories. The problem is that it doesn't know which memories are stored where. For it to function properly, the subject must be made to consciously recall those memories you wish to eliminate. This causes the corresponding neurons of the brain to light up, and in doing so lure the Mnemophage towards them. The process takes time."

Vasani isn't anywhere in her expression.

"How long."

"A little over twenty minutes."

Vasani screams and tries to lunge across the red paint circle. The second her fingers pierce that implicit barrier the light in the cell turns red, and segmented metal cords erupt from the wall to bind her arms and legs, pinioning her above her stool still shrieking with rage.

"Was *I* your subject, Vasani? You ruined me all the same."

Now that she's immobile, I feel safe enough to take a slow stroll around her cell.

"I don't think I was meant to see what I saw in your laboratory. That's war, I suppose. Mostly collateral damage. I always felt I was above murder, but it turns out I was really only distant from it."

Vasani tries to lunge again, but the cords hold her fast. She can only spit and snarl.

"In just a few moments you will lose yourself. All of you will be gone except the parts that did nothing wrong. An innocent woman will go to the guillotine never knowing why the world hates her. It will see what's become of her, and they'll fear to become her too."

I glance down. *Three seconds*, reads my bracelet.

Two.

One.

"All that," I say, "without a drop of blood."

The tears in her eyes blend with the froth around Vasani's defiant rictus. "You... you could have hidden what you saw, but you didn't, did you? No, no — you showed it to the Emperor because you knew I was right. You knew I was right, and you hated it! Admit it, monster: *you* should be where *I* am. Well execute us both I say, student and teacher! Let our heads roll together!"

Such are her last coherent words. The rest is all screaming.

My head is spinning when the cell-door slams shut behind me, propelled around and around by an alarm that roars like rocket-fire. Several guards are sprinting towards me but I'm twenty minutes past their saving and drifting further into negative time with every passing second. Without much thought I fish the phial from my pocket and hold it to my eye. Not empty, in fact; a drop or two still quivers at the bottom — one for each dosage it contained.

My knees give out, and the phial tumbles from my palsying fingers. It bursts open and rolls, describing its death-arc – a silvery thumbnail obliterated by oblivious bootheels.

One guard trying to help me up, another urging me to stay down, all inaudible over the blaring klaxon. Vision dimming, head sinking. Quick: what hope did I allow myself? My assistants have the Mnemophage formula now; it's theirs to make of it what they will. Maybe a new kind of death to those in need. A more selective one, taking only what you can't bear to live with. Maybe, if I've taught them wisely, but I'll never know. A guard is pelting off, calling for help. The Emperor will soon rue my failure. He'll punish me before I die, if uncreatively. Is that what I deserve?

I'll never know that either. Not with my mirror broken.

My thoughts are elsewhere.

Broken, mama!

Hands and knees now, sinking fast. *Vasri, my son, my littlest one.* God why did Vasani have to name him? Why shine his face so brightly on the surface of my memory? The Mnemophage can't pass him now. In just a few moments I'll no longer be a mother. My son will never understand why I don't love him anymore.

I can't stop myself from screaming, a wordless plea for my next self to please hurry and be me so that she can suffer instead.

This hurts as only a bloodless cut can.

See Evan Marcroft's story "The Bloodless Cut" online at Metaphorosis.
If you liked it, leave a comment. Authors love that!
Remember to subscribe to our e-mail updates so you'll know when new stories are posted.

About the story

Hitler is boring. So is Joseph Stalin, and all the ilk of their dubious caliber. We know what kind of evil these guys are. Everyone's old dad has read a million books about them and can probably tell you the names of their childhood pets. At this point, these towering evil personalities have been so dismantled by historical mechanics both amateur and professional that every great act of monstrousness they committed can be tethered to some innocuous event opposite the point where their actions crossed over into the deliberately insidious — Hitler's being rejected from art school and so on and so on. When we peel them open we see clearly the fibers of causality that bring murderers of millions into existence. What interests me more are the great vile inexplicabilities strewn across the path towards an ideal world without seeming to have been placed there. The mysterious moai of monstrousness who seem at times to have been hurled at the world by God or whomever, sometimes at meteor speed. I'm talking about your Zodiac Killers, your bronze-age Sea People, and not even that — I'm referring to your Mengeles, whose lives seem transparent to the modern historian yet don't causally seem to amount to the era-shaping influences they become. Where do these people come from? What invisible events, what unrecorded tragedies? This story is my way of manifesting one such character into a controlled fictional space where such figures can be scrutinized safely, even if by the definition of this archetype they can never fully be understood. All we can do is take what few details we've painstakingly gleaned and make judgments of our own, for that is all history is: a patchwork of assumptions, some informed, some less so.

A question for the author

Q: What five words describe you?

A: I don't think any individual five are going to be comprehensive, but I think the five-word phrase 'this can be even weirder' is a great summary of my writing philosophy.

About the author

Evan Marcroft is a speculative fiction writer from California currently making his lair above a laundromat in the heart of Chicago. Evan uses his expensive degree in literary criticism to do menial data entry, and dreams of writing for video games, but will settle for literature instead. His works of science fiction, fantasy, and spine-curdling horror have appeared several times in *Metaphorosis* and elsewhere throughout this dark and unruly internet. Find a complete list at evan-marcroft.squarespace.com

evan-marcroft.squarespace.com, @evan_marcroft

A word about Vanessa Fog

As with L. Chan, Vanessa Fogg appeared in one of our very earliest issues, with "In Dew and Frost and Flame" on 3 June 2016, a story of lifelong love and friendship and true devotion.

Vanessa also appeared in our first anthology, *Reading 5X5*, writing from the same prompt as L. Chan, but producing a story, "Kitchen", that's similar in some ways but very different in others. Plus, it's got homely kitchen magic and turmeric-spiced potatoes in pastry.

Over the years, I've made a point of mostly avoiding books by Metaphorosis authors. I like to review what I read, and what if I don't like it? Vanessa's book, *The Lilies of Dawn,* was a convincing argument to change my practice — a beautifully written story that's rich in imagery and metaphor, and in an intriguingly conceived world to boot. I'll let you (encourage you to) discover it on your own, but it's got enchanted and malevolent cranes.

Here's her latest for *Metaphorosis*, "The Cold Inside".

The Cold Inside

Vanessa Fogg

Anna's frightened when the ghost girl first knocks at her door: a hard, frantic hammering in the still of night. Anna's alone at the lake house, surrounded by forest and water, the nearest neighbor a quarter mile away. That's why she and her husband bought the place: the splendid solitude, the embrace of dark pines, the view from a bluff that leads down to a private rock-strewn beach. They could retire here, Brian said. And Anna had imagined that retirement—still a good decade or so off—coffee on the deck, the lapping rhythm of waves, the dazzle of light on the water as they had toast and eggs. They would hike in the nearby state park, and buy fruit from roadside stands. They would spend time in the nearby charming small town with its boutiques and restaurants and gelato shop, with its single bookstore housed in a historic refurbished log cabin and filled with an eclectic selection of books and gifts. Perhaps Anna would join the book club hosted by that book store. She and Brian would join civic groups; in their leisure years they would become part of a local community as they had yet to do during their busy city lives. And each night they would have this retreat, this cottage perched above Lake Michigan, this piece of miraculously undeveloped shore: forest and dunes and the light off the water, the lake's subtle tides an underlying music in their lives.

Anna and her husband bought the place together. But now she's here alone.

The knocking comes again, harder. Anna runs to the door, peeks out through a side panel of glass. There's a woman on the porch—a young woman, a teen. She's soaking wet, a white dress plastered to her skin, dark hair streaking down her back. In the porchlight's golden glow—triggered by the property's motion detector—Anna can see the girl's trembling blue lips.

She throws open the door.

The 'Woman in White' is a figure of ghost stories worldwide. Here in this northern stretch of Michigan, we have our own version. It's said that on a chill spring night, a teenage girl argued with her boyfriend. He broke up with her, just before a school dance or party. Distraught, she drove home alone and took a curve too fast; she plunged off the highway, off a high bluff, and into the cold waters of Lake Michigan. Her ghost haunts the region's lakeside communities, knocking on doors and trying to flag down cars on the road. She's always dripping wet.

Beware of touching her. Be especially wary if you're a young man. She's cold and still angry, and she's seeking warmth.

—from Haunted Tales and Legends of Lake Michigan's Shores,
Storm Bay Press.

In the space between turning away to grab a blanket for the girl and then turning back, Anna finds the girl gone. In the entranceway is only a puddle of water, slowly spreading across the hardwood floor.

Anna is often cold. Brian used to tease her about it. He was warm —so warm. She wore sweaters, wrapped herself in blankets, and snuggled hard against him in bed. Her head tucked into the space between his neck and shoulder. The softness of flesh, the hardness of bone. His warmth warming her through. He sometimes tossed off the covers at night, but he never complained when she pressed against him. His arms curved about her waist, pulling her close. Bare skin on bare skin. The warmth of breath. She fell asleep to his even breathing, the rise and fall of his chest.

And now he's gone, and there's nothing that can warm her. She has a weighted blanket. She piles her bed at home with pillows —heavy, body-length pillows on each side of her, enclosing her. Nothing helps. She has one of his old shirts. She holds it, presses it to her cheek, buries her face in it. She pretends that it still smells of him, even though she knows that the scent must be long gone.

She didn't bring his shirt to the lake house. She tells herself she doesn't need it, it doesn't smell of him. That in the house by the lake—the place he briefly loved—she'll be able to sleep without it.

She wakes from confused dreams, the blankets twisted around her. A memory of cold water, the beach at night. A lighthouse in the distance. She thinks she was calling someone's name. Shivering from cold. Sirens blaring on a highway above.

She walks into the kitchen and sees it: the blanket she tossed on the floor the night before, to soak up the puddle. It's still damp.

There was a girl here last night. It was real.

Numbly, Anna gathers up the blanket, tosses it in the laundry to wash later. She doesn't want to think of it. A girl wandering the woods and lakeshore, knocking on doors. Gone in an instant.

Anna makes coffee. Hot and black and strong. Mechanically, she scrambles eggs.

Only after does she remember the security camera. The one Brian set up last summer. Anna doesn't have the security app on her phone, so she has to log into the company's website to see the footage. She watches the porchlight turn on; she sees herself open the door. But she opens the door to no one.

Brian mentioned the ghost girl once. Anna remembers it now; an offhand remark—*They say not to drive too late on this road, not in the spring.* He was smiling. He didn't believe in ghosts, of course. It was just a bit of local trivia. He'd summered in the region as a kid with his family, heard some stories. A local urban legend: broken heart, car crash, death. He didn't mention it again. It never came up when they bought the house. Thinking back, Anna can't remember where on the highway they were when she heard the story. They drove up and down the coast on their summer vacations, exploring the little towns, beaches, lighthouses, parks. But in all their time together, they'd never come so early in the season. Now the beech trees are bare, the lake cold and gray. Businesses in the nearby town still closed, vacation homes empty.

There was a different emptiness in the city. The crowds streaming past her in the streets were filled with busy strangers, all walking briskly and engaged in their own purposeful lives. In her house, Brian's absence ballooned to fill every room. Anna had tired of it—she'd wanted to be alone and lonely in a different place. By the water, under open sky. Among bare trees and pines. To feel Brian's absence differently. His loss might have a softer presence here, she thought, spread throughout water and wood and sky. She found herself clenching the wheel hard as she drove out of the city, tension an ache in her jaw. Something loosened as the countryside opened up, as the miles stretched ahead. As the lake finally came into view. But when she opened the door to the silent, dark cottage, the grief hit her: a sneaker wave from a seemingly calm sea, knocking her off her feet, ripping away her breath, pouring in and through her in an endless flood.

He was only fifty-two.

She keeps thinking this, over and over. Even all these months later. When she first met him, they were in their twenties and she thought fifty-two ancient, an unfathomable age, the age of parents and professors and bosses. Old. And now fifty-two is young, far too young. Too *goddamn fucking young.*

'Jenny-of-the-Lake', she's called locally. She's been blamed for a string of purportedly mysterious deaths since the 1960s. A teen boy found frozen on the beach. Another who drove his car into a tree. A young man who never made his way home after a party, and was found dead in the woods. Perhaps the most disquieting cases are those of men found dead in their own homes. They either lived alone near the lake, or their families were away for the night. They were reportedly all in good health. And though there were no clear signs of foul play, they were found stiff with cold even though they died in warm rooms.

My friends and I all knew these stories growing up. 'Don't open the door to Jenny!' we said. It was a game among us, to ring a friend's doorbell and then hide or run away. 'Don't open the door to Jenny!' we'd say as we ran.

—recollections of Jack Dykstra, age 66, from the article "Rural Ghost Stories of the Midwest", published on the website *Modern Folklore.*

Anna drives into town. For once, after the disturbance of last night, she doesn't want to be alone. She orders a meal at one of the few places open. There's a scattering of local customers at the Blue Mitten Grill: two men at the bar, a few occupied booths, a harried mother scolding her young children. Anna orders a sandwich and fries and eats without tasting a thing.

She lingers over a drink refill she doesn't need. Watches as a family of four walks in. As the waitress flirts with a customer. Have any of these people met the local ghost? What do they know?

"Anything else I can do for you, dear?" the waitress asks her.

Anna doesn't know how to bring up the ghost. She doesn't know how to talk to people—not anymore. She feels like a ghost herself, watching the living people in this restaurant as though through a thick pane of glass.

"No," Anna says. "I'm fine."

The knocking comes again that night. Anna's been waiting for it. Curled up on the couch, trying to watch TV, yet not registering anything at all. Even though she expects it, the first knock makes her jump. She clutches her blanket to her. Holds still as the hammering comes again and again.

The ghost eventually gives up, goes away. Anna stays where she is, and her heart keeps hammering long after ghost's knocks have faded.

She doesn't check the security footage this time. She doesn't want to see. Or not see.

Daylight lasts longer these days, but there are still traces of snow in the woods, little mounds and streaks of dirty-white, even as green shoots push up from the earth. Anna's still cold; that hasn't changed. She's turned up the thermostat, built up fires in the fireplace. Taken long, hot showers and baths. Wrapped herself in her bed comforter. She puts on every layer she has when she goes outside. The cold is in her bones. It doesn't leave.

'Lady in White' ghost stories have common themes of abandonment, betrayal, and loss. There is almost always a tragic love story involved. The ghost sometimes loses her lover to mishap or war, but more often he cruelly leaves her. She returns to the scene of her grief or death—pacing the widow's walk of a stately old manor, haunting the backstage of an abandoned theatre; materializing in the bathroom of the girls' school where she hung herself, or walking the stretch of lonely highway where her car ran off the road. She's usually a sad, passive presence: a vanishing face in a window, a hitchhiker disappearing from the backseat when the driver turns around.

The story of Lake Jenny is an unusual example of the genre in that she isn't just a passively mourning spirit, a wistful figure in white. She takes on elements of a classic vengeance spirit: her grief is rage and desire with dire effects in the mortal realm. In her grief, she seeks and actively takes life from the living.

—from "Vengeance Spirits and Ladies in White: A Cross-Cultural Analysis of Female Ghosts" by Allison M. Lee in *Journal of Global Folklore.*

Anna spends most of the next day on the deck, staring out at the lake. Gray water under cold, gray skies. She lets the water, this vast inland sea, fill her sight. She lets her mind empty into the white-tipped waves, into the space where the water meets sky.

Her hands are numb when she finally stands, her whole body stiff.

She makes her way down to the beach. A flash of memory—bright sun, blue skies, and Brian turning over rocks at the shoreline, hunting for Petoskey stones, the state rock of Michigan. She can almost see him bent over in the water, the back of his neck reddening in the sun. She can almost touch him. They collected rocks together, piling them in little cairns on the beach, displaying them in glass containers. The glass containers are still here, sitting on shelves and on the kitchen table of the beach house. The little beach cairns are gone. She feels hot tears on her face. The wind is blowing. He's not here. He's not here, and all she wants is to hold him again, to see him, touch him, feel him. Talk to him. Tell him about the past few days, tell him everything, apologize yet again. Fling herself against him. She's cold. She's so cold, and she misses his warmth.

There's no knock on the door that night. The ghost has given up, Anna figures.

The ghost is knocking on other doors, haunting other houses. Walking the highway or beaches and dunes. Alone.

Over the next few days, the earth and air warm even if Anna doesn't. The sun breaks free. New green springs up from the forest floor, the understory leafing out beneath still-bare trees. The last traces of snow are gone, and birdsong fills the world. The sky is clear, and in its brilliant light Lake Michigan turns Caribbean blue.

The ghost is gone. Anna should be relieved. Instead, the hollowness in her chest only feels slightly bigger.

She spends an afternoon at the bookstore in town. Since Brian's death, she's had trouble reading for pleasure. Still, the presence of books is comforting—the shelves of stories around her, the heft of a book in her hands.

She finds what she was looking for. She takes it up to the counter.

"Ah," the owner says crisply as she rings up the 10th anniversary edition of *Haunted Tales and Legends of Lake Michigan's Shores*. "That's a classic. Has a few stories from right around here."

"Lake Jenny," Anna says, and she's surprised at how small, how childish, her own voice sounds.

"That's right." The store owner gives her a second look. She's a rather severe-looking older woman, gray hair pulled back in a bun. Anna doesn't think the other woman remembers her. She and Brian visited the store only a few times last summer. Last summer, the first season that they owned their first vacation home.

"Jenny is a sad story," the other woman says now, thoughtfully. Her demeanor has softened. "She's something of a boogeyman around here—something to scare kids with—but I always felt sorry for her."

Anna nods. "Me, too," she says.

Jenny doesn't return, but Anna can *feel* her out there in the darkness. Wet and freezing and desperate. Searching.

Looking for a lit window in the darkness. An occupied home on the empty lakeshore. Some sign of welcome or life. An open door. An outstretched hand.

Any offer of warmth.

Anna was especially cold last autumn.

Half-heartedly, she told Brian to stay away. To not kiss her. He didn't listen. She didn't expect him to.

She didn't *want* him to.

They never took particular care to avoid one another when sick. *I'll just get it, too,* Brian shrugged. Colds and flus—it wasn't really a big deal, was it? They still held each other. Slept in the same bed. Brian would grumble about the bunched-up tissues that she would leave scattered around the house, and clean them up. They would make each other soup.

This particular flu was the worst she'd had in years. A sudden headache, falling on her like a crushing stone. And then the bone-deep chills.

Her skin was hot to the touch, feverish. Her insides were ice.

She whimpered, snuggling into her husband's warmth. He held her from behind, spooning with her in bed, the heavy comforter piled on top. She couldn't get warm. He held her, he held her, one hand stroking her arm, her hair; she leaned back against him. In an aching, blurred landscape of pain and cold, he was the only warmth. She shivered and froze until she slept.

It *was* only the flu. The doctors verified this later.

They'd both had their flu vaccinations. They were both in good health.

Sometimes the vaccines aren't a great match for the circulating strains. A doctor friend once explained it to her: the science of how researchers try to predict which strains to immunize against each year.

Brian seemed to be getting better with his own bout of flu when his fever spiked. A deepening cough. Chest pain.

A bacterial secondary infection. Pneumonia, then sepsis. She should have gotten him to the doctor sooner. Insisted on it. A prescription of antibiotics would have stopped it, if they'd just gone in time. She should have urged him to get Tamiflu before the influenza—the first infection—could even take hold.

She should have stayed away from him. Not let him get sick in the first place. Locked herself in the guest room. Refused to let him touch her. Cuddle her, hold her.

It's okay, he said, holding her. *You know you're contagious before symptoms even show up, don't you? You've probably already given it to me.*

Survivor accounts of Jenny are generally reports of seeing her at a distance. A woman in white standing on the beach. A glimpse of her near the state park, on the highway, or in the parking lot of a motel. Contact isn't sustained; the witness doesn't see Jenny's eyes.

After the publication of the first edition of our book, we were contacted by many with personal stories of their own sightings of Jenny. An email from Ellen Rafferty of Chicago stood out, and we reached out to her for more. She claims that she was vacationing in the area with her family in 2019, staying in a rented home on the lake when Jenny knocked on her door.

"Rick and the kids had driven out to see a movie. It was one of those sci-fi action hero things, and I'm not really into that, you know? So I decided to stay in, have a quiet night to myself. It was around 10 when she knocked on the door. Scared the hell out of me.

"Of course I let her in. How could I not? I didn't know anything about ghosts. I just saw this dripping wet girl, this kid, who needed help.

"She never said a word. Just looked at me with these big, dark eyes that seemed to see and not see me. Even as I was babbling my head off at her, saying, Oh my god, what happened? *and grabbing her a blanket. She was wearing a skimpy white dress, sleeveless. Too cold for the weather, even if she weren't also soaking wet. She was shaking, and her skin was so pale it was blue.*

"She sat on the couch like I told her to, with my blanket wrapped around her. I said I would grab some dry clothes of mine for her to wear. But when I came back from the bedroom, she was gone.

"I still think of her. My family came home, and we called the cops to report a girl in need of help, but of course they never found her and there were no reports of anyone missing or hurt that night. Knowing what I do now, I'm glad I didn't touch her. I guess some part of me knew not to. But oh, she was lonely and cold. I could feel it. I really could. There was just.... cold and desperation coming off of her. Like hunger. I wanted to comfort her. I didn't touch her, but I wanted to—to wrap that blanket around her myself, hug her in it, *towel her off, make sure she was dry and warm. Give her a cup of hot tea.*

"I know that she's dangerous. I even knew it that night. But I still feel for her. I wish she were okay."

— from *Haunted Tales and Legends of Lake Michigan's Shores: Updated 10th Anniversary Edition.* Storm Bay Press.

Jenny haunts the area for only a few weeks of early spring. That liminal time when flowers bloom and songbirds have returned, but winter's bite still lingers. She returns like an ephemeral wildflower of the woods—a brief vision of white, here and gone before most can even notice.

Anna puts down her copy of *Haunted Tales.* She counts off the days left.

She's felt Jenny's silent call every night. That screaming need. Her hammering on doors that don't open, on empty vacation rentals and homes that ignore her. Cars that drive past.

Anna's dreams now are always of blackness and cold water. It's almost a relief; at least she's sleeping again each night.

The cold that she feels—it isn't all her own.

She normally leaves the porch light off, letting it turn on only in response to motion. But tonight she deliberately switches the light on. It's a sign that someone's home. A welcome. A beacon.

She leaves all the lights on in her house.

When Jenny comes, Anna has the thick blanket ready. She doesn't need to take her eyes off the ghost.

"I'm sorry," she told her husband when he first caught her flu. When it was still just a flu.

"I'm sorry"—when he was shaking with chills, and she was the one holding him and keeping him warm.

"I'm sorry," the doctors said. "I'm sorry," people told her after he died. *I'm sorry, I'm sorry, I'm so sorry for your loss.*

Her throat was blocked. She couldn't speak.

She could hardly look Brian's family in the eye.

Afterwards, Brian's sister kept calling her, texting her, checking up on her. Asking if she wanted to get together for a coffee or lunch. Anna came up with excuses, or didn't answer at all.

Finally, she fled.

It's a rare complication, the doctor told her. There were so many doctors at the end, but this one seemed to be the main one, the one in charge. He said, *Many wrong things had to happen in just the wrong way. I'm sorry.*

Jenny steps in, and she's what Anna remembers: a thin white girl with long black hair down her back. Blue lips and huge eyes. Dripping with water.

Anna gets her wrapped up in the thick blanket, not touching her directly. She hands her a cup of hot tea.

Jenny sits on the couch, sipping. Her eyes staring over the rim of the cup, hungry and dark.

She puts down the cup. "I'm still cold," she says plaintively. Her voice is a little girl's. A lost little girl.

"I know," Anna says.

Why did she let Jenny in? Did she really think she could warm her, comfort her? Do what the woman in her book could not? Cold radiates from the ghost, the chilling atmosphere from an entire planet of winter.

Jenny stands up, clutching the blanket around her. She takes a step toward where Anna is standing. "I'm still cold," she repeats. And her eyes lock on Anna's, pleading. Anna doesn't move.

Is this how Jenny has ensnared boys and men over the years? Not just seducing with beauty—which the girl certainly has —but with an appeal to compassion, to human warmth? To the vanity of thinking you could save someone else?

She could be Anna's daughter. If she and Brian had had a daughter. She's the right age. She even has Anna's coloring: the dark hair and dark eyes.

"I'm sorry," Anna says, as the girl takes another step. Water drips to the floor, and Anna smells lake water.

It's not vengeance. Anna knows that in her bones. Jenny has never meant to take revenge, to hurt anyone. She's just seeking warmth, in the easiest way she can. Anna understands. She knows what it's like to contain a frozen sea within. To starve for human touch. To crave it so badly she thinks she'll go mad. To yearn for just a simple brush of fingertips, an exhalation of breath, a heartbeat near hers. To live off the memory of past warmth.

Jenny's eyebrows lift slightly. "You're cold like me," she tells Anna.

"Yes," Anna says.

Like and not like. Anna's body still holds its human warmth. But oh, she's cold, and her cold is nothing to Jenny's. Anna deserves to be cold—she *deserves* it—and Jenny's is far greater than Anna can carry on her own. Jenny's is an endless tundra of cold, a fathomless lake: vast, immeasurable. Jenny's cold can swallow Anna whole.

This is what Anna wants. This is why she turned on the porch light, why she opened the door. She'd thought she was just reaching out—that she didn't want to be alone. And she doesn't.

What she wants, she understands now, is to join Jenny's cold. To disappear in it. To merge into that endless tundra, melt into her dark lake. To join the other souls Jenny's swallowed—to lose herself among them. To no longer be herself. No longer alone with the cold, bearing it all on her own.

She reaches out for the shivering ghost girl. She steps into her eager embrace.

See Vanessa Fogg's story "The Cold Inside" online at Metaphorosis.
If you liked it, leave a comment. Authors love that!
Remember to subscribe to our e-mail updates so you'll know when new stories are posted.

About the story

I'm fascinated by urban legends, our modern folklore. One such legend that shows up cross-culturally is that of the Woman in White, also sometimes known as the "White Lady". I think I was reading about her in late 2022. Around the same time, my family came down with a bad winter cold. It wasn't COVID (we tested), and we were all fine within a few days, but it was miserable at the time, as colds can be. COVID-19 was still very much in my mind, too, and I found myself thinking of the worst that could happen—of how it would be to feel responsible for someone you loved falling fatally ill. These things mixed in my mind and somehow created this story. Also, like Anna, I frequently feel cold when others don't.

A question for the author

Q: If your writing style were a bird, what type of bird would it be and why?
A: I like to think my writing would be a flock of starlings, individual words and sentences pretty but not overly showy, with subtle iridescence. And together, the starling-sentences would weave graceful patterns in the sky.

About the author

Vanessa Fogg dreams of selkies, dragons, and gritty cyberpunk futures from her home in western Michigan. She spent years as a research scientist in molecular cell biology and now works as a freelance medical writer. Her fiction has appeared in *Lightspeed, Podcastle, GigaNotoSaurus*, Neil Clarke's *The Best Science Fiction of the Year: Volume 4*, and more. She is fueled by green tea.

www.vanessafogg.com, @FoggWriter

Spring

A word about Saleha Chowdhury

Usually, there's been quite a long wait between when I first add an artist to our roster for potential work and when I first call on them. But when Saleha Chowdhury first contacted us in 2018, I liked her work so much that I drew on her right away. Her cover illustration for Arlen Feldman's "Graveyard" was so good that I also chose it as the cover of the our 2018 *Best of Metaphorosis* issue — and there was very stiff competition that year.

I brought Saleha back almost immediately, for the February 2019 cover, illustrating Catherine George's "The Bear Wife". That cover, with a woman and child nestled inside a bear's open mouth, is still one of my favorites — as most of Saleha's work is.

She appeared again on the December 2019 (Laura Duerr's "What Lies in Light") and January 2020 (L. Chan's "Sonata") covers. That also makes her a member of the Meta4osis club — the select few that have appeared in *Metaphorosis* four times or more — and we've been very happy to have her!

In this volume, she provided the cover art based on M.E. Bronstein's "Garden Teeth".

You can find more of Saleha's work at www.salehachowdhury.com

About Saleha Chowdhury

Saleha Chowdhury is a digital illustrator based in New York who enjoys working on a wide variety of projects including cover art, background art for games, and character design. She especially enjoys working on projects related to science fiction and fantasy.
salehachowdhury.com, arodude.tumblr.com

A word about R.W.W. Greene

R.W.W. Greene first came to my attention in 2018, with his story "The Stars Don't Lie" (which we published on 29 June of that year). It's a story about centaurides and magic and fitting in that I really enjoyed.

Greene reappeared in *Metaphorosis* two years later, on 10 July 2020, with a completely different story, "They Build 'Em Tough on Magna Mater", about farm robots repurposed for cage matches.

Both stories have in common a warm humanity concerned with more than just immediate consequences, which is also something you'll find in the next story, "The Wedding of Hope Garrison and Chevrolet Dodge Ford".

The Wedding of Hope Garrison and Chevrolet Dodge Ford

R.W.W. Greene

The farm looked like a lot of them did in them days, one part green to three parts dust. Twenty or thirty head of cattle worked the scrub to the west of the house. Rusted steel slumped on flat, rotting tires. A rickety-looking catfish tank sweated beneath the chicken coop.

The farmer pushed the much-mended baseball cap off his forehead. "How much you charge?"

"Depends," Hank said. "You got power?"

"Some."

"I need 110 to 120. Steady. I can hook my generator in as backup. Only charge you for the fuel."

The farmer took off his cap and wiped his forehead with the back of his arm. "What are we talking in all?"

Hank told him, ignoring the man's wince. "Not every day your daughter gets married, Mr. Garrison. Be a nice surprise for her. Half now. Half after the wedding. Plus meals and a bath."

Farmer Garrison studied his feet a while before tugging his cap back on and sticking out his hand to shake. "You need help setting up? My son knows a thing or two about juice."

Hank jabbed his thumb back at his motorcycle. "Got everything I need right there."

"Lucas!" The farmer hollered, cupping his hands around it. "Lucas!"

A fit young man in patched overalls jogged out from behind the barn. "Yeah, Pa?"

"Walk up and take a look at the water wheel. Make sure the crick's clear and everything's hooked up right." He nodded at Hank. "Man's gonna play music for your sister's wedding tomorrow."

Lucas showed a good set of teeth in his grin. "What's he play?"

"Vinyl," Hank said and tugged the cover off the motorcycle's sidecar. His deejay gear was arranged inside. "Where should I set up?"

The farmer showed him the barn where the reception would be held and helped drag a wooden table into place. "You can plug in there." He pointed to a rusted outlet. "I'll send my daughter in to see ya."

Hank unpacked his turntable and speakers and plugged them into the farm's power. He lifted the crate of records out of the sidecar — about a hundred albums ranging from pristine to warped as hell. He slid the best of the bunch, a copy of Michael Jackson's *Thriller* out of its cover, and lay the needle on side two, track one: "Beat It".

Eddie Van Halen's guitar work filled the dusty barn. According to a book Hank'd owned once, Van Halen's playing was so good the studio caught fire when he laid the riff down. He let the song play. MJ's voice warbled off tempo and key on the second verse. Hank checked the needle and the album for defects. They were perfect. The farmer's power supply was at fault. He ran a line out to the generator in the sidecar.

The record played fine after that, the generator barely a whisper inside the barn. Hank switched on the microphone and leaned in close. "Check. Check. Check," boomed from the speakers. The bride-to-be walked in on the echo.

"Daddy said you're gonna play music for my wedding."

"Best show in town," Hank said. "Get everyone up and moving. Make it a real party."

"Movin' ain't usually a problem with this crowd," she said. "What kind of music you got?"

Her no-color dress was frayed at the hem, and she had wavy hair that would need washing before the ceremony tomorrow. If she were pregnant, it weren't showing.

"Rock 'n roll, ma'am. Country. Mostly late last century." Hank handed her the *Thriller* album cover. The so-called Red-Blue War had left the boundaries of propriety muddy in the 'Messy Middle' states, and there was a chance she'd pitch a fit about being presented with a black man's music. She put the album cover back on the table without comment. "What else you got?" she said.

"Can you read?" He unfolded his catalog carefully and put in on the table.

"Course I can." She tucked her hair behind her ears and bent to puzzle out the list he'd typed out. She bit her lower lip as she traced out the words. Hank would have bet his fee that she hadn't heard anything but live music her whole life, most of that from drunken farmers on broke-down guitars and cigar-box mandolins.

"Do you want some suggestions?" She picked up a record. "He a real prince?"

They spent the next three hours spinning records and picking out her playlist. It was heavy on the Tom Petty, Johnny Cougar, and Bruce Springsteen sort, but she surprised Hank with some of her choices. "Let's Pretend We're Married" off Prince's *1999*. His sole Salt-N-Pepa album, *Hot, Cool & Vicious*, was badly warped, but the last couple of tracks on both sides sounded alright. Hank played "I'll Take Your Man" twice before she scribbled it onto her list. She also showed a fondness for seventies disco and asked him to put "La Freak," "That's the Way (I Like it)," and "Heart of Glass" in where it felt right.

"What do you want for slow songs?" he said.

"You pick." She fanned herself with the catalog and eyed his stack of records. "You sure got a lot of music."

Hank powered down his gear. "It's just about knowing where to look. Keeping your eyes open."

"Bet you've seen a lot of places."

"Some. Good and bad." The barn was getting warm, and his armpits were uncomfortably damp. "Half and half, I guess."

She sat on the edge of the table. "I ain't been anywhere but here."

And now she was about to get hitched and would likely never get clear. "Here seems nice enough," Hank said.

"It's tiresome. All do this and do that. Wash the clothes. Tend to the chickens. Take care of the kids."

Hank allowed that might get tiresome. "You're getting married."

She folded her arms. "Weren't really my idea. He did the askin'. My step mother said yes, but she ain't the one has to sleep with him."

Hank straightened the stack of records. Once she left, he could put his mind to picking out some slow songs she and her new in-laws might like.

"My name's Hope," she said.

Hank nodded.

"I work hard," she said, "and I'm stronger than I look. I got my letters and numbers. Betcha I could help out at your shows."

"Don't need much help," Hank said. "I got it alright."

"That motorbike of yours is big enough for two. We can pack all this up and be on our way lickety-split." She cocked her hip. "I got money."

"How much?"

She told him.

Not enough. "Sometimes you got to bloom where you're planted, miss."

Hope frowned. Her eyes were near green and life hadn't worn her features sharp yet. Her skin was smooth, except on her hands. She hadn't trued playing pretty yet, but Hank was mostly immune to farmers' daughters anyway.

"I'll do a good job picking out the rest of it, ma'am," Hank said. "It will be a pleasure to hear."

He didn't watch her leave. She might have been serious about running away, or she might have been hoping to see her beau get tough with a wife-stealing deejay. Neither option worked for him. He picked out a dozen or so slow songs, threw in some more fast numbers for the younger women, and typed up the playlist on his portable Royal.

The water pump next to the house ran off an old bicycle, and he had to hunt down the bucket. When he got back to the pump, Lucas met him with a tall glass of lemonade and a plate of food. "Wet your whistle," he said.

"Shouldn't you be getting ready for the rehearsal dinner?"

Lucas sat on the steps and tucked into his own plate. "All I got to do tomorrow is sit and smile. Don't need much practice for that."

The lemonade was cold and sweet. Hank pointed his fork at the pump. "Your doing?"

"Makes things a little easier on my stepmother." He stretched, lean muscles pushing at the fabric of his shirt. "You should let me show you my workshop."

"Got any electrical wire to spare?"

"Might." Lucas took their emptied plates back inside and led the way to a squat blue building on the other side of the house. "Ever see one of these?" Lucas handed him a silver disc from a shelf near the door.

"It's a seedee," Hank said. "Used to put music on them."

"Ever see one work?"

Hank's jaw dropped, half expecting the younger man to wave him over to a working player, but Lucas just laughed. "Me neither." He put the disc back onto the shelf. "Look over here, though." He directed Hank to the far corner of the building. "Nearly got it working."

The thing on the bench was shell-shaped, white on the bottom and translucent orange on the top. A white apple was stenciled on the side. It was attached to a keyboard like the one on Hank's portable typewriter.

"What is it?" Hank said.

"Watch." Lucas tapped the space bar, and a fan came on inside the shell. The glass front lit up and something inside the thing chimed. "Wait for it." A little drawing of an hourglass appeared and flipped over. And flipped over again. And again. And again.

"That all it does?"

"I get it working all the way, you'll see something!"

"Like what?"

Lucas raised his hands. "Name it. Games. Pictures. Music. Way more than you got. I can get the answer to any question worth askin' once this thing works."

Hank looked at the hourglass. It flipped over again. The screen flickered and went dark. The fan died. Something inside smelled hot. "What are you going to do when you fix it?"

"Sell it, maybe." Lucas grinned. "Buy a motorcycle and get rich making people dance at weddings. You wanna see what I got for wire?"

"Don't really need it." Hank followed Lucas out of the shed. "You really teach yourself all this?"

"Can't spend all my time tendin' the cows." He yawned. "I'm going back up to the house see if they left me any dessert. You?"

Hank shook his head. "Bed. Long day tomorrow."

"Suit yourself." Lucas crooked a half grin. "Holler, you get lonely."

Hank went back to the barn and climbed to the hayloft to sleep. He didn't come awake until he heard the wedding-setup crew stirring in the barn below. He rubbed the sleep out of his eyes and went up to the house to find some breakfast and a bath. The kitchen was full of girls about Hope's age, so he waited until he could flag down someone less likely to want to talk to him. She showed up in a gray dress and a scowl.

"Who you supposed to be?" she said.

Hank offered her his professional bow. "Dancin' Hank, the Wedding Deejay. I'm doing the music for this shindig."

She gave him the eye. "My husband hired you."

"Mr. Garrison and I shook on it yesterday afternoon. Price included meals and a bath."

"He dotes on that girl." She made a face like she'd tasted bad pickles. "You wait here, and I'll get you breakfast. Ask Lucas to show you the crick afterward. That'll do for you."

She ducked into the laughter-filled kitchen and came back out with a plate of beans and bread and a mug of coffee. "Eat it outside. Lucas should be coming back this way in a few minutes."

Hank took the food onto the porch and watched the sun clamber up the sky. Lucas came 'round just as he was sopping up the rest of the bean juice. "Your mama says to show me the crick," Hank said.

"Just about to go down there. Let me get my shave kit, and I'll show ya."

They detoured back to the barn so Hank could get his own kit and the suit he wore for working. Lucas led him away from the house, through the cow field, to a fast-moving stream. He pointed to a shed built over the water. "That's the water wheel. I recoiled the turbine yesterday afternoon so you won't need to tap your generator." He gestured downstream. "It gets deep and wide enough to swim there."

At the edge of the pool, Lucas stripped out of his clothes. His body was lean and strong, with a farmer's tan marking his smooth skin. He smirked, "Last one in's a mama's boy!" and dove in from the shore.

The stream was fresh and cold, and Hank flapped and blew until he got used to it.

"Reckon you're only a year or two older than me," Lucas said.

"Could be," Hank ran his fingers though his sopping hair to tease out the snarls, "but I'm wiser in the ways of the world."

Lucas laughed and play-tackled him, knocking him back into the water. Before Hank knew it, they were splashing each other and wrestling, warm slippery skin on skin. When it got to be too much fun, he pushed away and waded to the shore for his razor. "Got any soap?" he said.

"Over there in my kit." Lucas was floating on his back "Use all you want."

Hank lathered up with the good-smelling soap right there in the stream and rinsed off. He washed his hair and shaved carefully. Lucas watched him the whole time. "What're you looking at?" Hank said.

"Wanted to see if I could learn something new 'bout shaving and washing." Lucas ran his hand over his chest. "But nope. You do it same as me."

Hank toweled off with his dirty shirt. "You'd better get some practice in lest you look a mess for your sister's wedding."

"Think I'd rather float here and watch you."

Hank tried not to dress so fast that he looked nervous. His immunity to farm girls didn't extend to their brothers. He straightened his tie and slid on his shiny, silver jacket. "How do I look?"

"Like the Lord of the Dance hisself." Lucas had come up behind him while he dressed, his voice too close now, his body still cool and wet from the crick. He sniffed the side of Hank's neck. "You smell like me."

Hank cleared his throat. "I better get down there and make sure things are set up right."

"Suit yourself. I'm going back in the water again." Lucas's waist was narrow, his shoulders heavy with work.

"Where'd you learn how to swim so good?" Hank said.

The question stopped the dive back into the stream, as Hank hoped it would. "Hired hand we used to have taught me," Lucas smirked. "Taught me a lot of things." With a flex of leg and buttocks, he dove cleanly into the water.

Hank waited for his head to come up and waved to him. Lucas waved back and stroked away. Hank headed back up the hill.

It was a little too perfect. He might make a move and find himself invited to a game of Kick the Queer. He never won those games. He'd go on his way broke and nursing his wounds, or he'd get run off — still broke — for roughing up a local. Not starting from zero, exactly — he'd done that enough to know the difference — but maybe having to put a pencil line though parts of the map until things cooled down.

Hank wondered if Lucas knew his little sister wanted to cut and run.

The ceremony was set for noon, and Hank wasn't invited, so he went back to the barn to check his rig. He lay his shiny jacket on the table next to his records and spent a few minutes testing the sound again. Six months before and two-hundred miles south, a wire-chewing squirrel had cost him a payday when he dropped the needle on the first song and nothing happened. Hank check-checked the mike and got MJ to tell him to "Beat It" again. He dug a chunk of spruce gum out of his pocket and worked it soft with his teeth.

"Sounds alright." A shadow fell on the turntable. "How'd you hear about us, anyway?"

Cleaned up, Farmer Garrison was a couple of shades lighter. He was tugging on his shirt collar like it wanted to strangle him.

"Store clerk in Franklin," Hank said. "She told me about another wedding to check out next week. 'Bout fifty miles that way." He pointed north. "June and September are my best months."

"You make a living at that?" The farmer's gesture took in Hank's rig. "Showing up to parties and playing old songs?"

"I won't get rich, but yessir. I pick up extra work here and there, too. It suits me. I like to stay on the move."

Garrison nodded slowly. Likely he'd never been much of a traveler. He probably spent his whole life in the same twenty square miles, eyes fixed on a mule's ass. "What's she got you playing?"

Hank fetched the list from his jacket pocket and offered it.

The farmer waved the paper off. "Tell me."

Hank kept an eye on Garrison as he read the list, waiting for the farmer to holler or color up when he got to some of Hope's more scandalous picks. Farmers liked big butts, but they didn't always cotton to songs about them.

"I remember some of those," Garrison said. His face took on a faraway look, and he hummed a piece of something. "My mama used to sing that to my sister."

"Van Morrison's 'Brown-Eyed Girl.' I could sneak it in for you. Make it a father-daughter dance."

The farmer backed away from the table like it had something catching. "It's Hope's party. Let her pick the music. 'Sides," he smiled, "her eyes are green. Like her mama's were."

"Let me know if you change your mind."

He reached to adjust the cap he wasn't wearing. "What's it like out there now?"

Better on the edges than it is here in the middle. Or so I've heard. I've never been all the way west."

Farmer Garrison rubbed his leathery face. "My daddy fought for the Blue. Moved the family out here after. Said it was easier to try to grow your own food than wait in the lines." He looked at Hank sharp. "They still lines?"

"Some places. None of the cities came all the way back. Lot of the ones that didn't have a port emptied out. Others are okay. There's work if you want it. Food. Government has airplanes to move things around now. Trains."

"Lot of people died." Garrison whistled through his teeth. "Lot of people."

Hank didn't bother commenting. When the missiles started flying, both sides gave up claim to the word 'humane', maybe even to 'human'. Then the emps brought everyone back to the early 1900s and left them there.

"I wanted better for my kids, you know?" Garrison reached for his cap again. "Daddy always said he thought we'd get it back together quicker. Teevee, food, electricity for everybody like it grew on trees." He grimaced. "You're probably too young to remember any of that.

"Stories, mostly. Books and magazines."

"Didn't get much of it myself. I was five or six when the grid went down, and we came out here." He drew himself up. "Look at me jawing. Got me a daughter to give away. You know she wanted to be a singer? Talked about it all the time back when she was kid. Not much hope of that now."

The half dozen women still in the barn followed Garrison out the door. "Don't touch anything!" one scolded. They'd decorated with checked tablecloths and streamers and laid the food out on a long table.

Hank put on his shiny jacket and got hisself organized. He cued up the first song Hope'd hear as wife to... what's his name. Hank looked around for a clue to his identity. It would be mighty hard to call a wedding when he wasn't clued in to what to call one half of the happy couple. He finally spotted his name burned into a leather scrapbook on the gift table: "Chevrolet Dodge Ford and Hope Emily Garrison, June 7, 2023."

Hope and Chevy, together forever. A breeze made the tablecloths flutter. The sky darkened. Hank worked another piece of spruce gum soft and popped it into his mouth. It never hurt to have fresh breath.

About thirty minutes later, the ring bearer and the flower girl — the youngest Garrison kids — tore in like the devil was behind them. "Rain's coming!" the girl said. The little boy stuck his finger in the cake.

"Don't!" The girl fetched the boy a clout, and he darted under the table with a finger full of white frosting. The rest of the guests entered at a statelier pace, and Hank powered up the turntable. The B-52's "Love Shack" tumbled out of the speakers. It put the first few folks back on their heels, but the younger people picked up the rhythm and sort of bopped to their seats.

Hank didn't know the groom from Adam, so he kept an eye out for the bride. She entered unsmiling with a dark-haired man whose hairy wrists showed past the cuffs of his jacket. Behind them were Farmer Garrison, his wife, and two beanstalks that had to be the groom's parents.

Hank lowered the music volume and picked up the microphone. "Ladies and gentlemen," he said, "May I introduce Mr. and Mrs. Chevrolet Ford!"

The wedding guests stamped and hooted, and Hank got to work. His hands hummingbirded from record stack to tone arm again and again. Unsleeved vinyl piled up on both sides of him.

The guests tucked into the food and booze. Once in a while, Hank came out and shared some of the dance moves he'd learned from a book his mama had. The Funky Chicken and the Bump. The ladies ate it up and got some of the men to take a nibble, too.

Most of the boys weren't dancing, so Hank got a share of the bounces, flaunts, and coy come-hither looks from the single girls on the floor. He got some play from the married gals, too. Hope leaned low over the table a half dozen times, nearly falling out of her dress, to ask him to play something even faster and wilder. Her face was flushed from the exercise and the pint jar she was waving around. She pushed it into Hank's face. "Drink up," she said. "Can't both of us be sad at my weddin'!"

He told her he was the furthest thing from sad, but she insisted. The shine was bright and clear, almost peppery. He took a long drink and handed it back, sure he'd be flushed and foolish, too, if he had much more. Hope wobbled up on her tiptoes to kiss him on the cheek. She missed, with a little help from her new husband's outstretched hand, and landed on her knees on the floor. Her arm flailed into the turntable. The record needle scraped across three tracks of Tom Petty's "American Girl".

Big, strong Chevrolet Ford stood over his upturned wife, his right hand raised like he was about to slap a mosquito off her cheek. "I knew you wouldn't quit!" he said. "Momma told me you'd never—"

"Nice way to start the honeymoon," Hank said. He could see Chevy Ford was the kind of peckerwood that wouldn't let marriage get in the way of a beating. Hank's stepfather had been one like that.

Chevy shook his fist at him "You shut up, or I'll give you—"

Farmer Garrison hustled over to grab Chevy's arm. "She didn't mean nothing, Chev. She's just happy is all."

Chevy pulled away, nearly toppling his father in-law to the dance floor. "She's nothin' but trash!" He glared at Hope. "All you Garrisons are. Blue State trash."

Farmer Garrison's big right hand shut Chevy up quick. Chevy fell against the table and knocked it over. The turntable bust to pieces on the ground, and Hank's records scattered.

The edge of the table had caught Hank in the chest and knocked the wind out of him. He saw Chevy's pa come up behind Hope's daddy and rabbit punch him in the neck. Farmer Garrison dropped, and his wife flew at the elder Ford like a wildcat.

The dance floor changed tempo into a brawl. Hank got up and felt his ribs to see if anything was broke. He couldn't breathe so well, but he didn't need air to see the spit and boots flying around the barn. Hank stuffed his records into the milk carton and prodded Hope with his foot. "Let's go," he said, wheezing. "Get your money."

They made it all of fifteen miles down the road before a sharp rock let the air out of Hank's front tire and brought them to a halt. The spare was flat, too.

Hope ran the jack while Hank worked the tire off the rim. One patch didn't do anything to keep the air in, so he tried two. He was up to three patches when the ugliest thing he'd ever seen pulled up behind them. It looked like it might have started life as a pickup truck, but in its death throes it had bedded a tractor and a tarpaper shack.

"Looks like your horse came up lame." Lucas stepped out of the hole where the driver's door should have been. "Might be time to shoot it."

"You here for your sister?"

He shook his head. "Chevy and his pa are looking for her though. Daddy bought us some time by sending them south. He sent me this way."

"Don't suppose you got a new tire in the back of that thing." Hank mopped his forehead.

"Not that will fit, but I got a couple of old turntables we might be able to get working. I hear the job's easier with two. Hope could teach the dancing."

"What about your family?" Hank said.

"Four more where we came from. Step-mother's brood. They'll do alright."

"Maybe you and me will, too," Hank said.

Lucas smiled. "You're getting the right picture now."

The wedding up north wasn't for another week. Time enough to get into one of the abandoned cities and look around for a record shop.

"Help me get my bike on that trailer of yours," Hank said. "We'll all go see if we can find something new to play."

See R.W.W. Greene's story "The Wedding of Hope Garrison and
Chevrolet Dodge Ford" online at Metaphorosis.
If you liked it, leave a comment. Authors love that!
Remember to subscribe to our e-mail updates so you'll know when
new stories are posted.

About the story

Most weeks during the summer, my spouse and I hold an open-grill event called "Grill Friday". We have the backyard, a cooler, tunes, and the grill. People start showing up at 6 p.m. with a six-pack and something to share. A lot of our people are vegan and vegetarian, so one half of the grill is dedicated to that. A few years ago, a friend was cleaning out her basement, and she brought her ex's record collection along. It had been moldering for years at that point, so I took it upon myself to sort through it and deejay the event with whatever was playable. The story spun up in my head from there. I'm fascinated with the physicality of the older recording methods. You're literally carving the sound into a solid object, and you can get it back out intact as long as you have a needle, an amplifier of some kind, and the right spin speed. We picked up a gramophone recently, and I've been getting it back into working order. It's all springs, gears, and resonators. Not a circuit or power cable to be found. Old tech but once high tech. Maybe high-tech again someday. The rest of the story came out of that.

A question for the author

Q: What is the scariest or most disturbing story you've ever read?

A: The 'man's inhumanity to man' thing always gets me, and one of the best examples of that, in my opinion, is Shirley Jackson's "The Lottery". Just cold, community-supported darkness.

About the author

R.W.W. Greene writes SFF and lives in southern New Hampshire.
www.rwwgreene.com, @rwwgreene

A word about M.E. Bronstein

M.E. Bronstein appeared in the very first year of *Metaphorosis* (20 May 2016), with "Solomon and the Dragon's Tongue", a beautiful story rich with imagery and metaphor. Not only is the final story fantastic (in every sense), it was very good going in. Despite that, during the editing process, Bronstein rewrote the story essentially from scratch — twice! And it just got better and better! Bronstein's been my internal benchmark for hard work and devotion ever since — a near impossible one to match, and one I've tried to apply to my own writing (with far less success).

Happily, she came back to our pages a year later, on 16 June 2017, with "The Illuminator Leaves", a heartbreaking, but in some ways heartwarming story about the price you pay for art.

Bronstein's brother, Ben, by the way, provided art for three of our covers. Art runs in the family.

Here, Bronstein returns with "Garden Teeth", a story about learning what it is you really want.

Garden Teeth

M. E. Bronstein

Before she died, Ethel gave Julie a stapled packet of parchment paper, plump and noisy with seeds. "For your garden," she said. Julie didn't bother explaining that she lived in a tiny, one-bedroom apartment where she and her husband struggled to keep a box of pansies alive on the windowsill. (And they had only gotten those in the first place because 'pensées' had Charles's favorite double-meaning in French: 'thoughts' as well as 'pansies'.)

They were getting ready for the move — and both Ethel and the pansies had been dead about a year — when Julie rediscovered the seed packet. She tore it open and little yellow-white teeth bounced and clicked across the countertop.

"Oh no-no-no," said Julie, "Goddamnit, Ethel, no."

Julie was a preteen when her mother met Ethel at a women's reading group that formed at shul, and the older woman took the younger under her wing. Ethel started to show up at their apartment some afternoons, and Julie would find the pair of them in the kitchen together, laughing and drinking, Ethel's hand lingering on the seat of her mother's pants; Julie always mumbled an excuse about her homework and went to hide in her room. Ethel interrogated Julie sometimes, checked what she knew about history, literature, and music. She never seemed satisfied, and gave Julie lots of new books to read, which mostly went ignored.

Some days, when Julie's mother realized she'd have to stay late at work, she asked Ethel to pick Julie up from school and watch her for a few hours (or, occasionally, overnight — Ethel first told Julie about the teeth on one such occasion. Back then, Julie assumed that Ethel was just fucking with her).

Ethel was prickly and intense, but there was something mesmerizing in the low urgency of her talk; most of her sentences sounded like little incantations as they flowed out of her. Julie learned that, in her youth, Ethel had been an 'important' (or mildly infamous) scholar, known for her reinterpretations of biblical women — very much a feminist-of-her-moment, all about recuperating literature's Liliths and Delilahs and Jezebels.

Ethel was tall, hair and eyebrows thick and bristling and zebra-striped. She had veins so vivid they almost looked like scars. One flicker of blue forked between her left eyelid and her eyebrow — like lightning, her brain's sparks showing through her skin. She wore heavy jewelry, chunks of stone that clicked and clattered when she moved, a walking billiards table, one piece of her bouncing against another. She could not look motherly, even when doing supposedly nurturing things like cooking. Years later, Julie would retain a vivid mental picture of Ethel: barefoot by the stove in her dressing gown, a cigarette tucked between her lips as she shooed tendrils of smoke and steam out of her gaze and stirred a pot of bubbling purplish-red plum soup. Ethel tipped some leftover wine into the pot, then drank the dregs right out of the bottle.

People asked what Julie would do, when she and Charles went east, and they meant for work; Julie wasn't sure, but she said she'd figure it out. She would not miss her old job. She worked at an immigrant history museum downtown that had been a beautiful Moorish Revival synagogue, built in the late 1800s. When she first got the job she'd imagined she would get to spend more time with the building's crimson carpets, stained glass, the stars painted on the vaults of the sanctuary, but in fact she spent most of her days scheduling tours under the fluorescent lights of the office next door.

So, Julie didn't have much of a 'career' to speak of. She could see herself slipping into domesticity, knew she would become a housewife and occupy herself with the children, tend to the garden. Julie was the only one of her married friends who had taken her husband's last name. Sometimes, when she talked to old classmates from college and high school, they acted like something was wrong with her, like she should want to be bigger and louder than her own mother had been, and she tried to ignore them.

As she packed for the trip, Julie sewed the teeth into the lining of her jacket. They shifted and settled against her on the way to the airport. She half-expected the metal detectors to keen in response to the strangeness of her cargo, but they didn't. Sometimes she'd put her hand in her pocket and the point of someone's incisor would needle at her fingertip. She felt like a kid with a chick hidden in her clothes, checking to see if it was hungry, cold — did it need anything?

As the plane took off, Julie flipped through her planner. She had a list of things to acquire for the new house. And at the bottom of the list, she regularly wrote, erased, crossed out, and wrote again: *Garden???*

She had scrawled the list on one of several post-it notes that coated the pages of her planner like shingles: to-do lists and shopping lists and various other lists and reminders. Charles leaned his chin on Julie's shoulder and studied Julie while she studied her lists. He said, "What kind of a garden do you want, anyway? Like a vegetable garden? Or something pretty with flowers and stuff?"

"I don't know," said Julie.

"I don't get how you can want a garden and not know what kind of a garden you want."

"I'll know when we get there," said Julie.

"That's not like you," said Charles.

"What do you mean?"

"You like to plan things." He tapped the book in her lap. "Hence the planner."

Julie closed the planner. "I'm throwing caution to the wind. We're going on an adventure. Why not?"

'Adventure' had been Charles's word for it, a way of gentling the sting of temporariness when, after two crushing years on the job market, he had finally given up on his hopes of an immediate professorship and accepted what was a more or less prestigious postdoc in what seemed like a pleasant place. Charles took the book away and laced his fingers through Julie's, clearly relieved that she was trying to see things his way.

After the flight, they got onto a train that would take them into town, and a thin sheen of sweat glittered around Charles's temples as he struggled to hoist their bags up onto the luggage rack. Then he became a sleepy puddle, his sneakers propped up on the seat beside Julie's as she sat opposite him and played with his shoelaces. Light and dark flickered out the window as they emerged from a tunnel, passed trees and telephone poles.

"Charles…"

"Julie?"

"Have I ever talked to you much about Ethel?"

"Your mom's ex? The scary lady who died last year?"

"Yeah. I wouldn't call her 'scary' exactly. There was just something a little — jarring about her." How to say whatever it was she wanted to say? Julie could almost feel the teeth chattering against her skin through the thin cloth of her jacket, trying to speak for her, through her. "She told me the weirdest story once. It was about a family of witches who planted the teeth of their dead like seeds."

"Ick. Why?"

"In the story, the teeth grew into trees and flowers that contained the witches' knowledge and memories."

"They couldn't just write that stuff down? Isn't that what writing is *for*?"

"The women in the story weren't allowed to read or write," said Julie. She asked suddenly, "Have you ever heard a story like that before?"

Charles always knew where stories came from. He thought for a moment, then said, "Well, Cadmus and Jason both plant dragons' teeth, but those teeth don't actually grow into plants; they become people. Then there's that one Brothers Grimm tale — you know, 'The Singing Bone'? One brother kills another and buries him beneath a bridge, but his bone sings, 'My brother killed me'."

"Hmm. But that's about brothers. This one is about sisters. And mothers and daughters and grandmothers."

"I'll look into it, if you like. But I'm not sure I'll find a clear or exact source — maybe it was something Ethel just made up? Anyway, did anything in particular make you wonder about this?"

"I don't know. I just catch myself thinking about her sometimes, since she died." She reached for a reason he would understand. "She wanted to be remembered and I'm not sure anyone will remember her except me."

Charles leaned forward, pressed Julie's fingers in his. "I'll look into it," he said again. "You said she was sort of a scholar, right? Maybe she wrote about this story."

Julie nodded, though that seemed unlikely. Something about the story had felt very private and secret when Ethel told it to Julie.

"Listen," said Ethel, "there's a story I should tell you."

Julie tried to figure out a way to tell her she wasn't *that* little (like seriously, she was twelve), and she didn't need a bedtime story or whatever. Ethel settled at the foot of her bed anyway and tried to figure out a way to begin and Julie let her because she didn't know how to ask her politely to leave.

At last, Ethel found her way into her story: "Once, there was an old woman who lived in a big house with her daughters and granddaughters. People don't like women who live in big houses all together, especially when they have sharp teeth, which these women did. Their neighbors spread rumors that the old woman and her daughters and granddaughters put on snakeskin at night and slithered through town biting people, poisoning them as they slept. And this wasn't the first time people had said things like that about these women; the old woman had run away and started over in many, many different places over the course of her youth and she was getting tired of it. She and her daughters were never allowed to learn how to read or write. People were afraid of what they would do if they could write things down.

"Anyway, during the old woman's final years, two of her daughters died. I don't know if people killed them, or if they just died of some combination of hunger and sickness. Anyway, the old woman's youngest granddaughter noticed that as her aunts died, new flowers appeared in their garden. And the old woman explained to her, 'Your aunts are not truly dead. They are still here. They can still speak to us.'

"One day, the old woman gave her granddaughter instructions to go foraging in the woods, and she told her she should not come back for three days. The granddaughter asked why, and her grandmother wouldn't tell her. But the granddaughter was dutiful; she did as she was told, and when she returned home, she found everything broken and blackened; their neighbors had burned the house and garden down. The granddaughter remembered what her grandmother had told her, that her aunts could speak through the flowers. She worked around her tears and picked through the ashes of the garden, searching for at least one petal that might have survived. Instead, she found three teeth.

"She hid the teeth in her boot and spent many years drifting as her grandmother once had,. Some strangers who didn't know any better would take her in and let her work in their kitchens, their barns, until something crept out of her that frightened them: a glimpse of teeth just a little sharper than most people's are. And then she would run away again.

"Eventually, she found a little village where she kept her mouth shut and didn't bother anyone, and so her neighbors grew accustomed to her and let her be. She settled in a hut with a patch of dirt where she grew a new garden. And she collected a couple of beggar girls and made them her daughters.

"The granddaughter (now a mother) planted her family's three teeth, and they grew into a mulberry, a willow, and a fig tree. Sometimes, when she listened to their leaves, she heard whispers, but they never amounted to anything meaningful. But when she tore a switch from her willow and stirred her stews with it, or when she drank tea made of the mulberries and fig leaves, she started to understand; her garden gave her verses, rhymes, stories, prayers. In a nutshell: knowledge.

"And the granddaughter became an old woman in turn, and she remembered old spells and poems, and spoke in others' voices, in riddles. Once, she hadn't been allowed to read; later, she was too busy moving and surviving to learn; now, at last, she had time, but she was too old and tired. She never learned and so never taught her daughters. She decided it didn't matter; they had their gardens instead.

"And one day, she told her eldest granddaughter, 'When I die, you must pluck the teeth from my skull and plant them in your own garden.'"

Ethel watched Julie for a reaction. Julie said, "Gross."

An old friend of Charles's had worked for a few years as a lecturer at the university, but since he had at last managed to snag a tenure-track job at a small college upstate, Charles and Julie inherited his townhouse at the edge of campus. The situation was far from luxurious (the floors linoleum, the walls peppered with the scars of previous occupants' nails and thumbtacks and the inverted shadows left by their posters), but it was still more space than Julie had ever been able to pretend ownership of since she started calling herself an adult. Charles's friend left a faded aroma of lavender and gin in his wake. In spite of the bright summer weather, it always felt chilly as a cave indoors, no matter how much Julie fiddled with the thermostat, and she often walked around beneath a heap of blanket.

About a week after their arrival, they were having their breakfast together in the new kitchen, Julie stirring instant coffee that smelled like dog food. Charles had a fat book out on the table, and Julie peered over his shoulder. It took her a moment to process the author's name at the top of the page: Ethel Milgrom. Her attention darted down the page:

Lilith makes a sideways, skittering appearance in Isaiah 34:13-14:

'And thorns shall come up in her palaces, nettles and brambles in the fortresses thereof: and it shall be an habitation of dragons, and a court for owls. The wild beasts of the desert shall also meet with the wild beasts of the island, and the satyr shall cry to his fellow; the screech owl also shall rest there, and find for herself a place of rest.'

The English I've just provided is from the King James Bible (venerable standard and monolith that it is). But you might notice that something is missing. Where, oh where is Lilith? I promised we would find her here.

I'll tell you: she's hiding (she does that). The KJV's 'screech owl' replaces the Hebrew 'lilit'. The Vulgate Latin likewise dances around Lilith and dubs this mysterious creature the 'lamia'. And so we have two phases of erasure, in Latin and in English.

Ever since, Lilith has hidden in various literary corners. In accordance with this pattern, I read her as hidden in Keats's Lamia; *picture her, coiled underground (under the page), waiting ...*

And then there was more stuff about the Keats poem, which didn't mean much to Julie, since she had never read it.

There were two pictures reproduced in black-and-white on the verso: Dante Gabriel Rossetti's *Lilith*, brushing her lustrous heap of hair, and John William Waterhouse's *Lamia*, on her knees before her unsuspecting knight, crumpled snakeskin hidden in a corner of the scene.

"I've been looking into Ethel's work," said Charles needlessly. "I haven't found anything about teeth yet, but it appears dear old Ethel had a serious thing for Lilith. And other snaky-demonic temptress ladies who eat children and lure silly men to their deaths."

"And what do you think? Of Ethel's work?"

"Oh — it's interesting? Entertaining? This fever-dream kind of theorizing isn't really my style, I guess. I'm a stodgy and traditional researcher and I like my clear and explicit arguments and evidence, thank you very much. I don't really get this stuff that was in fashion a few decades ago where you can almost smell the weed on the pages. But you should read and see for yourself."

Julie almost laughed; she knew already it would hurt to follow the windy path of Ethel's thought through her early-morning brain fog. "Maybe later," she said.

She stepped toward the sliding door beyond the kitchen table, and it stuttered on its track as she shoved it. She hovered on the threshold and let a breeze twine around her hair and ankles. Much more rousing than the coffee. Charles came to her side and they studied the lawn: a little stretch of grass with a chain-link fence around its perimeter. There was a big planter box with a pale wooden frame, poorly sanded and ready to give them splinters.

"Well?" said Charles. "What's it going to be? Vegetables or flowers or rocks or sculpture? That should about cover all possible gardeny things, right?"

"Flowers," said Julie.

Charles agreed, "Flowers."

The bedroom Julie sometimes occupied at Ethel's had clearly belonged to another girl once. Someone about her age, maybe a couple years younger — but precocious, smarter than Julie. Julie felt around the sharp edges of an old tragedy, which explained something about the way Ethel looked out of windows on rainy mornings, as though willing the day to complete itself. The meaningless tasks she gave herself: scrubbing already-clean surfaces, disentangling old skeins of yarn she would not use anyway, sifting through lentils and picking out the brown and pebbly ones. The kinds of tasks an evil stepmother would assign her stepdaughter, but Ethel was the stepdaughter and stepmother in one very garbled package.

Asking about the other girl would be wrong, invasive. And yet Julie kept running into pieces of the room's shadow occupant. She found ancient and moon-pale pads of gum wadded on the underside of the desk. There were bright scraps of tissue paper glued to the window in a child's facsimile of stained glass, so that looking outside meant looking through the wing of a giant, demented butterfly, all patchwork crimson, teal, and amber.

Julie benefitted from the yellowing paperbacks left on the room's shelves and got to know her predecessor's handwriting in the margins. The two of them were often at odds with each other. The other girl disliked quietness. Julie wanted to write a retort whenever she found a frowny face in a book's margins. The other girl wrote *boring* a lot when authors waxed too descriptive and went on about landscapes or architecture.

I don't believe you, thought Julie, one eye on the colorful window. Whoever she was, the other girl had been in the habit of wishing herself elsewhere — even if she didn't like to admit it. Julie could feel her restlessness brined in the room's murky light.

Julie was not a natural gardener. Once, in her early twenties, her uncle had trusted her with housesitting while he was on vacation, and she killed his potted geraniums and spider plant with over- and under-watering respectively.

Not that being a decent gardener mattered much. The flowers were just a big and showy thing to distract potential naysayers from her real project: the teeth. Still, Julie bought a pile of gardening books and looked up whatever was seasonal and local and more or less straightforward to take care of. Which meant flowers with names that sounded like they belonged to debutantes in pearls and silk gloves: dahlias, peonies, clematis.

They went to a nursery and collected dahlias with fat pink and orange heads. It turned out they had plump tuberous roots, and Julie wondered if you could eat them like potatoes and parsnips. Fleshy, mandrakish. Julie read that they liked bone meal. She roasted a chicken, picked the fat off its bones, boiled them clean. She turned the bones brittle in the oven before wrapping them up in a plastic bag, and when she smashed them with a meat tenderizer, Charles ran in to check that she wasn't murdering someone.

Later, Julie sprinkled bone dust into holes in the planter box's soil, hefted the flowers and set their tubers gingerly in place. Each time she did so, she'd glance back at the house, the windows, to check if Charles was watching her — he sometimes did, amused by the spectacle of her and dirt, which did not ordinarily go together.

Her husband's absence confirmed, Julie would slip a tooth out of her pocket and put it into the earth before she planted a dahlia to guard it.

Some of the flowers needed to lean on stakes to hold their fat heads upright. Once she had planted about five of them, Julie stood back and admired the effect. Her radiant and crooked children.

Meanwhile, Charles occupied an office at the university and made friends with a handful of new colleagues. Once they had settled in sufficiently and cleaned the house, he invited them over for dinner, and they discussed university politics; Charles compared 'back home' and here. Julie wasn't sure why he kept calling the other place 'home' when it seemed unlikely they would go back. She made ratatouille for dinner with a colorful array of tomatoes from the farmers' market, and Charles's new colleagues praised her cooking and asked what she did, which Julie and Charles jointly deflected by making jokes about the garden, it being Julie's new 'project'. They took their guests to the yard, where they shivered in the early evening chill. Twilight burnt the deep blue sky orange at the edges, early stars and satellites blinked above the trees' shivering silhouettes, and the little dahlias looked very squat and simple next to that.

"My Lilith," said Charles, one hand on her shoulder.

"Who?" said Julie. "Me? What? No. What do you mean?"

He said, " 'The rose and poppy are her flowers.' "

Rossetti. "No-no," said Julie. "Away with you. No roses or poppies here."

"In spirit."

"Not in spirit. Dahlias. Dahlias in actuality."

"That's harder to fit into iambic pentameter."

Julie got self-conscious then, especially because of the bright and promising young professor who'd asked what she did in the first place, and the way she squinted at Julie, and Julie could almost hear her thinking, So, *she cooks* and *gardens*, as she checked Julie's back for a wind-up key.

Julie pressed her shoulder blades against the house's clapboard walls.

She listened and listened. Not to Charles and his new colleagues — who talked about Rossetti, Keats, poets and painters and their flowers — but to the garden.

Waiting, always waiting, for it to start talking.

One day, Ethel unearthed a cigar box hidden behind old, dark bottles of whisky and amaro in the liquor cabinet.

Inside the box were several little muslin bags, each tied shut with a pale string. Ethel took one of the bags out and handed it to her. Julie loosened its opening and carefully spilled some of its contents into the palm of her hand.

There were bits of dried flower, fragrant and brittle. And a few shriveled pods. It all smelled like earth and roses and decay.

Ethel gestured for Julie to give the bundle back to her. She transferred its contents into a tea ball, which she submerged in a mug of hot water.

She gave it to Julie. "Drink," she said.

Julie hesitated. She remembered the story. The granddaughter who stirred her witches' brews with willow wands and nibbled like a silkworm on mulberry leaves, and was changed by what she consumed.

"Drink," said Ethel, and Julie didn't know how to get around the clear note of command. The tea was still very hot and it burned her tongue. She waited, terrified, expecting to croak, for toads and snakes to fall out of her mouth like the wicked girl in that one fairy tale.

Ethel watched her until she drank the whole mug of tea, then took it from her and dropped it in the sink amid a mounting pile of dirty dishes.

Julie kept waiting. But nothing happened, and that almost disappointed her.

That is, nothing happened until much later — a few days after drinking the remains of some old garden of Ethel's (or Ethel's grandmother, who knew?), Julie was in her English class, staring at a pop quiz, and at first she couldn't remember what 'ossify' or 'nacreous' meant, but then it came to her. Not only that, but she knew both words' Latin roots, even though she'd never studied Latin.

Later, Julie poked around corners of her memory and discovered fragments of other languages. And stories. And spells and riddles.

In her dreams, she smelled flowers and her teeth were sharp as thorns.

The dahlias had been in place about a week when they started to wither. Pink petals turned orange, then brown, and curled into themselves. Julie thought of dead spiders with their legs coiled into their abdomens, salted leeches, burning paper.

Their heads drooped. Every single one.

Charles said maybe something underground was lunching on their roots. He suggested pesticide and Julie said no.

The first weeds appeared a few days after the dahlias died.

Julie made no connection between the weeds and the teeth at first. The books had informed her: look out for weeds, they will sneak in.

Julie tore out creeping, twining threads of green and brown and their little leaves. They kept coming back. Some weeds she knew (buttercups, clover, groundsel), others she didn't. She took pictures and sifted through her books. Corncockle and feverfew and chickweed. They looked innocuous, pretty even — little purple and white flowers, tiny and starry. But then they spilled out of the planter box and spread through the yard.

The garden knotted, tangles of color resurging almost as soon as Julie eradicated them. When she retreated to the kitchen and guzzled a glass of water, Charles held her face, rubbed at a smear of soil on her cheek and said she looked like she had come back from a fight with a dragon —

And then something clicked.

Dragons, serpents, lamias. Witchy, snaky women with sharp and needling teeth.

It all felt so much like a trick they would play. She gave them a home and they gobbled up her dahlias.

Could it be? She couldn't confirm without digging and inspecting the teeth to see if they had burst open and all this life had started crawling out of them. And Julie couldn't do that, wouldn't upset or disrupt them.

That evening, she woke up after midnight. Charles didn't stir as she crept out from their sheets, tugged on a sweater, slunk downstairs, to the yard, shivered and studied her handiwork. Hoped to catch the teeth in the act overnight, when they didn't expect her.

And then, a strange call — low and hollow. It stretched out and then stuttered, repeated after itself. Probably just an owl. They had weird calls out here. There was one species that locals said chanted, "Who-cooks? Who-cooks-for-yooouuu?"

And Julie might have accepted that it was just an owl, might have gone inside again, if not for the yellow flowers.

It could have been a trick of the gloom and starlight, that they seemed to glow and pulse, flower heads that had been closed for the night opening to peer at her. And Julie stepped backward, hovered on the threshold. In another frame of mind, she'd have laughed at herself. Quaking before a bunch of glinting weeds.

She retreated, hand rattling as she slid the door shut and locked it, like the weeds would creep in after her if she wasn't careful. She went back to bed and wondered if Charles would notice when he woke up that they had new neighbors, a little coven of dandelions that hadn't been there the day before. Weedy lions' teeth bristling out of the earth.

After Ethel made her drink the tea, the voices stayed in Julie's head for maybe a couple of weeks, and then they faded and Julie became herself again. The scraps of language and knowledge she'd imbibed got lost somewhere. And so Julie resumed being Julie, a mediocre student, listless and inclined to stare at the window instead of listening to the teacher.

Julie thought about asking Ethel for more of her tea. She could feel Ethel waiting for her to ask for more.

In a really stupid way, the voices that had traveled from the dried leaves and petals into her brain had been her only friends, these past few months. The only people who really paid attention to her — not like the girls she ate lunch with in the cafeteria, who only ever wanted to talk about bad pop groups and parties Julie hadn't been invited to.

But those little voices whispering at the back of Julie's head had scared her, too. Their attention sometimes felt hungry, desperate. Like wayward mountain lions, coyotes, hunting for chickens in their neighbors' backyards.

One lingering memory explained the underlying principle: that a tooth's fruit could be tamed and tempered a little; a flame and boiling water could cook just a little of the voice out of it so that it would sit in her gut without devouring or clamoring over her. So, Ethel had been protecting her, by giving her a taste of the garden-as-tea; that made consuming the garden a little safer. But still: the threat of being overtaken. It was there.

They had lain dormant for a long and lonely time.

Julie had been old enough by then that her mother trusted her more on her own. She stopped asking Ethel to look after Julie, who didn't see Ethel for months at a time. Though sometimes her mother still gave Julie books and said they were from Ethel, and Julie would open them up and pressed flowers would fall out from between the pages and into her lap. She flushed them down the toilet.

Dandelions' yellow and white heads dotted the planter box and the surrounding grass, a lacy froth of petal and pappus. The planter box had turned into an overflowing pool of weeds — greens and tawny golds, shocks of purple and white and yellow — that spilled out and softened the boundary between the box and the rest of the yard.

Charles approved. "The other flowers — what were they again, dahlias? — that was all wrong, I see it now. Manicured, artificial. This feels... wilder. More natural. It's pretty."

But he only said that because he couldn't hear them.

Not that Julie could, either, really. But she almost could. Maybe they had been quiet for so long, they'd forgotten how to talk, and so they couldn't communicate in any identifiable language — but there was an intensity about the garden, a ghost of noise, like a faraway growl of thunder, an itch buried deep in Julie's skull. She gathered dandelions, tucked them into her hair, arranged them in mason jars and left them to wilt on the kitchen table. She kept them nearby. She listened.

And still they wouldn't talk.

Later, Julie wouldn't be sure what took her so long, why she hesitated.

One day, she had spread a picnic blanket in the yard and had a sunhat on and lounged with a magazine in her lap. Some of the flowers were heavier than they should've been, their petals brittle. Almost like they were tiny, very accurate sculptures of flowers, rather than the real thing.

Julie closed her book and plucked a pale globe of dandelion. She twirled its waxy strand of stem between her fingertips. She tried not to fidget it to death, but it still shed feathery seeds across her lap. She listened.

The dandelion has many uses. Its petals can produce a delicate yellow dye. It's also been called piss-a-bed (after its French name, pissenlit) because of its diuretic value. It can soothe troubled stomachs and teeth. But to most of us, it's an invader, bright and annoying. So, what else would Ethel's child choose, to grow out of her soul's soil? It had to be her.

Julie remembered that if you consume the fruit of garden teeth thoughtlessly, it will eat you up from the inside out, sprout out the top of your skull and speak its own poetry.

And then she ate the dandelion's head off. She gagged a little (it tickled).

It chattered as it fell through her.

She remembered that some people believe the dandelion's airborne seeds are like will-o-the-wisps, souls of the dead drifting on the wind.

Even after Ethel and Julie's mother grew apart, they still talked a lot, and Ethel always asked how Julie was doing and still sent her too many damn books (no more flowers pressed into them, though, like maybe, just maybe, she was conceding defeat on that front). Julie visited her a handful of times over the course of her adult years.

The very last time Julie saw Ethel before she died, Ethel had covered the windows up with heavy curtains and lived in the dim, and Julie caught herself tiptoeing around patches of molten light that slipped inside, like she'd burn herself on them if she weren't careful.

Ethel brusquely swept coats and old skeins of yarn off the couch before she let Julie sit, then brought out a tarnished tray cluttered with old porcelain. She stirred her tea with a silver spoon even though she hadn't put honey or anything in it.

Ethel said, "You're grown up now."

"I don't feel very grown-up," said Julie mechanically.

"And you're married?

"Yes," said Julie. She rushed to add, "If there had been a real wedding we would have invited you. Charles was busy, and neither one of us wanted it to be a big thing, so we just went to the courthouse with a couple of friends for witnesses."

Ethel nodded and sipped her tea. "Little Julie," she said. "I can't believe it."

And Julie showed her pictures from the courthouse — half to prove the truth of what she'd said. It was nice at least to talk to someone about it who wouldn't probe about her husband or ask if he meant to convert (not that Julie's mom gave a damn, but too many aunts and uncles did). Julie had worn a short-sleeved dress, pale champagne silk. Julie told Ethel about Charles. "You'd like him," she said.

"I'm sure you'll be very happy," said Ethel, as if the prospect bored her. "Cheers." She startled Julie then by asking when they would have children. She didn't ask *if* they wanted children, but *when* — as though the children in question were an expected infestation, like cicadas, and Ethel had only forgotten where they were in the cycle, how many years were left until they swarmed aboveground again.

"That's kind of a personal question, Ethel."

"Can't I ask you kind of personal questions?"

"I guess. Well, the answer is, I don't know. Soon. Before long."

And then, Ethel startled Julie again by talking about her own daughter.

"We used to have a garden," said Ethel. Her daughter used to dig holes in it. She said she was digging a well. She'd come inside and fill a plastic bucket with water, take it out (sloshing all over the place), fill the hole she'd dug, then would get upset when the water just faded into the earth, and it darkened and softened.

She loved dandelions, but only after they'd turned pale and feathery, and she'd breathe them to pieces. (She didn't know that some people think dandelions are prophetic: blow and then count the leftover seeds, and you will learn how many years you have left to live.) She loved the buttercup game but always held them too close to her chin and crushed them.

Ethel's daughter spent less and less time in the garden as she grew up. Ethel had been trying to think about ways to entice her back into the garden when — well, you know. Forcing her would have backfired anyway; she was the kind of daughter who would scream and squirm if made to do anything she hadn't decided on herself.

They shook hands as Julie left. Ethel's fingers felt so small and dry, but she clutched Julie's hand so tightly, her heavy rings became signets, marking Julie's skin like wax.

The dandelions grew and spread beneath Julie's skin.

Julie and Charles were getting ready for bed, hovering around the sink as they brushed their teeth. Charles spat and stared at Julie, and she said, "What?"

He reached and touched her throat; his fingertips traveled, traced her collarbones. Julie studied herself in the mirror, tugged at her nightshirt to better see the skin of her neck and chest, and she found a sequence of yellowish patches: dark at the center, a starburst around the edges. Something between a bruise and a flame caught beneath her skin.

"How'd that happen?" said Charles.

"I'm not sure," said Julie. "Must have been while I was gardening."

"It looks like someone threw rocks at you or something."

"Yes, the neighbors come and stone me when you're not around," said Julie, then regretted joking when Charles's mouth flattened. She had buried herself in gardening, hadn't started to look for work or any foothold in the local 'community'. What was the point, when they would just leave in a couple of years anyway, when Charles went on the job market again? Putting down roots felt foolish. The dahlias had taught her the illogic of that.

"It's probably some kind of rash," said Julie. "An allergic reaction. I must have touched something funny in the garden, then scratched myself."

It didn't hurt or burn or itch, though.

Charles nodded, gnawed his lower lip, visibly chose to believe her — for now. The dark way he studied her through lowered eyelashes said he'd check soon whether or not the mysterious bruises faded or lingered, and Julie found herself strategizing already, mentally picking out turtlenecks to wear that lay buried at the bottom of tightly taped boxes of winter clothes they hadn't even bothered unpacking.

The next day, Julie went to the farmers' market and came back with a basketful of plums, which she cut in half and pitted, and Charles came home and looked over her shoulder at her bubbling pot of purple and said, "Oh my, a witch's brew!"

"A recipe from the Old Country," joked Julie — and only then realized that it was Ethel's recipe, not something she'd grown up with herself. She said that plums were in season, and he asked if she needed help, and when of course she didn't, he set up his books on the table and kept up whatever work he'd started earlier in the day at the university.

While Julie leaned over the pot and its steam curled up in her hair, he spoke.

He said, "What's that?"

"What's what?"

"That tune," he said.

"Tune?"

"You were whistling something," he said. He considered, then added, "I don't think I've ever heard you whistle before."

And now that he'd interrupted, Julie could feel the song leaving her lips, but could not for the life of her retain whatever it had been.

Julie forgot to answer sometimes when Charles said, "Julie? Earth to Julie?" She forgot, again and again, that that was her name. It had gotten lost somewhere in the petals she gathered and sugared, then mixed into her oatmeal.

She went foraging in the woods near campus for yellow chanterelles (she knew where to find them now) and didn't come home until midnight, her forearms scratched and bruised.

She dipped a needle in ink and drove it into the flesh of her thigh because she remembered an old design that used to live there — a stylized dog rose — and she missed it, knew it had kept her safe.

They had the same conversation over and over. Charles said things to the effect of *You're making me nuts. Are you trying to make me nuts? Are you trying to punish me for taking you away?*

But he hadn't 'taken' her anywhere — she had come because she wanted to. Julie had followed him, because that was Julie's thing. To find someone to trail after, because she didn't know what to do with herself otherwise.

He had asked many times if she was okay with it.

"I know, I know," said Julie.

She hadn't been happy, back west. Or that was how Charles put it. News to her — but she got what he meant. She hadn't been thriving.

"And you thought I would do better here?" she said. In new soil? Did he think the fresh, different air would clean the shadows out of her brain? (She giggled, and Charles said, "Are you *laughing*?" And she said, "No I'm giggling.")

He had been thinking of their future, the family they were planning, and they needed money, he needed to have something resembling a career to realize their plans, since Lord knows Julie wasn't showing much motivation in that regard, and that should have made Julie angry, but it didn't. She thought of Ethel. Perhaps Ethel had in fact chosen her because of her dullness and normalcy. All Julie wanted was a family, and so she would give the teeth daughters to talk to, and more teeth to put underground in turn.

Charles said, "I just want you to be happy. Please tell me what will make you happy."

Then it rained and rained and Julie sprouted a fever and Charles took care of her, brought her tea and pressed wet towels to her forehead. He stayed home from the university and lingered by her side.

Julie could not remember smelling things in her dreams before the teeth. But now bursts of perfume and musk wafted through her sleep. Pretty scents like jasmine, honeysuckle, rosemary, but also the dry-erase funk of soft brown apples, cherries, plums melting and fermenting in sticky puddles of sloughed off skin.

And she heard whispers.

The lamia, the serpent in the garden, sows her own teeth to grow a garden of memories.

If you hear your child laughing at you know not what, perhaps your little girl has devoured the fruit of some witch's garden teeth, and you must touch her nose and intone, "Out, Lilith!"

(If you want Lilith out, that is.)

Once there were a grandmother, a mother, and a daughter. When the grandmother died, the mother sowed her tooth, which grew and became an apple tree, and the good and dutiful daughter ate an apple, and so the grandmother took root in her granddaughter and spoke out of her mouth.

When the mother died, the granddaughter sowed her teeth, which became a blackberry bush, and she fed blackberries to her own daughter in turn.

You see how this goes. A pattern, an unending braid of the same three women, over and over. Eating, becoming, birthing each other.

Apples and blackberries and and and.

Cloves or maybe clematis or cardamom.

Around goes the daisy chain.

Sometimes, a young girl slipped through Julie's dreams. About nine or ten years old. A flash of dark hair, wavering behind a tree. Playing hide-and-seek. Julie stepped toward her; a branch snapped beneath her weight. The child giggled and lurched away. She ran uphill, and Julie followed her.

She was losing her, the girl going too fast.

Julie wanted to call after her, demand that she stop. But she couldn't. She touched her own mouth, pried her lips apart. Pulled on her tongue to make sure it was still there.

"Rose!" she called, because that, it turned out, was the girl's name.

And Rose stopped. She had led Julie to a clearing in the middle of the forest with a house in it. An ugly, squat little gray building, but surrounded by a colorful and very weedy gated garden. The gate was open and Julie stepped through.

The garden was full of dandelions and bees and flies and life. It turned out to be much more expansive than it had seemed from just outside the gate. Tall grasses brushed against Julie's skirt, thorns prickled against her skin. She followed an avenue between densely gathered shrubs and low trees with twisting branches. The scene darkened as she got lost in it, the swampy green dim interrupted only by starbursts of dandelions. Behind her, Rose said,

How to entangle, trammel up and snare
Your soul in mine, and labyrinth you there
Like the hid scent in an unbudded rose?

They took one turn, then another, and another. Julie realized she wouldn't be able to make her way out of this place again without Rose's help. The girl laced her fingers through Julie's and led her deeper into the maze of trees and dandelions, and Julie let her.

When she woke at last, Julie stayed languid and clumsy. She kept knocking things over by accident and cut the soles of her feet on broken glass. When Charles suggested they make a doctor's appointment, she insisted no, she was all better, she just needed time to find her legs again, and she did not tell him that there were a few minds stuffed into her head beside her own now, and they weren't used to the weight and length of her body.

She fell back into the rhythm of her life, more or less. Except she kept getting that life just a little wrong as she forgot how to put on an accurate performance of 'Julie'. The Julie Charles knew always complained about the cold and kept the windows shut; the unbudded rose in Julie kept opening the windows and letting flies and wasps and moths inside. Charles hated things that tasted like licorice, and Julie knew that, and yet she kept putting caraway and anise in their food. She forgot to turn the gas off, and Charles shook her and said, "Jesus, Julie, wake up! Where the hell is your head?"

How to explain that she was just filling in the gap of a young girl's death? While the other women faded in and out of her, Julie had given Rose a permanent maze to hide in. And it was frightening to realize how much she liked that, liked dissolving, becoming someone else, someone more important than Julie.

Charles suggested again and again that Julie look for work in the area, even though his stipend was generous enough to support them both; he didn't like all the time she was spending alone (he didn't know that she wasn't *really* alone).

Julie had an old necklace of Ethel's with a chunk of jasper for a pendant: striped orange, polished and cool in her hand. She gathered henbane from the garden, purple veins crackling through its white petals. She made a nest of flowers in a bowl, laid the jasper at its center like an egg, and Charles slept very soundly that night. He woke up later and more slowly than usual, smiled foggily at Julie. He kissed her forehead and left her to her gardening.

As autumn came and the garden wilted, Julie wrapped bouquets of dandelions in twine, pressed buttercups between the pages of Charles's books, sealed nettles and mallow blossoms in jars. She brewed teas and broths and sifted through thoughts that weren't hers.

She had a faint recollection of pliers, cotton, a little plastic bottle of rubbing alcohol. And blood on white porcelain, fading to pink as it mixed with water.

Ethel, tugging out one of her own teeth before she died.

Faded memories of her mother came and went, too: how Julie's mom stared at Ethel with wide eyes, how she called her 'brilliant' and 'sharp', like she was a sunrise or a cliff face, not a woman, even though sometimes, all Ethel really wanted was to be soft and muted with someone.

Charles started to apply to jobs again. Last time he had gone through this process, he asked Julie's advice, made her read his dossiers, probably just so she felt involved even though she didn't always understand the point of his work.

This time, however, she became much more interested. She scribbled questions in the margins of his writing samples. She dashed off check marks when Charles said something surprising or creative. She wrote *boring* when he went on too much and made basically the same point over and over. Charles laughed and said, "Harsh. But okay, I see what you mean."

Julie whispered to the dried garden by moonlight, and offers came in the spring as the garden bloomed again.

They started to talk more about the things they used to dream up together. They talked about children. What they would call their daughters. They talked about these things even when the henbane and jasper started to wear off, and Charles looked at her so warily sometimes, like he didn't recognize her. Julie knew his uneasy sense that she wasn't (quite, or just) the person he'd married would slowly push them away from each other, the way creeping weeds and ivies can become part of a wall and then dismantle it.

Sometimes Julie felt her canines with her tongue and imagined that they were just a little bit sharper than they used to be. Or maybe that was Rose, crawling on all fours beneath the dining table, pretending she was some kind of wildcat. When Ethel peered down at her, Rose hissed, and Ethel said, "What the hell are you up to, you crazy kiddo?"

Julie remembered Ethel (she remembered *being* Ethel), her pen starring the page as she hunted for signs of Lilith in Keats's *Lamia: Her throat was serpent, but the words she spake / Came, as through bubbling honey, for Love's sake.* Ethel, who mixed and muddled her literary interpretations with biblical apocrypha and kabbalistic sources, noticed that the *Zohar* described Lilith in rather similar terms: it compared her tongue to a sword, her words to oil, her lips to roses full of sweetness. Ethel saw kinships between all these women with lions' teeth, snakes' skin, and owls' wings, who lurked in forests and gardens and swamps.

Julie remembered being Ethel, sitting at the edge of Rose's bed, and then Julie's, telling her a story. And Julie remembered — no — Julie could *foresee* (it was hard to tell the difference between remembrance and foresight when you were just part of a daisy chain of mothers and daughters, of Liliths and Lamias) how she would do the same damn thing, tell the same story to a resistant daughter, who would maybe become a little less resistant over time.

It was hard to imagine Charles, who had once loved her docility and quietness, being or staying a part of that picture. Best to hide as much as she could from him.

Julie remembered and foresaw as she washed the dishes; she'd hung a crystal-and-brass suncatcher by the kitchen window and flakes of iridescent shadow wavered up and down her arms. Charles paced in the next room, describing two competing job offers to his parents over the phone. After their talk petered out, he rejoined Julie, dried the dishes she had already cleaned. He reported on the call, then asked, "So, what do you think? Where should we go next?"

Julie said it didn't matter — they could go anywhere.

So long as she had space for a garden.

See M.E. Bronstein's story "Garden Teeth" online at Metaphorosis.
If you liked it, leave a comment. Authors love that!
Remember to subscribe to our e-mail updates so you'll know when new stories are posted.

About the story

I'd say this story started with dragons' teeth before anything else. I've been intrigued for ages by Ovid's account of Cadmus sowing the dragon's teeth (which Charles alludes to briefly in the story), and the image of teeth-as-seeds just felt very dark and witchy, and so other associations started to spring up. That's often where stories begin for me, with weird images and chasing whatever connections feel intriguing. So, in this case: dragons' and serpents' teeth, dandelions (i.e., "lions' teeth"), and mythical women often associated with serpents, like Lamia and Lilith.

A question for the author

Q: What is your favorite fairy tale and why?

A: I always struggle with "favorites"! But I am a sucker for Beauty and the Beast and its assorted variants, especially Cupid and Psyche (the Crafts' gorgeous picture book was a major childhood favorite). As for why: that's a little difficult to articulate... but I'm often drawn to stories that capture something ambivalent about women's experiences, rather than insisting that they must be absolutely passive or agentive? Plus there's all the dense, very pretty symbolism. I also once taught a course on Beauty and the Beast and Bluebeard, as well as various retellings (broadly construed), and the unsettling ways the two story types can resemble each other.

About the author

M.E. Bronstein is an academic and creative writer who studies medieval translation practices and writes various kinds of horror and dark fantasy. Her very first short fiction publication appeared in *Metaphorosis*; since then her writing has also appeared in *Beneath Ceaseless Skies, PodCastle, khōréō magazine*, and elsewhere.

mebronstein.com

A word about Laurel Beckley

We first published Laurel Beckley on 22 October 2021, with her story "Tell the Crows I'm Home", about an older woman in rural Oregon trying to come to terms with a changing world. I loved the story from the moment I saw it — this was the kind of story *Metaphorosis* was created to house. If you haven't read it, you should put it at the top of your list. You'll be grateful you did.

Happily, Beckley also participated in our most recent original anthology, *Museum Piece*, a collection of stories about unusual museums. Beckley's story, "The Museum of Perpetual Service" offers a grim warning about the incentives that can pervert faith and loyalty into meaningless spectacle — but also about how to take charge of your own destiny.

Here, she's back in our pages with "But No Man Moved Me Till the Tide", a completely different story about embracing your true self despite pressure from others.

But No Man Moved Me Till the Tide

Laurel Beckley

Myrna met him on the bluffs above the cove after dinner.

It was a moonless night, the height of autumn. A night for sea monsters and storms. She closed her eyes, letting the presence of ocean wrap around her, as if she were the island being caressed by waves, as if she were swimming through the depths in her true form, currents whispering across her fur.

The wind whipped her curly brown hair, tickling and tangling while its icy touch nipped her exposed cheeks and ears. The approaching storm sat offshore still, kicking up the white-caps and pushing the stench of salt and fish guts and rain. It seemed like each year the storms arrived earlier and earlier, and with them the dangers of the deep.

Myrna opened her eyes. Fog enveloped everything but the piercing beam of the lighthouse above.

Flash. Four seconds. Flash.

She smelled Gabriel's human-musk before he crested the bluff. He was freshly shaved, hair slicked down with orange-scented pomade and wearing his nicest suit, which happened to be his lighthouse keeper's uniform. His hands, however, held his day's work embedded within each crease of skin.

"Hello, Miss Coates," Gabriel said.

His eyebrows bunched together as he eyed the pelt she carried in her arms, cradled like a child. She'd brought her pelt at her mother's insistence, tucking the grey-speckled fur so it resembled a jacket, the paws clenched tight in her fists so he could not wrest it from her. This was nothing like the uncivilized days when humans stole otterkin pelts and forced them onto land, but Myrna remembered the old stories. She didn't hand it over. Not yet.

As an otterkin, Myrna had known this moment would come. But unlike her cousins and older sisters, who'd spent their girlhood afternoons crafting scrapbooks and dreaming of the mysterious spouses who would arrive to bind the wild thing lurking inside all otterkin, Myrna had stared into the white-capped waves surrounding their island home. They'd grown up and found spouse-keepers, while Myrna had refused each human placed in her path. She'd always preferred the ocean to land. Her soft fur to pink flesh. And now her fate was here, in the form of her most persistent suitor, who would propose to her at any moment. He'd ask for her pelt and half her soul, and she'd have to obey, because that was what otterkin did.

Myrna clamped her lips tight to keep the brewing cry of refusal from erupting across the sea. The wild thing inside her scraped her chest, wanting out. Silence stretched between them, interrupted by the squawking of a gull.

"Would you like to walk along the ridge?" Gabriel asked.

Myrna nodded, not trusting herself to speak without screaming. She could do this—for herself, and for her family. Gabriel was a kind man, a man who rescued jellyfish and fixed broken seagull wings and treated her younger cousins as children, but what person *wanted* an otterwife? A woman bound forever, a woman who was strong and loyal and could never leave, even in the most isolated of postings? A woman shuttered?

Their boots crunched sand and hallowgrass and rocks. Each step felt heavy as tradition and her family's increasing expectations weighed upon her, heavier than the cloudy night sky. Her family hadn't seemed to mind the loss of half of themselves. They had welcomed it with sighs of relief, as if they'd spent their whole lives waiting for the wild thing to be tamed. Her sisters would say she was lucky to have such a kind man wanting her. Her mother would tell her to stop protesting and submit, because this was as good as it got, and far better than she could have expected. But how would it change her, to give her soul to another's keeping?

Gabriel stopped at the trailhead leading down to the cove where her family swam each moon night, the only time their spouses allowed them to assume their true forms. Waves passed over the pebbled beach. The rocks trilled as the water ebbed back into the ocean, the sound rising through the fog.

"I know it's fast and we should have brought a chaperone, but we worked together all summer and I thought—I um, I want to do things proper, for you." Gabriel paused, fiddling with the lapels of his jacket. "My posting here ends in the spring. My next station is to the north, in Alanshaw. It's a single keeper position."

A single keeper with a spouse, if they had one. Without a spouse, he would be alone for the two-year tour. This was why he wanted a wife. Why he pursued Myrna.

It was a shame, Myrna thought, that she was the only one of marriageable age.

Gabriel bent, one knee resting on the rocks and sand, and looked up at her. Her breath caught. It was happening.

"Myrna, I—" Gabriel began, stretching a hand toward her.

His fingers brushed against her pelt. She jerked back from the touch, a lump clogging her throat, stoppering the scream, forcing it through her body instead of out, until she felt like she would explode if she didn't, if she—

"Myrna—"

His eyes were wide, pleading, the color of the ocean on a summer day, but reality was staring at her too and even though she was expecting it, she couldn't—*she couldn't give it up*. She took another step backward. Then another and another, one after the other, down past the rock outcroppings and the verbena and the sand as the waves crashed harder against the shore and the pebble-song screamed across the rocks and the storm wind picked up into a howl.

She ran until cold water kissed her shins, and then she wrapped her pelt about her shoulders and dove into the sea.

The fog and frigid water swallowed her whole, engulfing her in a harsh and angry and cold world as an undertow snagged her, dragging her down and down and down to the silt and rock bottom.

Myrna shed her boots with a kick, giving them to the ocean and shoving her feet into her pelt. She never swam in her human form—how ungainly, how slow, when she could be *majestic.*

Something brushed against the thick fur on her back. She yelped, spinning to catch the silvered flicker of a giant sea bass slicing into the deep. She twisted her body, hooking one paw around an algae frond as an anchor while she oriented herself, eyes adjusting to the dark.

She had been dragged further and faster than she had expected. She was no longer in the shelter of the cove, with its fields of coralline algae blooming in red and brown and mud-green, but had been pulled beyond the jetty, where the bottom dropped and the tall kelp grew. Where she was forbidden to go alone. Her heart hammered. She needed to get back to shore. To face—

Myrna did not know what fate waited an unwed otterkin. She'd only known of one. Eyde, who'd left the island when Myrna was a toddler and was only mentioned in whispered conversations among the oldest otterwives on winter nights when the shutters shuddered from the howling storms.

Myrna had broached the subject of not marrying once, and her mother had told her otterkin always wed because that was what was done, and that she'd better be quiet or the sea monsters would take her. In marrying, an otterkin severed her ties to the sea and wildness and bound herself to humanity and civilization, and that was that.

Since she had turned eighteen, her mother had shoved men— and later, women and a few people who were neither man or woman—onto her daughter with increasing desperation and irritation.

None of her family understood Myrna's reluctance. They had been happy to give away their pelts, to set themselves firmly on land and a life of marriage and babies. They treated their monthly excursions to the cove as honoring their history, but while the sea was the source of their livelihood, it wasn't their life. It didn't sustain their souls, not like it did Myrna. She craved the wildness with a yearning she couldn't quite put into words. In the sea, she was free. She didn't want to give any part of herself away.

Myrna closed her eyes to stop her tears. The ocean didn't need more salt. She had to go home, and face her mother's disappointment.

She had taken only one stroke toward shore when she heard it.

The song rippled through the waves, soft and cooing. It came from beyond the tall kelp forest, the sound wending through the fronds and the stipes. Thoughts of her family, of Gabriel and expectation, fell away. Longing screamed through her, tearing away thought and reason and rationale and pulling all of her wants and desires just out of reach. The singer *yearned*, just as she did. There were no words, but she knew this desire, this need for something beyond…beyond. This desire to fill the hollow in her chest, to heal wounds scraped raw and bleeding.

The ocean's bottom plunged away as she emerged from the kelp forest.

Myrna kicked backward and grabbed a frond with her paws, the cold undercurrent threatening to sweep her into its depths.

The song faded. Myrna clutched the frond, straining to hear. The ocean was quiet and her heartbeat thrummed in her chest and her chest ached from the need for air and the song grew louder once again. The singer was right over there and—

The song turned sword-sharp and bloodthirsty as thick tentacle whipped up from the depths, spearing toward her.

Myrna screamed as another tentacle rose to join the first. She thrashed through the fronds, retreating through the forest toward shore as fast as her paws could pump.

Her vision greyed. Her lungs burned. She had to breathe.

She burst to the surface, and sucked rain-clogged air through her sharp teeth. The waves rolled high and vicious and the downpour of rain mixed with the tears streaking her fur-covered cheeks. When she caught her breath—she'd been in one place too long, far too long, surely the monster should have caught her by now—she plunged back into the water.

There was no sign of pursuit.

The monster had vanished, leaving only its song wending through the fronds of the forest, once again softly yearning, laced with such sorrow and regret that Myrna nearly swam toward it again. She fought the song, fear keeping her oriented to the shore. She swam the entire way without stopping, until she emerged onto the pebbled beach, never noticing the gills that had sprouted beneath her ears.

The storm raged about her as she cried and coughed the saltwater from her lungs. Her sobs mixed with the crash of waves and the howl of wind. She'd grown up hearing wintertime stories of sea monsters and the dangers of the deep waters. The past few years of winter storms had brought the sea monsters closer to the island, but there was ocean's breadth in the difference between hearing about a danger and facing it. Even on shore, she could feel the song echoing through her bones, and she did not know if her tears were of relief, or regret.

Not one of her family had ever said the sea monsters *sang*.

Gabriel kept up his courtship as if the night on the bluff had never happened, leaving flowers and a pink ribbon and a mewling grey kitten, as if the gift of a living creature would endear her to him. Myrna avoided him and hid her pelt in the carved space of a dead tree and tried to forget that the night of his proposal and the monster had ever happened.

Myrna heard the song again as she helped her youngest niece crack a mussel during their next moon night. She'd volunteered to watch the youngest girls, to teach them to pull their pelts about their shoulders, how to find the best rocks and tuck them into their foreleg pouches, how to surf the streams into the kelp meadow and forage for the tastiest sea urchins. She'd hoped that in teaching them she'd find that spark of motherhood, that desire for creation and nurturing that seemed to reside in everyone but her. Instead, she felt nothing but frustration.

The song was faint, and lonely, and before she knew it she'd drifted to the edge of the meadow and was between the first stipes of tall kelp. She pulled herself away—her otter limbs felt long and sinewy and strange—and dragged her niece to the surface, checking over her shoulder to see who else in her family was captured by the monster's siren song.

"Did you hear that?" Myrna asked her niece.

"Hear what?" the little asked, nibbling on a clump of seaweed.

A hiss nearby, from the cluster of teenage cousins floating in the middle of the cove. Their teeth bared in silent accusation for stringing Gabriel along when *they* would have been a much better match, if only they had been old enough to marry.

At the weight of their stares, Myrna pulled her niece to shore, fighting the song's pull with every stroke. No one else seemed to hear it. There must be something wrong with her, something that made her different enough to hear the sea monsters when no one else could. This difference scared her, because she didn't know what it meant.

As fall turned to winter, Myrna retreated into herself, avoiding her family as diligently as she did Gabriel.

She tried to ignore the gossip surrounding her, from her aunties, who gathered in clumps by the fireplace at nighttime, muttering, *Not like Eyde, no, not like her.* She tried to avoid her married cousins and sisters, but they sought her out while she was in the middle of her chores, telling her it was time to stop staring at the sea and get married to Gabriel already. They never said it outright, but she knew they thought it was past time for her to give her pelt into a human's keeping. Taming their wild thing was the civilized thing to do. As much as she dodged her cousins, Myrna couldn't avoid her mother, who just eyed her with a mix of frustration and pity.

Myrna bottled herself up, suppressing the wild thing that burned in her chest. She craved escape, but unlike before, when she could flee into the water whenever her family's expectations for her future became too much, now a sea monster waited for her in the depths.

She knew it was still there, because it stalked her.

Its siren song reached out to her on land, humming incessantly in her ears. The further she pulled from her family, the more the song tugged her, strumming along the tip of her tongue, leaving her irritable and filled with a yearning she could not explain because she did not have the words. It infected her soul, and she could not tell anyone because she didn't think anyone else had ever felt like she had before. Surrounded by her perfectly content aunts and cousins and sisters, Myrna felt like an island in a vast sea, besieged by fierce storms on all sides. It made sense that the sea monster targeted her. She was different. She was wrong. And the monster's song was her punishment for staying unwed and turning her back on tradition.

For keeping the wild thing inside her instead of giving it away.

Rain lashed the roof. Wind clawed the wood siding. The lighthouse's foghorn trumpeted, warning ships away. The monster's song shrieked above everything else, high and vicious and hungry.

Winter was sea monster season, when storms pushed the creatures closer to shore. This year was different. Four wrecks this month alone, each with survivors who spoke of tentacles wrapping about the masts, hurling their ships against the rocky shoals. The Head Keeper told his otterkin wife that he had never heard the ocean sing during a storm before, and she had told him it was just the wind over the rocks. But these stories brought the aunts together, whispers of *Eyde* and *never so bad before* and once, just when they thought she was out of earshot, *not Myrna.*

It was all a circle, from Gabriel chasing her to her aunt's outraged stares to her mother's sighs to her cousin's whispers to Myrna berating herself, asking what was *wrong* with her. Why couldn't she just say yes? Why couldn't she submit, like the rest of her family?

The monster's song changed, from vicious cry to sweet coo, warm and welcoming.

Myrna pulled her pillow over her head, trying to drown out thought and sound with goose down and cotton.

Her bedroom door banged open. "Abigail is missing," Myrna's mother said.

They rushed outside, Myrna urging her youngest siblings to stay *inside*. Her aunts and eldest cousins were already racing toward the cove, their white nightgowns clinging to their strong bodies, turning them into wraiths attacking the night.

Abigail was halfway down the beach when they found her, bent double and sobbing as she staggered toward the churning black water.

One of Myrna's aunts grabbed her arm, but the girl flung her off and was almost in the water when another aunt tackled her. It took all of them to hold the girl down, her eyes rolled white and her mouth open in a scream of need as her heels drummed the pebbled beach. Someone clubbed Abigail across the temple and the girl sagged. Her limp arms stretched toward the water, as if even unconscious she yearned for what the song promised.

Myrna stepped away from the thrum, rubbing her bloodied nose. She was on the verge of tears and didn't know why. The song caught her, its crackling desire meeting the wild thing inside, and she took three steps toward the water without even realizing it when the sharp sting of a slap brought her back to reality. Her oldest cousin grabbed her arm and dragged her back to her house, snarling that Myrna shouldn't have come, that this business was *married* women's work.

The aunties gathered at Myrna's mother's house that night, clustering about the hearth. Myrna boiled water for tea. She knew she wasn't allowed at this meeting, but she thought if she made herself useful and kept quiet she might learn why this was happening.

Myrna arrived with the tray right as her eldest aunt jabbed a finger at Myrna's mother and hissed, "Tell that girl to get her head straight and accept the boy already. We *cannot* have another Eyde."

She couldn't stop herself. "What happened to Eyde?"

Her aunts turned, their eyes dark and vicious, their teeth flashing otter-sharp from the light of the fire. "Go back to bed," her mother said.

Myrna fled.

Another storm hovered on the horizon.

Myrna grabbed her jacket from its peg by the door and left the house, ignoring her nieces' stares as they stopped flipping through last season's fashion magazine to watch her. Their whispers started the second her back was turned. Myrna wished they knew that she was just as scared as they were, that she didn't know why the storms were so bad this winter and why something lurked in the cove beyond the breakers. She wished they knew all these things, and yet she couldn't tell them, because speaking the words meant she'd have to admit she couldn't marry Gabriel, and to admit that meant that she was wrong and broken and the cause of everything.

She was the reason her family suffered. She knew she had to fix it, but she didn't know how. The only option she saw was unacceptable. Surely there was a way to keep her family *and* her soul? To keep herself for herself, and herself alone?

She walked straight to the shore without pausing to check her pelt in its hidey hole.

The waves were tall and vicious, sea foam whipping off the white caps and flying toward shore. The pebble beach's song screeched like hunting birds, even as the whisper of the sea monster's song caressed her cheek. Myrna wondered what it would be like to give in to the song, to dive into the waters. To sing instead of listen.

"Myrna?"

She turned away from the water. Gabriel stood at the top of the trailhead to the cove. His head bowed against the wind, his arms wrapped protectively around something the size of a winter jacket. Her stomach clenched.

He closed the distance the second he saw the horror on her face, thrusting her pelt toward her with both hands. "Your mother gave it to me."

Rain stabbed her cheeks, ice cold and spear-sharp. She didn't take the pelt. She couldn't move, couldn't speak.

So.

Her family had chosen for her, had gone back to the old days of pelt stealing. It was done. She had thought she'd feel *something* —that love her mother mentioned, or resignation or revulsion or anything at all, but her family's betrayal emptied her, excavating the wild thing that had lived inside her until she was a hollow shell.

Above her, the lighthouse beacon flashed. Four seconds. Another flash, cutting through rain and clouds and reminding her that anything she had wanted was just a dream—untouchable and nonexistent.

Words tumbled from his mouth, spilling like sea foam across the pebbled beach. "I really did want to wait. I had no choice. I'm being reassigned early." His hands clutched her pelt, his fingers smoothing and straightening it with as much gentleness as he had shown that newborn kitten. She'd given the kitten to a younger cousin, but she couldn't give this away. His voice dropped to a whisper, barely audible over the shrieks of the approaching storm. "I'll give it to you whenever you want, not just on moon days." He looked up at her, his face earnest. "I will love you. And you—you will learn to love me, too?"

As if she had any choice in the matter, anymore. "I will be whatever you wish of me, husband." Her voice was a croak, the word *husband* tasting like rotten fish in her mouth.

Hurt danced across Gabriel's eyes, and he tucked her pelt against his chest. It lay in his arms like a dead animal. He opened his mouth and took a step forward, but his eyes widened as he took in something behind her. "Oh, seas," he gasped.

Myrna turned to see what it was, and he grabbed her arm, jerking her toward him.

A fierce howl pierced the crash of waves. There was a flash above, the lighthouse slicing through the fog, and Myrna turned in time to see a massive tentacle lift out of the waves to wrap about the boulders at the edge of the cove. Another scream, a hunting song, angry and hungry.

The sea monster had come to shore at last.

Gabriel lunged for her. Myrna tried to sidestep him, tried to flee, but he grabbed her upper arm and whipped her around to face him. "No," he gasped. "I won't let you go."

Myrna stared into his eyes and saw her future unspool before her. Marriage and babies and expectation and all the things she could never do. Perhaps there would be pockets of joy and laughter with Gabriel, but she would never throw off the shroud of imprisonment. If she stayed, she would never refill the hollow inside her. The fear that had been building ever since that night in the kelp forest vanished, leaving only resolution.

The sea monster's song rose into the air, a triumphant battle cry, but she was not afraid. She did not want to die, but better that than the future that awaited her if she stayed with Gabriel.

He tried to pull her ashore, but she stepped away, jerking her pelt from his unresisting fingers. "I was never yours."

He did not reach for her again.

The song softened, the sea monster shifting away as Myrna took step after step down the uneven edge of the jetty. With the fog shifted, there was a woman standing at the end, wearing her nudity with the unconscious grace of an otterkin. And Myrna knew she *was* an otterkin, for despite her shark-sharp teeth and the kelp streaking her curly brown hair, she was the mirror image of Myrna's mother.

"I have grown tired of waiting for you, niece," Eyde said.

Myrna lifted her chin, trying to hide her confusion. "I thought the sea monster was here to kill me."

"There is death, and death." Eyde remained where she was, unafraid. "Did you ever wonder where the sea monsters came from?"

Myrna hadn't. Sea monsters had always existed, ruling the winter seas. "I don't understand."

Then she did. It was obvious, in retrospect. Sea monsters and otterkin were the same. She could not see through the fog, but she imagined Gabriel stood on shore still holding her pelt. Beyond him were her family and everything she knew. They were the ones who chose to bind themselves instead of embracing the wild thing that lived inside.

"They know, but they are afraid," Eyde said, her voice soft and gentle. "Why do you think they honor marriage and tradition as they do? But some of us cannot fit into their world, no matter how hard we try. And so we choose another way."

The lighthouse flashed above, its beam cutting through the fog, reminding her of the island and family and tradition. A wave crashed over the rocks, sea foam swirling about her legs, the ocean promising her adventure and a life bound to herself and the sea alone. Myrna was caught between sea and shore, but the hollow in her chest felt just a little bit less empty. Because for the first time in her life, there was a choice beyond what she'd always known.

Myrna turned back to her aunt. "There are more...people like us?"

"An entire ocean full." Eyde stretched out her hand in silent offer.

Freedom, but in exchange, she'd become a monster. She would lose her family, and everything she'd known. But she would gain herself. She would *live*. She would be among others just like her. Myrna glanced toward the shore one last time. And perhaps, eventually, she could return and make her own way back to her family. Both her, and the wild thing that lived inside.

She took her aunt's hand, and together they leapt into the sea.

*See Laurel Beckley's story "But No Man Moved Me Till the Tide"
online at Metaphorosis.
If you liked it, leave a comment. Authors love that!
Remember to subscribe to our e-mail updates so you'll know when
new stories are posted.*

About the story

The seeds of "But No Man Moved Me Till the Tide" started, oddly enough, in 2012 when I visited Chincoteague, VA. As a longtime fan of Marguerite Henry, I'd always wanted to visit, but surprisingly, the ponies were not the things that stuck out to me. I was intrigued by the Assateague Lighthouse (repainted since my visit), the isolation of the island itself, and also by a docent I met at the museum who was very kind—and who I didn't realize had written a book on the community of Chincoteague until I was at a bookstore an hour later and saw her name on one of the books.

However, the story itself was supposed to be a secondary world steampunk-ish fantasy novel about a journeyman lighthouse keeper who was 100% human. Because it had no plot, I stalled out at 45k words, and *The Keepers* has sat untouched on my computer since 2016. In 2021 I wrote a short story called "Terrible Tilly Hunts the Cadborosaurus" (*All Worlds Wayfarer*, Issue X), which resparked my thoughts of lighthouses, otter-shifters, and islands. In 2022, after reading a brilliant *Little Mermaid* retelling (I can't remember who wrote it) and feeling trapped by the anti-LGBTQ+ legislation being pushed throughout the US, I started playing around with a short story called "Otterkin", taking pieces of *The Keepers* and transforming it into a story about tradition, queerness (specifically, asexuality) and not fitting in with rigid societal expectations. I'd also been reading a lot of folklore about cryptids (specifically, animal-brides), which is where the otterkin people came from.

I tend to either know the titles of my writing right off the bat, or give it a working title like "Otterkin" or *The Keepers*, and then scour the internet for something in the public domain that catches my eye/fits the vibes of the story. "But No Man Moved Me Till the Tide" is a line from Emily Dickinson's poem, "I Started Early — Took My Dog".

This story took a lot of editing—I've ripped this story apart and pieced it back together more times than I can count, both by myself and with feedback from *Metaphorosis'* Morris and my short story writing group—to figure out what I was trying to do with this piece, to the point where the words stopped wording and my brain was no longer braining (this happens more often than you'd think). Many thanks to Morris, my writer's group, my wife and my friends. It really takes a village. Thank you, dear reader, for picking up this work out of the millions out there. And, museum docent Myrna, thank you most of all.

A question for the author

Q: Do you read more fantasy or SF (hard or soft)?

A: Both science fiction and fantasy are going through a huge renaissance right now, and it's just a great time to be an SFF reader. I'd love to say that I read both equally, but my reading spreadsheet reveals the lie. I read a lot more fantasy than science fiction, although science fiction is my favorite genre. I'm not really into hard sci-fi, although I will read it—I'm a mood reader to my core and I read a little of almost everything. The actual science and technology matters far less to me than political/social allegory, plot, character development and world-building, which is probably why I am a huge science-fantasy fan (the squishiest of soft sci-fi).

Since I'm a librarian, here are some recently-ish published favorites I recommend. Sci Fi: *Light From Uncommon Stars* by Ryka Aoki, *The City We Became* by NK Jemisin, *Gideon the*

Ninth by Tamsyn Muir, *How High We Go in the Dark* by Sequoia Nagamatsu, *An Unkindness of Ghosts* by Rivers Solomon, *Some Desperate Glory* by Emily Tesh, and *All Systems Red* by Martha Wells. Fantasy: *Saint Death's Daughter* by CSE Cooney, *The Spear Cuts Through Water* by Simon Jimenez, *Jade City* by Fonda Lee, *The Bone Orchard* by Sara Mueller, anything by CL Polk, *The Dawnhounds* by Sascha Stronach, and *The Unbroken* by CL Clark.

About the author

Laurel Beckley is a writer, Marine Corps veteran and librarian. She lives with her wife, fur creatures, and a collection of gently neglected houseplants.

thesuspectedbibliophile.home.blog, @laurelthereader

Summer

A word about Philip McCulloch-Downs

Philip is a vegan artist based in Somerset in the UK. He has spent all his adult life exploring and refining his creative skills and has learned how to process the varied experiences of everyday life through his art, video-making, novels and poetry.

Since 2014 his artwork has entered the world of veganism and animal rights. His series of uncompromising paintings 'Moving Pictures' attempt to dignify the creatures we abuse and to bear witness to their suffering by recording it with accuracy, empathy and compassion. He also produces vibrantly coloured and highly detailed pieces in ink and acrylic paint that celebrate the beauty and majesty of free-living wildlife.

He has exhibited his art prints at *Vegfests* and vegan events all over the world, including the *International Animal Rights Conference* in Luxembourg. In 2020, he and fellow artist/activist Helen Barker created the online gallery "Agitate Art" on Youtube, as a showcase for all forms of 'Protest Art'.

www.philipdownsart.co.uk

instagram.com/vegan_artivist

A word about Michael Gardner

Michael Gardner is a member of the elite Meta4osis club — authors who've published four or more stories with us. We didn't accept his first story, but the second became "Renewal", published in September 2017. From then on, we published "This Side of the Wall" in January 2018, at 15,362 words, the longest full story we've ever published; "Nana Naoko's Garden" in October 2018; and "All That Remains", in August 2020.

We like Michael's work so much that he's one of just five authors whose work we've published in serial form, with "Infinite Possibilities" published from September to December 2022.

One of Michael's strengths is an ability to take outlandish situations and not only make them plausible, but show the human and emotional trials of the characters that confront them. The following story, "Colossus", is a perfect example.

Colossus

Michael Gardner

Alexi Vanderbilt lived in the upper right thigh of the Colossus. Floor to ceiling windows built into the flesh of the mummified giant afforded him a handsome view of the ocean. It was angry, and lashed the coast on which the Colossus stood with foam crested waves. On the horizon were dark clouds, lightning spiderwebbing their underbellies. A storm that was predicted to reach landfall before it exhausted itself, something the colonists had no record of.

Alexi had originally found the forecast hard to believe, but the wind had risen violently during the last hour and now rattled the window in its frame. He felt the drop in temperature through the glass. Alexi's days were largely indistinguishable from each other, so the prospect of something new caused his skin to tingle with anticipation.

The apartment system chimed softly. "Show message," Alexi said, his attention still with the storm. There was a gentle clicking sound, then Miriam's message with details of his next job appeared in green text within the glass of the window. It brought him quickly back to mundanity. He sighed, read it. Excessive heat in one of the premium apartments. Mr Rowbotham's residence. He had the vague recollection of doing some work there last year. Maybe the year before. If he recalled correctly, Mr Rowbotham was an elderly man that insisted on being called Commander.

"Remind me of the location," he said. The text dissolved, became an image of the complex and in red, a rectangle showing him a large apartment, top centre in the chest. "Log the job. I'll be up shortly."

The image faded. A gust of wind spattered the outside of the window with fine droplets of rain. It stopped as quickly as it started. Alexi leaned closer to the glass, ran a dirty finger along the window surface, leaving a smudge. He shook his head, smirked. Unbelievable.

After taking a last glance at the storm, he collected his bag of tools from the kitchen bench and left his apartment.

The Commander led Alexi to the kitchen. "You feel that, son? It's like the oven's running."

Alexi frowned, peered over the kitchen bench to confirm there was an oven and it was indeed off. Alexi didn't use an oven. Too old fashioned. And expensive. The Commander's kitchen opened into a spacious loungeroom with expansive windows. They offered panoramic views that took in the ocean, the sprawling terraformed gardens that surrounded the Colossus, and the barren desert beyond. He wondered how the Commander had afforded such a prime location, such a large space. He appraised the man with a sideways glance. Straight back, tall, grey crewcut. "It is warm," Alexi admitted.

The Commander gave a curt nod. Alexi placed his bag of tools on the ground, removed a flex screen, unfolded it. Moving his fingers swiftly across the thin glass, he brought up the diagnostic program, attempted connection to the Commander's home system. He was prompted for approval. He passed the screen to the Commander, who raised it for an eye scan, handed it back.

"The kitchen is running five degrees above your preferred settings. The air conditioning system is attempting to compensate but is failing. The kitchen is the hottest room, but your entire apartment is warmer than average. This is odd. It's possible the storm is interfering with our systems." Alexi glanced across the loungeroom and out the windows to the purple-grey clouds that filled the sky. There were now several columns of hazy rain falling in the distance over the water.

"Huh," the Commander said, an exhalation of breath. "Perhaps. Or perhaps it's age. Some days I feel this complex is degenerating more quickly than me. You should have seen it when it was new."

Alexi looked up from his screen, found the Commander regarding him with sharp eyes. "You were here when this was first built?" Alexi asked.

A smile flickered across the Commander's lips. "I was. I was the first person to move into the Colossus."

"You don't look old enough," Alexi blurted out.

The Commander chuckled, an odd, staccato sound. "Oh, I'm plenty old enough. I'm first-generation. I've had some regenerative work, but the best tip I can give is stay active, physically and mentally."

"I will, sir. Do you mind if I ask what you did?"

"Engineer. I helped build the offshore mining rigs after we landed, but my proudest contribution was solving our permanent accommodation issue. We overcame the lack of natural resources by utilising this," he said, gesturing to the apartment.

Alexi whistled softly. There weren't many first gens left. Alexi found it hard to imagine what it had been like for them. Life seemed so routine now. Dull, even.

In contrast, this man had volunteered for a one-way trip in stasis. Had woken over a decade later to establish the colony and build the laser array to propel the light sails of the fleet that followed. Millions of people had relied on them. Without the colony's propulsion system, the carriers would never have achieved the speeds necessary to reach the new home world with sufficient fuel and supplies.

The first gens had known they wouldn't follow the fleet. Everything they brought with them was used to construct the mines and laser array, including their ships which were broken down and repurposed. The first gens epitomised sacrifice for the greater good. Their reward was to watch the carriers pass, to celebrate and farewell them with blasts from the array, then to exist as best they could. Yet Alexi sensed pride emanating from the Commander. A sense of purpose and contentment.

What did Alexi have in comparison? He hadn't contributed to the great mission. The salvation of humankind had been achieved long before he was born. The biggest event in his life had been choosing a career of maintenance over mining. Some days, he wondered if it would have made any difference had he simply chosen to sit around all day doing nothing.

He noticed the Commander waiting, watching. "Thank you for your service, sir," Alexi said.

The Commander smiled, nodded. Alexi cleared his throat; conscious he wasn't paid for chit chat. "Do you mind if I check your service hatch?"

"Of course."

The Commander led Alexi from the kitchen into a short hallway. The silver hatch was built into the far end. The Commander unlocked it with an eye scan, and Alexi pulled it open, leant inside, then jerked back like he'd been slapped.

"What's wrong, son?" the Commander asked from just behind.

"The heat," Alexi said. But that wasn't the whole truth. When he'd thrust his head inside the hatch, he'd heard something: a low thump. A sound like a soft strike of a bass drum. He eased his head back inside the hatch, found it silent. He used his flex screen to turn on the dull strip lighting in the hatch. He examined the mummified, grey flesh of the Colossus hidden just behind the apartment walls. It was marbled with fibre and copper cabling, reinforced with steel beams. But something was odd. The flesh, which had always been dry, glistened. He ran fingers along the surface, found it warm, damp. He removed a thin silver probe from his jacket, pierced the flesh, watched readings flicker across his screen.

He read them in disbelief.

He read them again.

"Find anything?" the Commander asked, and Alexi jumped. He took a breath, removed his head from the hatch.

"Maybe. But I need to run further tests." He looked around for his tool bag, realised he'd left it in the kitchen. "I'll just grab my bag." He turned to go, but stopped when the Commander said, "What the hell is that?"

Alexi turned and found the Commander pointing. He followed the outstretched finger toward the thin probe that Alexi had left impaled in the flesh wall. From it ran a thin trickle of something darkly red which looked very much like what it couldn't be. Blood.

"There are five more complaints about excess heat on floors eighty-six, seven and nine. There are also two complaints about noise on floor eighty-three," Miriam said through the transmitter.

"We have a problem, Miriam."

"You're closest to the Armitages', should I alert them that you will attend to them next?"

"Are you listening? We have an issue. Something strange is happening."

A pause. "What do you mean?"

Alexi took a breath. "The heat in Mr Rowbotham's apartment is not a result of faults in the wiring or air conditioning. The heat is being generated by the flesh of the Colossus."

A longer pause. "I don't understand what you're trying to tell me. We have complaints lining up. We need to address them. That is your—"

"I know what my job is," Alexi interrupted. "I'm telling you the heat is not a fault in the system. It's the... it's..."

"What?"

He sighed. Gathered his thoughts. "The inner wall was bleeding."

It was a long time before Miriam spoke. "But that's impossible."

"I'll send you my readings."

"Okay. But while I review them, make yourself useful. Check the central climate control system. Just in case."

Flurries of rain slapped at the windows that lined the corridor. Alexi stopped and pressed his face to the glass, looked down. He saw rain falling for the first time upon the terraformed gardens around the Colossus, and the large desalination plant that supported them. Up to now, rain had seemed a distant phenomenon, something that fell well out over the ocean. He shook his head, set off again toward the access panel. The wind buffeted the apartments.

Alexi unlocked the access panel, pulled it aside, stepped through into the vast space beyond. The sound of the rain grew softer.

The climate control system had been built on the remains of the Colossus' diaphragm. The space in which it sat was cavernous, gloomy. Grey flesh infused with fibre cables, copper, criss-crossed steel beams. Yellowed ribs encased huge lungs that hung loose and deflated like ancient curtains. The room smelled of dry earth.

The huge cavity was poorly lit, so Alexi switched on his torch. He aimed it toward the middle, where the light feathered across the steel housing of the distant climate system. It was large, about the size of one of the smaller apartments in the calves of the Colossus. He stepped carefully across the uneven floor of muscle, began the trek toward the system. The floor felt spongier than he remembered.

When he reached the system, he found the casing covered in moisture. Alexi ran a finger along it, raised the liquid toward his nose, sniffed. It smelled of nothing. Water, he presumed.

He opened the access panel, connected his flex screen, which told him that the system was working overtime to compensate for excess heat throughout the building. Alexi found no faults with the system itself. He disconnected, closed the panel, had turned to go when he heard a loud thump from above. He jumped, swung his torch up, the beam wavering.

He ran the light slowly over ancient, rubbery arteries. The usually deflated white casings were semi-engorged, crimson beneath. He shone the torch on the monstrous grey heart, usually withered. Not now; it had swollen. As he watched, it clenched. Alexi nearly dropped the torch, regathered, tried to hold the beam steady. He saw the heart release and the sound it made was a deep thwomp. The vessels around it shivered, red pulsed, stopped. Everything was still again.

Miriam sat behind her white desk, eyes closed, nose pinched between thumb and forefinger. Her office was immaculately clean, smelt lightly of bleach. There were no decorations on the walls. The only furniture was the desk, the bank of computers, the two black chairs opposite her in which Alexi and the Commander sat. Behind her, glass panes allowed a view of the desert, the corundum mine visible on the horizon.

"That's impossible," she said again.

"I know."

She opened her eyes, let her gaze drift from Alexi to the Commander, who sat ramrod straight. "And why are you here?"

"The Commander was with me when we discovered the blood. He also designed these apartments. I thought he might be of assistance."

Miriam cleared her throat. "Okay. If there is light to shed here, please do, because presently I'm at a loss to know what to do with this information."

Alexi turned and looked hopefully at the Commander. For a beat, all he saw was an old man, but then something hardened in the Commander's eyes.

"I can't explain why the Colossus has begun to regenerate. It's as unfathomable to me as to you, ma'am. But for whatever it's worth, I can provide a little history.

"I was on the first ship of colonists to arrive, and the presence of the giants was a shock. Our scouting crafts and probes had no record of sophisticated lifeforms, and yet we discovered six colossal, sexless bipeds, somewhat reminiscent of huge Neanderthals. This had either been a terrible, improbable miss, or evidence that the giants had been first hidden, then mobile in the years between our initial explorations and the arrival of the mission.

"We were initially very wary. But investigations revealed that the giants were lifeless, even though the corpses exhibited few signs of natural decay. It was like they had been unnaturally preserved; their poses staged."

"Which is impossible?"

"Yes."

"So, if you knew so little about them, why take the risk of utilising them for housing?"

"We were only twelve years ahead of the interstellar fleet and our primary objective was the laser array. The successful settlement of humans on the new world—El-Salalong—depended on an operational array propelling the light sails of the fleet as they sling-shotted around this planet.

"We had sufficient materials to build the array, the corundum mines, and temporary accommodations. Long-term arrangements were left to our ingenuity. But as you can see from that view behind you ma'am, natural building resources were not readily available.

"The giants presented a solution. We had ample sand for glass, we had some iron supplies, but there were no trees, just scrubby bush and seaweed. The giants offered an existing structure that we could utilise for our homes."

"I'm assuming you triple checked they were dead before you moved in?"

The Commander snorted a laugh. "I can absolutely assure you they were. The readings we took suggested they had been dead longer than we knew was possible given previous observations of the planet. The flesh had dried and hardened into something reminiscent of timber, the bones like concrete. The idea that they are now softening, well..."

"Yes, well..."

There was a long silence, which Alexi chose to break first. "What do we do?"

Miriam sighed, closed her eyes again, shook her head. As she opened her mouth to speak there was a groan, the floor of the office jolted hard, and the glass behind Miriam cracked from base to top. The three looked at each other with wide, stunned eyes.

"An earthquake?" Alexi asked.

"I think," the Commander said quietly, "The Colossus just moved."

Alexi stepped out of the giant's foot and into driving rain. The wind gusted strongly, and he had to lean into it. He squinted against the deluge, raised his hand. He was soon drenched, cold. The scent of salt from the ocean overpowered the usual dusty smells of the desert.

Lightning flickered overhead, followed closely by the low rumbling of thunder. The waves of the sea were white capped peaks, lashing the shore a few hundred metres away. Date trees swayed in the storm, and the shrubs around the Colossus cowered close to the ground, beaten down by the rain.

Behind him, the building moaned. Alexi spun round, looked up and shielded his eyes against the stinging rain. He tried to spy what had caused the sound, tried to check his memory of the creature's longstanding pose. The task seemed impossible. It was difficult to take the creature all in at once, and as he scanned the Colossus from top to bottom, shoulder to shoulder, he realised that for years Alexi had taken its presence for granted. An inert structure, blue tinted windows cut into the flesh. But now, outside, with the image of the creature's beating heart in his mind, he looked upon the form anew. It stood tall, proud, one foot slightly ahead of the other, arm raised and pointed to sea. Yet the grey, dried skin around the glass seemed ruddier. And although he could not sense any significant change in the giant's position, he felt it leered down at him. He shivered.

Another moan. Alexi's eyes darted about, finally settled upon a trickle of broken glass that fell from high up. The glass glinted as it fell, the sound of it striking the sand obscured by the downpour.

He engaged the transmitter in his jacket, called Miriam.

"There's evidence of more damage outside," he yelled over the din of the storm. "There're broken windows, and glass is falling. I'm worried about the structural integrity of the building." And he was worried the Colossus was waking, which was what he refused to say out loud. The thought was equally frightening and exhilarating.

"What do you suggest?"

"Ultimately, it's your call. But I think we should evacuate. Otherwise, we'll find ourselves stuck in this thing."

He heard soft breathing from Miriam. "Do you think it has something to do with the storm? The electrical activity?"

"I don't know. I honestly don't."

"Where would our people go?"

"The mine."

"Let me put in some calls to the other colossi. If they're not exhibiting the same changes, they might offer better options then the mine."

"And if they are?"

"Just let me make the calls. You prepare the vehicles."

Alexi drove the fourth transporter up out of the subterranean car park and onto wet sand when Miriam's voice broke into the cab. "It's not just us," she hissed. "The Warrior has collapsed. The Lady is trying to fucking stand. Some of the apartments have been crushed. They estimate twenty-two colonists dead, more injured."

Alexi sat in the cool cab of the transporter, breathed heavily. "Dead?"

"Dead, Alexi. The giants are coming to life and crushing the inhabitants."

"Why didn't your colleagues warn us?"

"They were pretty fucking busy trying to save themselves."

Alexi felt time slow for a moment, then it snapped back fast. He blinked a couple of times, rubbed his hands furiously over his face to clear his head. "We need to evacuate, Miriam. Now."

"Okay," she said. Alexi heard a siren wail from inside the Colossus. He opened the transporter doors, stepped out into the rain. He looked up, saw more fragments of glass falling to the ground. He took in the outstretched hand of the Colossus, saw it clenched, not finger extended as it should be. The skin was a deep brown hue. There was new hair on the knuckles, on the forearms, curling over the blue glass in its wrist.

Alexi tore his gaze from the giant, ran into the building.

As the residents emerged from the stairwell Alexi directed them outside and toward the transporters. The residents looked frightened, panicked, so Alexi did his best to maintain calm. But it was difficult with the building—he had to stop thinking that way— the leg of the giant shaking.

The foyer jolted suddenly, the walls cracked loudly, and Alexi stumbled to the floor, plaster showering down upon him. He waited on all fours until the shuddering stopped. Waited a moment more. When all seemed still, he rose, helped a middle-aged man to his feet, ushered him outside onto the wet beach. When he returned to the foyer, he found it empty, but then Miriam appeared on the stairs, her face bleeding, a bruise forming on her temple. She lurched across the foyer, and Alexi grabbed her by the arm, steadied her, looked into wild eyes.

"Everyone except us and the Commander is outside. We need to go."

"Wait. The Commander?"

"I tried, Alexi, but he refused to leave. Muttered something about this being his creation. He said he wanted to see it through to the end."

"We can't leave him. He's an old man."

Miriam broke free of Alexi's grip, stumbled when the foyer rumbled again, but held her feet, as did Alexi. "He's made his fucking choice. We have a responsibility to the rest," she said, then ran outside without looking back.

Alexi watched her go. Just above the sounds of the storm, he heard a transporter roar to life. He took a step toward the exit, stopped. Looked back. He didn't owe anything to the Commander. The last vehicle was outside waiting for him. But the Commander and the rest of the first gens hadn't owed anything to humanity either. And still they had risked their lives for the betterment of those that came behind. The chance for millions to reach a habitable new world, while they remained here on this shitty outpost. Sacrifice. When had Alexi done anything so meaningful? His life was maintenance. Keeping the status quo. Where was his purpose?

He glanced at the door, the elevators Miriam had shut down for safety, the warped staircase. "Shit," he muttered to himself, then ran toward the stairs.

Alexi stood on the sixty first floor landing, bent over, hands on knees, dry retching. He regained control, sucked in a huge breath, cleared his throat, spat. The saliva hit the cement with a splat. His breath was ragged, his chest burned.

The stairs beneath him groaned, the walls of the stairwell shuddered. With a squeal, the landing beneath him buckled, cracked, then most of it fell away.

As the floor went, he leapt on instinct, grabbed hold of the balustrade still connected to the wall of the stairwell. His body jerked against his grip, nearly loosened his fingers, but he held on grimly, feet dangling over nothing. He refused to look down, but heard the cacophony of the stairs still collapsing. Dust filled the air around him with the acrid scent of cement. He gritted his teeth, pulled, his muscles aching, and slowly eased himself up onto what remained of the broken staircase.

The Colossus shuddered. Alexi gripped the railing tight. When it steadied, he sucked in a breath. Here was that adventure he'd been craving, he thought, grinned. He fought back the urge to laugh manically, began his ascent again.

Breathing hard, Alexi buzzed the doorbell as the building around him shivered. He held on tightly to the door handle to stop himself toppling. As he waited, it hit him that the stairwell was gone, that escape was no longer simple. His stomach constricted painfully; his throat went dry. He swallowed to stop from panicking, forced himself to think.

Several service tunnels linked the upper floors. There might yet be a way to use them to get down to a point where the stairs remained intact. It was worth a try, he thought.

The door swung inward suddenly and Alexi fell with it, lost his grip, and slid across the floor past the Commander, who was pressed hard against the foyer wall. "What are you doing here, son?" the Commander asked, staring at Alexi as he tried to scrabble to his feet. The floor shifted again.

"You need to get out," Alexi said.

"I've already made up my mind. I told Miriam."

"You're fucking crazy. You don't know what you're saying," Alexi screeched, rose, staggered toward the Commander, then fell painfully upon his knees as the apartment lurched.

Alexi swallowed down the hurt, looked up at the Commander. "This fucking thing is alive. We need to go. Now."

"It's incredible, isn't it? I spent my life working on the Colossus, moulding it, reshaping it, living inside it. All the while wondering what it had been like when it was alive. I don't have to wonder anymore, Alexi. I'm going with it. A final adventure."

Alexi opened his mouth to argue, but was cut off by an incredible rending sound, so loud that Alexi thought his eardrums would burst. He lifted his hands from the floor to cover his ears, but as soon as he did, he slid again across the floor of the apartment, now tilted alarmingly toward the large windows.

As he careened toward the glass, he saw the view was changing. Instead of storm clouds, he saw roiling waves crashing against the beach. Then he saw the Colossus' foot and ankle buried in the sand.

Alexi smashed hard into the glass, which shuddered in its frame. The jolt knocked the wind from him. He clawed at his neck, tried to force air in. The Commander slammed into the glass beside him a moment later. Spiderwebs of cracks appeared, ran across the surface of the glass. The old man whimpered, went limp.

The Colossus continued to shift. An armchair tumbled across the room and smashed into the window, which groaned and cracked more. The window tilted further, until Alexi found the glass beneath him instead of the floor.

A giant, haired arm encroached on Alexi's view. The arm pushed down with force, the hand speared into the ocean with an explosion of water. The Colossus shuddered, but the arm steadied the giant's fall. The apartment stilled. Air seeped back into Alexi's lungs.

Gingerly, he tried to rise, but as soon as he placed weight on the glass, it moaned, and splintered. He quickly lay back down, distributed his weight, then slid slowly toward the Commander. He shook the old man's shoulder.

"Commander. Wake up."

But the man didn't move. The glass groaned again, a piece the size of a dinner plate breaking away from the corner of the frame. Alexi watched it tumble toward the water, which seemed very far away even with the Colossus bent over. The sounds of the storm intensified. A gust of wind invaded the apartment.

He grabbed the collar of the Commander's shirt, moved away from the middle of the glass, pulled the Commander after him. He made his way slowly toward the edge of the window, wrapped his free hand around the window frame where the glass had broken away.

The apartment shook again, the Colossus began to rise, the view shifting up. The window squealed in protest as it was wrenched and twisted, then all at once, it shattered, and the Commander slipped out into the air.

Alexi held on with all his might, arrested the Commander's fall, but he was heavy. Alexi's grip on the window frame, all that stopped them from both tumbling to their deaths, was sweaty, and he felt it slip. Wind and rain assailed him, blew glass fragments into his face. He squinted against it, gritted his teeth, tried to pull the Commander back into the apartment, but it was no good. He couldn't hold them both.

"I'm sorry," he screamed, as the Commander slipped from his fingers. Tears stung his eyes as the old man tumbled away and was soon swallowed by the sea. Alexi wanted to scream with frustration. He thought his purpose had been to save the Commander. Like the Commander had saved so many of their kind. But he'd failed. Perhaps he just wasn't cut out for anything noble.

Alexi wrapped his other hand around the steel frame, ignored the pain of glass slicing his palm. He held on grimly, blood trickling down his wrist.

Rain slapped him as he dangled. Thunder boomed in his ears. His arms ached, he was at his limit, yet just when he thought he couldn't hold on any longer, the Colossus reached its full height and the apartment levelled out. With the last of his strength, Alexi pulled himself back inside, lay panting prone upon the floor.

The Commander's apartment, being set in the chest of the giant, remained relatively intact—the window was shattered, the floor badly warped, the walls scarred and cracked. Yet it held. Alexi could only imagine the damage wrought to the lodgings in the arms and legs of the giant.

The storm roared, the wind licked at Alexi's face, his clothes. The rain seemed heavier now. It blew in through the destroyed window, drenched Alexi until he shivered.

The building groaned again. Panicked, Alexi lurched toward the window frame, took hold of it once more. It vibrated under his hands, and when he looked down, he experienced vertigo.

The building swayed left, jerked hard forward, and to the right. Alexi wrapped his body around the steel support, held on tight. Below, there was an incredible splash, a jolt. Alexi looked down and saw the Colossus had wrenched its right leg free of the sand, had planted it in the water. The apartment swayed right, jerked hard forward, and left. The left leg. The giant was wading into the ocean.

A crack of thunder left Alexi's ears ringing. He squinted against the icy rain. He couldn't stop shivering. The surface of the ocean drew closer as the giant waded deeper. Lightning forked, struck the giant's arm, shattered glass and left hair sizzling. It didn't slow. Alexi watched in amazement as the burnt patch healed before his eyes, leaving scarred skin behind.

The giant stopped abruptly. It turned right, looked out to sea as if searching for something. Suddenly, it spun, and moved quickly toward the shore, but toward a point much further north than where it had stood for the last sixty-two years. Alexi's transmitter beeped. Miriam.

"Where are you? We had to get the transporters moving when that thing pulled itself from the sand."

"I'm in it," Alexi said, yelling to be heard above the wind.

There was a pause. "You're what?"

"I'm in it. I went back for the Commander. He wanted to stay. I tried to get him to leave, but I couldn't. He's dead, Miriam. The giant stumbled, and I couldn't hold him. He fell and... and..."

"Okay. It's alright. You did your best. Let's just focus on you now. Can you get out?"

"I don't think so."

"I'll send someone back for you. Maybe—"

"No, Miriam. It's no use. It's... It was great working for you."

"Don't say that. You're still alive, right? Plus, you're my best caretaker. I can't replace you."

Alexi chuckled without mirth. "I don't think we have anything to take care of anymore."

"Just hold on, okay. Look for a chance to escape. It might stop, it might let you get down. If it does, contact me. I'll ensure someone is there to get you. I'm sending vehicles after you as we speak."

Alexi knew in his heart that wouldn't happen. But he appreciated Miriam saying the words. "Okay," he said.

The giant reached land again, and without the water to hold it back, it picked up speed, began to jog, then run, each footstep pounding the earth, shuddering the apartment, which groaned and creaked. Alexi held on tighter, his muscles burning, his body hurt and bruised. He jerked and jarred every time the giant's feet slammed into the desert, but he held on gamely. As the ground sped below him, he was struck by a thought that pierced the tumult and terror. No one, ever, had experienced anything like this before him. No one.

"What's happening?" Miriam asked. She sounded so close.

"It's running into the desert," he said. "It's ridiculous and incredible. This thing is... I don't know. It's unfathomable. It makes me wonder about everything we did. The why? What was the point, Miriam?"

"I don't know what you mean."

"We didn't have a purpose like the first gens. We existed because that's what people do. But I wondered sometimes if there was more. Whether there was a reason we were here. Today, I thought that maybe I was destined to rescue the Commander, but I couldn't. So maybe I have no purpose. Or maybe it's this. To hold on, and to bear witness to the regeneration of these beings. I know that sounds crazy... but..." Alexi trailed off, uncertain how to finish. Uncertain how to articulate what he really felt as the wind and rain stung his frozen skin.

In the distance, Alexi saw something huge loom over the horizon. At first, he didn't understand what it was. There were no hills in the desert. But then he recognised it as another giant, running toward him. "There's another one," Alexi said, breathless. "We're going fast now."

"Hold on, okay?"

"I'm trying, Miriam. But it's difficult." Each footfall rattled Alexi's teeth, shook him to his core. Each time he thought, *this one, I'll lose my grip and tumble this time*, but he didn't.

It was the Lady. The giants were sexless beings, but her physique was curvier in shape, so the Lady was what they had dubbed her. She moved with grace, power. A lithe being almost floating across the desert sand, rushing toward the Colossus, who seemed to lumber in comparison.

"She's coming," he said almost to himself, his eyes wide with awe. "She's coming."

"Who's coming," Miriam asked. But he didn't respond. The two giants covered the ground fast. They flew toward each other through the storm. Through the wind, and rain and swirling sand. The Lady soon filled Alexi's vision of the world. She was close, arms outstretched, face euphoric.

He didn't know if they were charging at each other to fight or fuck. He didn't understand any of it, but he wasn't supposed to, he realised. The giants lived on a plane separate to his. Alexi and the colonists were inconsequential when compared to these timeless beings.

He muttered a prayer to himself. Then the Lady was upon them.

A thunderous clap filled Alexi's ears, he was thrown hard backward across the loungeroom, and he smashed through the kitchen bench. Bones shattered, flesh tore, pain touched every nerve ending, and his vision filled with dust and red. The world rocked like it had been torn in two, and something new had been birthed. Something immense.

The world spun; debris engulfed Alexi. But he didn't feel it anymore. He didn't know which way was up, or down. Everything was crushed under yielding grey-brown flesh.

For the briefest moment, his mind caught hold of an idea that made everything seem clear. Then it disappeared amidst the crush of the giants.

See Michael Gardner's story "Colossus" online at Metaphorosis.
If you liked it, leave a comment. Authors love that!
Remember to subscribe to our e-mail updates so you'll know when new stories are posted.

About the story

Like a lot of my stories, "Colossus" started with the concept. I had previously written a short story where the houses in the world I created could only be built if people were walled into the foundations of the home. These people continued to live in a preserved, semi-aware way. In "Colossus", I inverted that idea. Instead of preserved people walled into a house, I began to wonder what it might be like to build homes into a preserved creature.

This story was also inspired by a masterful short story I've read many times by Clive Barker, called "In the Hills, the Cities". This is an odd story, where two remote towns in the former Yugoslavia have an annual tradition where the townsfolk lash themselves together to form giants that battle each other. Nothing goes smoothly, and horror ensures. What always stayed with me was the way Barker imbued his giants with a sense of awe, wonder and mysticism. I don't pretend to have his skills, but I hope my giants are also memorable.

A question for the author

Q: What made you start writing?
A: The short answer is a love of speculative fiction, and an imagination that never turns off.

The longer answer is that these factors took a long time percolating before I started writing regularly and submitting my stories to magazines.

I wrote short stories in high school, and at university produced a bunch of chapters for a tedious novel that I never finished. Part of the issue was I didn't know what to do with these stories. Occasionally I'd share with friends, but otherwise I was writing just for me. Which is important for a first draft. But you don't edit that first draft over and over just for yourself. You edit because of a desire to have others read your work, too.

Things changed for me several years ago when, as a birthday present, my sister sent me to a one-day writing course. The presenter was a local Australian author, Ian McHugh. He was a great presenter (and his collection of short stories, *Angel Dust*, is excellent). I came out of that course inspired to turn more of my ideas into short stories and to send them out into the world.

About the author

Michael Gardner is a writer of fantasy and horror who masquerades as an economist by day. His work has appeared in *Writers of the Future Volume 36, Aurealis, Bourbon Penn,* and *Metaphorosis Magazine*. He is also a three-time finalist for the Aurealis Awards. You can find out more about Michael and his work at: www.michael-s-gardner.com

www.michael-s-gardner.com

A word about Lisa Short

There are people who are good writers, people who are a joy to work with, and people who are both. Lisa Short definitely falls in that latter category. While I tend toward the dour and gloomy, Lisa, in my experience, is at the other end of the scale — the people who are sunny and optimistic, who see silver linings when the sky is overcast.

Lisa's first story for us, "The Season of Withering", in October 2019, caught my eye with it's complex, intriguing fantasy world. As a commenter said, 'What a compelling story, tremendous world-building!' Lisa followed up on that in October 2021 with "Genesis", showing that she's just as comfortable and effective with science fiction (and that a sunny disposition doesn't necessarily mean utopian settings). Lisa's third story for us, "Salaatu", in October 2023, creates another intriguing, nuanced world populated with engaging, interesting characters.

When I solicited a fourth story, Lisa mentioned in passing that all her stories for us had been published in October. It wasn't intentional then, but this time it is. Enjoy "Far Horizon", on which our cover art is based, below!

Far Horizon

Lisa Short

Carollene Jonaitis braced herself against the astrogation console as the *Ostatny* dropped out of its *i*-space bubble and engaged its drives with the usual bulkhead-rattling roar. The *Ostatny's* ineradicable, mildewy stink always seemed to intensify when the drives came online—*revalidating its reality in its own special way*, Carollene reflected sourly. The *Ostatny* reeked, this *job* reeked—

"Jonaitis? Anything on the board?"

Carollene winced at the sharp edge in the captain's tone—*Captain* Zhenya, ha! Like the *Ostatny* rated an actual captain—but she dutifully pried her hands off the console's frame and called up the *Ostatny's* external sensor interface. The forest of yellow *Warning! Caution! ALERT!* messages blooming beneath her rapidly moving fingers weren't anything new; she no longer bothered mentioning them. "Nope."

"Could you be a little more specific, Jonaitis?" She could almost hear Zhenya's teeth grinding behind her and she smothered a smile—not that difficult, given that she was sitting in a rickety deathtrap surrounded by hard vacuum. The temptation to simply toss him another *Nope!* was almost overwhelming—almost, but not quite. During the few months she'd been aboard the *Ostatny*, she had learned just how far she could push him.

"Sorry, Captain. By *nope*, I meant no comm traffic in-system." Carollene squinted down at the flickering pools of data displacing the last of the yellow ALERT! messages. "No comm traffic, no beacons, no noth—oh, wait a minute."

HostName=FarHorizonRF01-SeMI-00
    HostID=c615d983-a399-44a0-8111-e906ae39c482

DateTime=232112030003
RunJobs 2025/0000/COUNTER
2025/0001   DIAGNOSTICS   powergrid1.   2025/0002
DIAGNOSTICS environmental2. 2025/0003 DIAGNOST—
ping \<general address>
ping \<general address>
ping \<general address>
STANDBY
::Restricted:: HostApplication=INITIALIZE ::Restricted::
ping \<general address>
ping \<general address>
ping \<general address>
SANCIA
SANCIA
SANCIA
I'm awake.

"What?" That was Bellows, behind Carollene at the auxiliary engineering console—the best place for him, as it was barely ever needed. That edge in his tone was usually a lead-in to a prolonged whine about something or other, but for the moment at least, Carollene didn't care. Her fingers flickered across the console, her eyes tracking the shifting numbers. She hadn't bothered switching on the console's graphical interpreters when they'd dropped out of *i*-space, as sure as she'd been that this run was yet another waste of both her and the *Ostatny's* time. She quickly did so now, the stab of irritation at giving Zhenya something to legitimately complain about lost in her growing fascination with the console's sudden wealth of data.

"Huh. Something *is* out there—something besides a star and a handful of planets nobody gives a crap about, that is. Or at least, something *was* here, at some point." Carollene swiveled around in the astrogation console's chair, remembering its broken left support just in time to stomp her foot down before the whole thing collapsed sideways under her, and squinted up at the captain. "C'mon, Zhenya, give. Why'd you drag us all the way out here?"

Zhenya's narrow gaze shifted away from Carollene's console to her face. He had edged up closer behind her, presumably to get a better look at the console screens. For a long moment, she didn't think he was going to bother answering her—and he didn't *have* to, of course—but then he said, "A new listing on the salvage boards."

Carollene's brows contracted; she spun back around and ran her hands over the console again, then craned her head back over her shoulder to give him a pointed stare. "No way," she said flatly. "There's definitely nobody in-system besides us, except for whatever the *Ostatny's* sensors are picking up. As long as it took us to get here, if there'd been something new up on the boards, this place would be crawling with other ships by now."

Zhenya's lips pinched together until nothing was left of them but a line bisecting his face. Carollene couldn't help thinking how reptilian it made him look. Bellows, the third and least of the *Ostatny's* three-person crew, was only annoying; Zhenya actively creeped her out, from his clean-shaven scalp all the way down to his overpolished boots. "I heard about it before it hit the official board listings," he said at last. "So we have time to pick over whatever's here before anyone else shows up."

Carollene wrestled briefly with her conscience, or what was left of it ever since she'd picked the wrong corporate horse to back —not much anymore, really. That realization stung, even numbed by repetition as it was. "Great," she muttered, turning back to the console's busy display. "Just super."

HostName=FarHorizonRF01- SeMI-00
HostID=c615d983-a399-44a0-8111-e906ae39c482
DateTime=232112030138
RunJobs SUSPENDED pending Administrator login
>username:Administrator\SANCIA login:*************
Login SUCCESSFUL
>Power on: PASSIVEDETECTION
>Power on: PASSIVECOMM
SANCIA ping general address UNKNOWN. Passive detection systems self-check OK OK OK OK OK. Passive detection systems ONLINE. Query PARAM?

You know what to look for. Remember when the station lifeboat left? Think of that as a template—this may not look exactly the same, but the pattern of electromagnetic and gravitic disturbances should be similar.

SANCIA 'SIMILAR' =? = <> ?

Run comparisons at 10%/20%/50%/85% of baseline and overlay.

It's okay. You've got this.

It's probably nothing.

"It's over there," said Carollene, gesturing at the bloated, gaudy sphere taking up a good quarter of the bridge display. Zhenya had taken up position just behind her left shoulder, oppressively close. "You can't actually see it from our approach angle yet. The signals are coming from the moon that's just about to rise over that gas giant. Well, barely a moon really, more of an asteroid that happened to get snagged into planetary orbit—but that's the source of what the *Ostatny's* sensors picked up."

"So, what *did* they pick up?" Zhenya's eyes had drawn down into slits in his colorless face.

"Radio emissions, too structured to be natural phenomena. Once I triangulated on those, it was easy enough to find a suspiciously stable heat source as well—that gas giant ain't no Jupiter, it's too far out from the primary. It doesn't generate any heat at *all*, it's cold as shit on that moon's surface...except for where that EM noise is originating from."

"Did you ping it?"

Carollene rolled her eyes. "Of *course* I pinged it, as soon as I spotted it. Nothing. So... what *was* that listing? On the board?"

Zhenya's gaze was flat; apparently she hadn't toned down the sarcasm enough. "Research station," he said finally. "Just shut down."

Did he actually think she would buy that? A recent shutdown would still have a hell of a lot more in-system traffic than this one did, even if there were no longer any official residents. But she wasn't going to argue with that snakelike stare. "Sure. Well, let's see if I can get more of a response if I try..." Her fingers flew across the console screen. "Maybe an SOS, or—ha!" She started to lean back in the chair, then hastily straightened up again at its ominous creak. "There's something. Huh. That...looks like a SeMI? Seriously?"

HostName=FarHorizonRF01-SeMI-00
        HostID=c615d983-a399-44a0-8111-e906ae39c482
        DateTime=232112030201
        RunJobs 2025/0003/COUNTER: PAUSED
        SANCIA parameter overlay RSD >5.0000 INCONCLUSIVE
        Take out all the specific mass data and recalibrate.
        1100/0001 RECALIBRATING

SANCIA parameter overlay RSD < 0.3701 QUERY?
I don't know.
It could be a ship.
A real ship.
<ARCHIVE   FILE   5664135.txt><transcript>
(datatag:Administrator\SANCIA)
(DateTime=231701030201)'WE<sp>JUST<sp>HAVE<sp>TO<sp>HA
NG<sp>ON<sp>UNTIL<sp>THE<sp>RELIEF<sp>SHIP<sp>COMES'
It's not a relief ship.
SANCIA verify metadata tag (KEYID:UNK_1) IS NOT
'RELIEF<sp>SHIP'?
No. It's been too long.
It's something else.

Beside her, Zhenya twitched—Carollene couldn't think of any other way to describe it, but before she could do more than take note of his suddenly rigid expression, Bellows yelped, "*What?* No way!" He scuttled over to Carollene's other side, ignoring her pointed glare as he leaned over her shoulder. "Where? I don't see anything."

Bellows's rebellion against Zhenya's obsessive level of grooming, besides resulting in an unkempt growth of hair and beard, also generated a certain odor. Surreptitiously breathing through her mouth, Carollene pointed at the upper right corner of console display. "See that? That's a hard feed address—that particular set of prefixes is restricted to SeMI usage only." She paused, peering down at it. "Though it's weird it's not answering— the hard feed address is just something the sensors can read automatically, not an actual pingback from the source. Maybe it's in low power mode, or...something?"

"I don't believe it," Bellows muttered. "Nobody'd leave one of those things behind, I don't care *how* fast they needed to get out of there. They're too fucking expensive." He straightened back up, putting a very appreciated meter of space between himself and Carollene.

"They're not that easy to decommission. I'm sure they just figured they'd come back for it later, after whatever happened to the station got fixed..." Carollene trailed off. "Uh, that might be a problem, if they show up while we're in the middle of salvaging it?"

Zhenya's shoulders jerked in an irritable shrug. "They shouldn't."

"How do you kn—"

"Look, Jonaitis, I'm sure nobody's showing up! Just get back to work."

"Fine." *Unethical, sneaking*—he probably *was* sure, and she was equally sure she didn't want to know why. Her conscience sent up another feeble protest; Carollene slapped it down and turned back to the console. "Now that I have the hard feed address, let's see what we've got in ship's archives." For the next few minutes, the bridge was silent except for the soft wheeze of the *Ostatny's* environmentals. "Yep, it matches a real SeMI, all right. *Semi-Autonomous Machine Intelligence RF-01,* registered with some outfit called *Far Horizon.* Never heard of 'em. Not that that means anything, I probably haven't heard of at least eighty percent of all the little startups out there. Though they usually *don't* have SeMIs... No info on when it was commissioned *in situ,* either. Just a manufacturing release date on the SeMI, pre-installation. Six—no, seven years back, looks like."

HostName=FarHorizonRF01-SeMI-00
    HostID=c615d983-a399-44a0-8111-e906ae39c482
    DateTime=232112030315
    RunJobs 2025/0004/COUNTER: PAUSED
    1100/0030 Initiating self-check on external sensor array from STANDBY. 2025/0004 self-check complete. POWERGRID low-optimal.

Is it landing?

SANCIA 'LANDING' =? = <> ?

Approaching the station on a trajectory tangent to the lunar surface. Or possibly intersecting it, if it's about to crash. Run a kinematic analysis of position, velocity and acceleration versus time.

    2025/0005 ADHOCJOB00: OK

SANCIA ship is approaching station PROBABILITY >90% LANDING LANDING LANDING query SANCIA

    SANCIA

    SANCIA

    SANCIA WARNING! Initiating self-check on health monitor SANCIA

I'm fine.

    SANCIA

    >Administrator\SANCIA: Disengage hypothalamic inputs on DELAY TIMER=0s

SANCIA ERROR! Dataflow: insufficient. Health monitor: 89% incomplete/unstable

>Administrator\SANCIA: Reengage hypothalamic inputs on DELAY TIMER=300s, /p throttle 50/50

SANCIA WARNING! Health monitor: 90% and PAUSED/stable. SUBOPTIMAL

You'll get over it.

The *Ostatny* wasn't really designed to land on any surface, lunar or otherwise—it had been built with orbital docking facilities in mind, and if the research station's moon had had more than the most meager gravity, Carollene and the *Ostatny's* automatics wouldn't have been able to manage it at all. As it was, she was pretty sure they'd bent a support strut coming down. A lightning-quick peek at Zhenya's face didn't reveal any awareness on his part of that minor calamity, in spite of the distant, screeching *thunk!* from the ship's belly.

A faint, sharp smell of armpit wafted over to her nose; Bellows was clearly back to hovering over her shoulder. Carollene ignored him, staring at what had to be the source of the steady heat and EM from the moon's surface on the bridge display. It wasn't much—a small, standard-build modular station buried in a rock spire, almost lost in the shadow cast by the gas giant looming on the horizon. It certainly *looked* abandoned—no running lights, no faint haze of atmospheric venting, no nothing.

The *Ostatny* didn't rate a locker room—the envirosuits were stowed in its cargo bay, perpetually ten degrees colder than the rest of the ship. Carollene shivered her way into the suit's clammy, bulky embrace. She especially hated their interior plumbing; every time she'd ever used it, including the very first time, she'd wound up with a raging UTI. *Fuck it,* she thought, and left the plumbing disconnected. She'd just hold it. Or pee down her leg if it came to that.

Stepping out of the *Ostatny's* grav field, twitchy and unreliable as it was, onto the moon's barely tenth-gee, made her stomach lurch and bile sting the back of her throat. She ignored it as best she could and grimly shuffled forward. Zhenya took the lead, striding out in a reasonable facsimile of an experienced spacewalker—Carollene felt no need to scurry any faster in his wake. He could just damn well wait for her to catch up after he reached the station. Staring out at the too-short, too-sharp horizon or, worse, the too-black sky beyond, dominated by the crushing bulk of the gas giant, sent shudders of agoraphobia down her spine; she kept her eyes focused determinedly on the station as they approached.

Zhenya ignored the station's cargo airlock in favor of the smaller personnel lock. The manual controls embedded in the exterior wall were functional, if stiff with disuse—no corrosion, at least; hard vacuum had few advantages as an environment, but that was one of them. Unfortunately, also no power—Carollene had cherished a faint hope that their approach on foot to the station would trigger some kind of automated entry protocol, but it clearly hadn't. It took all three of them to wrestle the outer door shut again and seal it; the interior of the airlock was black, silent and, from the unwanted pressure of Zhenya's and Bellows's suited arms against hers, barely large enough for the three of them.

"Bellows, turn on your helmet light." Zhenya sounded calm enough. A faint *click* as Bellows obeyed, then a bright white glare splashed out across what was obviously an interior airlock door in front of them and, thank God, another manual access at waist-height. This one, however, was locked down tight behind a panel. "Jonaitis, can you get that open?"

"On it." Carollene unhooked the standard-issue toolkit from her utility belt, letting it bob around on its anchoring tether while she rummaged inside it—the envirosuit gloves were clumsy, but the toolkit had been designed with that in mind. A few minutes later, the panel cover popped off. Carollene straightened back up, rather pleased with herself, as the door swung silently outward. Beyond it was a corridor—*not* pitch-black, a pleasant surprise; emergency lighting cast a faint red glow across the floorplates, which led straight to another airlock. Zhenya moved forward; Carollene opened her mouth, then closed it with a shrug—if there was any kind of unknown hazard ahead, Zhenya was absolutely the one she'd prefer found it first.

As they approached it, Carollene realized that the far airlock wasn't a heavy-duty exterior model like the one they had just come through; it was just an interior door, an airlock only in the sense that it hermetically sealed the environment on both sides. It even had portholes, three of them in a central cluster just a little above Carollene's eye level. She couldn't quite make out any details of what was beyond it, but it was clearly lit by something more than just emergency floor strips. As soon as Zhenya got within a meter of the door, its outline flared green; Bellows jumped back a few paces. "Jonaitis?" snapped Zhenya.

"It's fine," said Carollene hastily—she'd managed to disguise her own start under the muffling layers of her suit. "I've seen this before. It's pretty common in these modular research stations. It means—" She stopped abruptly. "It means there's *air* on the other side. I mean, pressure of some kind—no guarantee it's actually *breathable* air, but—"

"Good enough for me," said Zhenya, sounding as close to happy as she'd ever heard him. "Does it open automatically, or—"

"Usually, yeah. When you get close enough."

Zhenya edged forward. The door pulsed green once more; with a hiss audible even through their envirosuit helmets, the vents imbedded in the walls above their heads began shooting out a fine white vapor. A heartening sign that *some* sort of automatics had been left intact by whatever calamity had chased the station residents away—Carollene relaxed a little inside her suit. A few seconds after the last of the vapor had vanished, the interior door slid obediently open. Zhenya took a brisk step across the threshold, then abruptly doubled over, grabbing the doorframe. Carollene's stomach clenched in on itself and she sucked in a huge gasp of canned suit air.

"What?" Bellow's voice wasn't much short of a shriek.

"Nothing, it's nothing—it's gravity. Just gravity." Zhenya pushed himself back upright and turned to face them. *"Jonaitis, report!"*

Carollene already had the toolkit open, yanking out the handheld analyzer, then stepped gingerly through the doorway herself. She wobbled for a minute, then planted her backside against the nearest wall, flicking a gloved finger over the handheld's display. "Doesn't feel *exactly* like full gravity, but it's close—" She squinted down at the numbers rolling across the tiny screen. "About eight-tenths gee. And we *do* have atmosphere. O2 pressure and concentration are a little on the low side, but it's definitely breathable. I don't see any trace chemicals that could do us harm—no radiation either—now, *biological* contamination, unfortunately, I can't really check for. Not with this thing."

"We'll stay in the suits for now." Zhenya tilted his helmet towards the center of the room.

Carollene tore her attention from the handheld and took her first real look around the room they stood in; her lips parted, but no sound emerged. It was relatively small, maybe ten meters in diameter, but Carollene instantly recognized it for what it was—a *fishbowl*; a combine corporate showroom, designed to impress visiting investors. Gleaming black and chrome surfaces, blank projector panels everywhere interspersed with abstract art sculptures in crystal. What had she so offhandedly called it, back on the *Ostatny, some little startup*—well, she'd been dead wrong about that. Shoestring-budget startups didn't have fishbowls.

And Zhenya had known about it. He *had* to have known all this. *What am I getting into now?* wailed an inner voice—one that Carollene was pretty sure she should have listened to in the past, far more often than she actually had, and probably shouldn't be disregarding now. But what other choice did she have, really? They were here, and the *Ostatny* was the only way *out* of here, and the *Ostatny* was Zhenya's. *Yeah, that's what you always think, what choice do I have, what choice do I have...how's that turned out for you so far?* She gritted her teeth and headed for the bank of consoles.

HostName=FarHorizonRF01-SeMI-00
    HostID=c615d983-a399-44a0-8111-e906ae39c482
    DateTime=232112031026
    RunJobs 2025/0005/COUNTER: PAUSED
    SANCIA
    SANCIA Health monitor: 90%. ALERT <adrenaline serum levels 1000 ng/L><cortisol serum levels 100 mcg/dL><BP 180/120> ALERT
    SANCIA
    Stop it, okay?
    SANCIA JOBQUERY JOBQUERY JOBQUERY
    I'm thinking!
    ...
    ...fine. I'm scared. I don't know why they're here and I'm scared.
    <ARCHIVE FILE 10359863.txt>
    datatag: ***FAR   HORIZON   Facility   Security Protocol_v1.0.0_Issue date 20170101***
    <'FACILITY SECURITY PROTOCOL is a critical component of an effective security program. The guidelines contained in this document are based on recognized industry best practices and provide broad recommendations for the protection of FAR HORIZON facilities and employees within them.'>
    <'THREAT ASSESSMENT is the process of identifying or evaluating entities, actions, or occurrences (natural or man-made) that possess or indicate the potential to harm or destroy FAR HORIZON assets.'>
    You make me laugh at the strangest times.
    SANCIA OK = <> ?

Yeah, I'm okay. We can do this. Come on, let's see what they're up to.

Carollene eased her suited behind down onto one of the console chairs, in far better shape than the one she usually occupied on the *Ostatny's* bridge, and ran her gauntlet over the nearest screen. Hard-packed dust rose in neat little furrows on either side of her gloved fingers, then lifted up into the air, whipped away by the faint, constant breeze of the facility's air circulation system. Which was what should have already happened to *all* the dust, long before it ever got a chance to settle down and form a crust on the console's surface. "Zhenya? How long did you say this station had been shut down, exactly?"

A pause, then, "Not long."

"*How* long?"

"A month or two, Probably. Look, I don't really know."

Carollene turned her frowning attention back to the console. Was two months really long enough for this much dust to settle? And possibly an even more pertinent question—why had the environmentals ever switched back *on?* Because they *were* on now, obviously, and—she glanced at the handheld—the room itself was holding steady at ten degrees C. Cold in terms of human comfort, but considerably warmer than the surface of the moon outside... and not something it could have achieved even if it had activated as soon as she'd pinged the station from back on the *Ostatny*, not with less than a tenth of a degree of variability.

"So? Can you get in?"

"Hmm...probably. I mean, this likely isn't a secured area. Like, this is all just window dressing...so what I can get into might be limited, but I should be able to get *something* out of it. Gimme a minute." Carollene waved her right suit gauntlet over the console's screen, which promptly lightened to a pearlescent gray. "Good sign...okay, okay, let's see—" Brightly colored graphics flashed beneath her gloved fingertips, a swirl of galaxies zooming down to a single circuit board, then closer and closer until every transistor was a skyscraper, every etched copper tracing a superhighway—then a brilliant explosion of light, resolving into a fashionably archaic font spilling across the screen. "Oh, *here* we go. *Welcome to Far Horizon, paradigm-changing technology for future generations!* blah blah blah, typical marketing crap, zero actual details on what the hell they were *really* doing here—"

"Biologics?"

"Ha, found the general facility floorplan! No, it doesn't really look like it. No cryo storage, no bio lab infrastructure that I can see —huh. Actually, I don't know—wait, what are you *doing?*"

Zhenya didn't dignify that with an answer, simply finished unclipping his helmet from his suit and pulling it all the way off over his head. Carollene stared at him in unfeigned, horrified fascination. Zhenya crossed the fishbowl to its only other exit, another interior door presumably leading to the rest of the facility, then motioned at Bellows. From what Carollene could make out through his faceplate and hers, Bellows had zero interest in doing any of the same. "Bellows, take your damn helmet off. There's nothing here that's going to hurt you."

After a long pause, Bellows did so, then glared openly at Carollene. Carollene spared a glance at her gauntlet readout— about ninety minutes of breathable air left in her suit tanks. Chances were that Zhenya was right—and also, that he knew a lot more about what they'd been working on here than he was letting on. Chances were also one hundred percent that Zhenya the Self-Absorbed would *never* deliberately risk exposing himself to dangerous, unknown biological agents. She couldn't help sniffing surreptitiously at the air as she unsealed her helmet, though. Certainly it smelled better in here than in the *Ostatny*...or rather, it didn't smell much like anything at all.

"Look, before you two head out, let me at least verify that the rest of the facility is pressurized, with grav and temp control online." She stripped off her gloves and got to work on the console. "Yeah, looks like it," she said, looking up a minute later. "That was my last freebee, though—it's locked me out. Now it wants an access code. Don't suppose you happen to have one, Zhen?" Zhenya, not surprisingly, ignored that. "Okay, let's just try the guest access route first. Oh good, *that* worked—it's not offering me the keys to the palace, but it's fine with letting me surf around the basic menus." She cocked an eyebrow at Zhenya. "It's not acting anything like a SeMI, though. Just an ordinary, run-of-the-mill facility management system."

"Good!" Bellows burst out, startling Carollene into dragging her attention off the console and cranking her head around to look at him. He hadn't moved off the far wall, in spite of Zhenya's impatient prompting; now he was hugging himself, gauntleted fingers drumming in a tight, nervous tempo on each suited elbow. "SeMIs creep me out."

"What?" Carollene said blankly. "*SeMIs* creep you out? Why? Bellows, please tell me you're not one of those whackjobs who think the SeMIs are real, honest-to-God AIs just sitting around waiting for their chance to enslave all mankind. SeMIs are just really smart, *really* specialized computer systems, but they still just do what they're told, they don't, like, *want* to do anything else —"

"Yeah? And who says they don't? The combine corporations that make trillions off 'em? Of course *they're* gonna lie about it—"

"Oh, for fuck's sake, *I* used to work for a combine, remember? Believe me, they'd love for that to be true—do you have any idea how much money they'd make off *real* artificial intelligence? They'd be the last people to keep it a secret if they actually had it—"

"Enough," said Zhenya flatly. "Bellows, come on, or I'm cutting you out of the salvage bonus."

"Fuck you! You can't do that!"

"I can and I will." Cold black eyes flicked sideways to Carollene's face. "And keep looking for that SeMI."

Bellows, flushed and furious, shoved himself off the wall and scurried across the fishbowl to stand behind Zhenya. Zhenya stepped forward and the facility door whispered obediently open; Carollene watched the door slide closed behind them, its bright green outline winking out, then turned back to the console.

HostName=FarHorizonRF01-SeMI-00
        HostID=c615d983-a399-44a0-8111-e906ae39c482
        DateTime=232112031312
        RunJobs 2025/0005/COUNTER: PAUSED
        >Administrator\SANCIA: ADHOCJOB00:
Videofeed06:MainCorridor01. Reroute to directsynaptinput01.
ADHOCJOB01:   Audiofeed06:MainCorridor01.   Reroute   to
directsynaptinput03.   ADHOCJOB02:
ConsoleScreen07:Fishbowl/LINK
        2025/0006 ADHOCJOB00: OK
        2025/0007 ADHOCJOB01: OK
        2025/0008 ADHOCJOB02: OK

The video feed shows a bright flash of gray, then darkens to near-black; the door at the far end of the corridor has closed. Movement—two suited figures, helmetless, the taller one holding the only light source now visible to the camera lens, a small, circular pool of radiance at the smaller man's feet. The figures begin to walk forward, steadily,

"Cap'n! Something there, up ahead!" The taller figure points with the hand not holding the light—a patch of darkness near the

middle of the walkway, several meters from where they had paused when the taller one shouted.

They approach it warily. "Ugh," says the tall one, as the harsh brilliance of the light plays over the huddled shape on the floor plating. It is a body—a long-dead body, half-skeletal, half-desiccated, wearing a coverall of some faded color. The most remarkable thing about it is its hair—long, dark, lying in glistening ropes across the bony shoulders, arms, skull. "I don't smell anything, though—"

"No, you wouldn't." The shorter figure, speaking for the first time. "Whatever started decomposing her, died along with her when the station was shut down. Come on, let's keep going."

It was a lot quieter in the station's fishbowl than it ever was aboard the *Ostatny*—the station environmentals were clearly in far better shape, even if they were running on the low side of optimal in terms of absolute pressure, temperature and O2 concentration. Or *were* they running on the low side...?

Carollene reached for the console screen, then hesitated—just viewing the station environmentals was one thing; asking whatever-it-was that she was interacting with what the specific setpoints were, might require a deeper level of access. Well, nothing ventured, nothing gained—Carollene tapped out a search query.

After a pause that felt slightly too long, probably due to her stretched-tight nerves, the console returned a scrape of the facility environmental status screen—not real time, just a snapshot from a handful of seconds before, right about the time Carollene had queried it. And it *wasn't* running low—for whatever reason, when the station had come back online from whatever length of time it'd been shut down, it had changed the pressure, temperature, O2 and gravity setpoints to ones that no actual person would have been willing to tolerate for long.

Weird enough, but that scraped status screen bugged her even more. Unless it had some scheduled job to periodically save scrapes, which made no sense at all given that it was certainly archiving all that data in far more efficient and machine-accessible formats, why would it have *this* ready to show her? That scrape was a really specific answer to her query, while still making sure no genuine access to the system was being granted to her.

"SeMI?" she wondered aloud, then flinched—now that the fishbowl was empty of everyone except her, it had acquired a faint echo. Her back was to the facility door—her scalp twitched and she glanced quickly over her shoulder. At a closed door and nothing else. "*Stop* it," she mumbled. "It's *not* creepy. It's just empty. And you're not alone here, Zhenya and Bellows are still close by."

Weren't they? Carollene glanced down at her suit gauntlet resting on the console; the suit-to-suit commlink indicators blinked reassuringly back at her. She was hardly going to call them up just because she was nervous or, God forbid, for some casual chitchat—with *them?*—what she really ought to be doing was getting back to work.

Maybe a list of most recently accessed files—she managed to squeeze into the root directory, though she didn't even try to fool herself into believing she was seeing anything but the most obvious and innocuous of the system files. She tried sorting them by date and quickly realized that the system had masked most of the file properties, including *all* its date-time stamps—*numberViews* looked fairly promising, though. She selected it and watched the various filenames flicker past as the query neatly resorted them. The top file was fairly large—she didn't recognize the extension on it at all. Well, she had to start *somewhere*—she tapped the filename, an unenlightening set of seemingly random numbers, and waited resignedly for the facility management system to tell her ACCESS DENIED or NO APPLICATION TO READ FILE AVAILABLE or—

The screen abruptly darkened, then flared to life once more, a wild kaleidoscope of images that flickered past too rapidly for Carollene to process. One image froze, a broad, high-walled facility corridor, packed with people. Carollene leaned forward, unconsciously chewing on a fingernail, as it began to play forward at normal speed. It was a video of some kind, with a date stamp in the bottom right corner. *11-01-2316*—five *years* ago?

The video lurched into motion with an accompanying roar of sound; Carollene recoiled involuntarily at the wall of noise coming from the console. A klaxon wailing, interspersed by panicked shouting—the crowd of people were moving, shoving at each other, eddying like a river around two larger figures in some kind of combat armor, both clutching what looked like shock sticks.

But something else was breaking the rapid flood of stationers towards whatever was out of sight at the bottom of the screen—a woman, clad in pale blue coveralls, with a swirling cloak of heavy dark hair, was fighting her way through them, heading in the exact opposite direction from the rest. As she struggled past the two armored men, one of them reached out and grabbed her arm.

"Where the hell are you going?" His voice barely managed to override the din surrounding them. "Get back!"

"My daughter!" the woman screamed—her voice, high-pitched, cut through the crowd's roar like a sonic knife. "My daughter, she's only twelve, she's in the infirmary, she can't get out —"

"They're evacuating the infirmary, just *go!* They'll catch up with you—"

"Get out of my way!"

Small as she was, the woman still managed to shove him hard enough to send him staggering back into the roiling boil of pushing, shoving people, long enough for her to dart past him and plunge back into the crowd. Then the video froze, the audio dying along with it—in the cold silence of the fishbowl, Carollene stared blankly at the screen. The woman was still barely visible near the top of the vid, a flash of long black hair and one blue-clad arm flung out, reaching for something outside the camera's range. Then the video slowly dissolved, leaving the blank gray screen undisturbed once more.

The commlink beeped. Carollene started violently, then snatched up her suit gauntlet. "Here," she said, hoarsely, then cleared her throat. "Here!"

"Jonaitis?" Something about the facility walls must have been interfering with the signal; the sound quality was terrible, but it was still recognizably Zhenya. "Have you found the SeMI yet?"

"Uh, not exactly, no. I did find footage of the station evac, though. Looks like a real clusterfuck. No clue exactly what happened here, maybe some kind of facility-wide catastrophe." Her tone sharpened. "And I don't think it happened any few *months* ago."

"I don't care. I want that SeMI, Jonaitis."

Carollene folded her arms tightly across her chest and glared down at the commlink. "What, the SeMI we're still not sure exists?"

"It exists. You found its feed address, remember?"

"Look, what are you going to do even if I find it? It's not like you can just, just rip it out and *sell* it—it IS the installation, that's how they work, they're always distributed physically throughout—"

"What? Why the fuck would they do that?" Bellows's voice cut in, even tinnier than Zhenya's.

"It's more economical and it gives the SeMI more of a feel for the facility as a whole—"

"A *feel?* I thought you said they weren't AIs!"

Carollene rolled her eyes. "Jesus, they're not, okay? That's just a figure of speech. SeMIs aren't my field of expertise, Bellows. I only know that if you want to use one to run a facility, they work better if their components are installed in more than one physical location."

"I just want the core." Zhenya's voice crackled over the commlink. "*Find* it, Jonaitis. I mean it."

HostName= FarHorizonRF01-SeMI-00
HostID=c615d983-a399-44a0-8111-e906ae39c482
DateTime=232112031437
RunJobs: 2025/0008/COUNTER: PAUSED
SANCIA 'Core' Query PARAM?
...I think they want to steal you.
DBQUERY: 'Steal':<'take (property) without permission or legal right and without intending to return it'>
>Power on: EXTATMOSPHVENTSYS
ARCHIVEJOB00:   Station   decontamination   protocol
BIOHAZARD LVL 4
2025/0012 ARCHIVEJOBJOB00—
Wait!
SANCIA NOK NOK NOK
>Administrator\SANCIA: MOBILITY APPARATUS engaged.
Videofeed10:MedBayCorridor02   /Audiofeed10:MedBayCorridor02
LINK TO/ConsoleScreen07:Fishbowl OVERRIDE engaged
Let me at least try talking to them first.

I just want the core—"For what?" Carollene said irritably, to the room at large after making sure her suit gauntlet comm wasn't sending. "You can't *do* anything with a SeMI core, not unless you have the—" She stopped. Not unless you had the primary code keys, which *nobody* had except the manufacturer—not even the purchaser was given those keys, because while SeMI raw materials were certainly costly, and its neural network construction and training could take not just months but years depending on what use the SeMI was intended for, the handful of combine corporations that manufactured them still made a sale profit in the tens of *thousands* of percent compared to the build cost. The code keys were the *real* secret, what kept just anybody from building their own SeMI and the devil take the combines' monopoly on them.

Which meant that Zhenya most certainly had *not* seen the listing for this place on any salvage board. Zhenya was, had to be, under some kind of private contract. To retrieve this SeMI, this *particular* SeMI, for its original maker. Though that *maker* was no longer its *owner*—the SeMI now legally belonged to any surviving board member of Far Horizon, of which Carollene seriously doubted there were any or she wouldn't be sitting there in a layer of dust a centimeter deep watching five-year-old vids of its station's final days, or those board members' heirs. Who probably had no idea this station even existed, much less its SeMI, or they'd have shown up long before now.

Bellows was buying the salvage job story because he didn't know crap about SeMIs except that they were the kind of expensive that most people could only dream about, which meant that the typical ten-or-twenty-percent-of-value return from salvage was worth the time and effort. But Carollene knew better. Possibly Zhenya even *knew* she'd know better, that she'd figure it all out, but didn't care because—

—because it's not like you're exactly famous for your personal integrity, is it? He knows you're for sale too. Even if he doesn't list whatever he's actually going to get paid for this job on the boards, whatever he does list is going to be a lot, *and you're going to get your piece of it. He's counting on that to keep you on script. Keep you toeing the line.*

The console suddenly beeped; Carollene started back violently, fingers jerking up off its smooth glass plane. Plain, fine black letters shimmered to life on its blank gray surface.

Hello.

Carollene gaped down at it, hands frozen in midair.

I'm sorry. Hello.

Please.

What the hell was this, a joke? Only believable if either Zhenya or Bellows had had any sense of humor at all, not to mention the technical know-how to sneak a message into a strange station's facility management system. So, not even *remotely* believable.

Is your name Jonaitis?

Carollene scrabbled for the screen.

Yes! Carollene Jonaitis.

I'm Sancia.

What the hell kind of SeMI was named *Sancia*—*no* kind, that was what, and in the course of her abortive corporate career, Carollene had interacted with more than a few SeMIs. This was *not* how they communicated. "A survivor?" whispered Carollene, into the echoing emptiness of the fishbowl. "Oh, shit. A *human* survivor? But how? No way, no fucking *way*—" Her fingers flew across the console screen. *Where are you? How are you? WHO are you?*

The console screen shimmered, then split—virtually split: one half still the text conversation, one half another facility video feed. Not the same corridor as before, though, at least she didn't think so—it looked narrower, with a lower ceiling. The console speaker crackled, then transmitted a faint, rhythmic crunching sound—then, on the video side of the screen, two suited figures, helmetless, stepped into view from the bottom of the screen, the crunching noise in time with their steps. "Hey!" Carollene said sharply, but the suited figures didn't pause—the audio was apparently only one way.

The door at the end of the corridor flared green; Zhenya and Bellows stopped a handful of meters short of it, Bellows jerking his arclight up to shine on the door. Just as the beam of light touched it, it slid soundlessly open; a silhouette stood framed in the doorway. *"Shit!"* cried Bellows. *"Oh*—oh, wait. Is that...some kind of maintenance bot or something?"

The door was too far away from the camera for Carollene to make out any real detail, but she could tell why he might have thought so—the outline was uniformly, inhumanly tall, thin and angular. It stepped out of the shadow of the doorway—no, *rolled* out; the leglike appendages were mere stilts, set on tractor-style treads. Carollene wasn't sure why her own pulse was hammering in her ears, why she felt almost lightheaded, as if she couldn't find enough air to breathe.

"Hey," called Bellows experimentally. "Hey—"

"If it's a bot, do you really expect an answer?" Even processed into tinniness by the audio feed, Zhenya's tone was sharply sarcastic. "Come on." He started walking again, towards the slowly rolling apparatus.

A flicker of motion caught Carollene's eye; she glanced sideways, down at the text window. New letters had appeared. She read them, then read them again. Then a third time.

I'm there.

That's me.

Bellows's suited form lifted his hand; the arclight splashed up and over the moving figure's trunk, then up to its head.

Carollene jammed her fist against her own mouth—the scream ripped out of her anyway, beyond any conscious control, muffled by the knuckles she'd mashed into her lips. She pried her fingers off her face and slapped them down on the console.

Why? Her fingers stumbled across the screen, tracing out gibberish; she clenched them into fists, took a couple of deep, gulping breaths, then tried again. *What happened to you? Why?*

We had to. The station was shutting down. I had been messing around with one of the loaders in the storage bay. I wasn't supposed to be there. I had an accident, I broke an arm and both my legs. I couldn't leave the facility when

**53414e43494120737375726766976616c2070726f62616269
6c69747920302e303030302**

couldn't have kept me alive the way I was before until

**657374696d617465642074696d6520746f207265747572
6e206d696e696d616c6c6c20656**

Full shutdown, not even minimal life support. Ran out of everything

**68616420746f66669782053414e434941206d616b65206
86572206f6b206f6b206f6b2**

station finished all the repairs and started everything back up. There had to be

**737572676796363616c20636f6e736572766174696f6e206d6
178696d756d206566666963**

less of me and I had to be vacuum resistant

The residual dust left muddy streaks on Carollene's shaking, sweat-soaked fingers. *But what do you mean, WE?*

An image shivered to life, superimposed on the text window. A paper, dense with text and charts, the small, bold header in the sort of font Carollene had been used to seeing in high-level exec briefings. *"'A new approach to true AI: Experimental integration to enhance semi-autonomous machine intelligence using a coma patient's subcognitive potential,'"* she read aloud, numbly. *"Far Horizon Research Facility One."*

I wasn't in a coma. But the SeMI thought it might work anyway, and then I could help it figure out how to save the facility, how to save me—it knew everything about the facility, everything about human physiology, but it didn't know how to use what it knew and it couldn't act outside of certain constraints without a directive from an authorized administrator anyway. There was no other way. I would have di

73746f700a

STOP!

Carollene had quit looking at the video feed—partly from pity, partly from revulsion—her gaze jerked back just in time to see Zenya's hand flash through the beam from Bellows's arclight, something small and chunky wedged tight into his gauntlet. It had a handgrip, reflecting dull silver, with a short, thick tube protruding past his fingers.

"Wait, what are you *doing?*" Carollene yelped. "Zhenya, wait!"

Abruptly the fishbowl's audio feed snapped online. "*—wait!*" echoed, jagged as cut glass, from the vid, her own voice now tinny and unreal. Bellows jerked back and the gun-thing in Zhenya's hand paused its upward swing. "That's a *survivor!*"

"Are you outta your fuckin' *mind?*" Bellows, in a panicked screech. "It's some kind of monster! Captain, shoot it!"

Thankfully, Zhenya lowered the gun's muzzle. "We're not here to hurt you," he said, slowly and clearly. "I just want the SeMI. If you tell me where its core is located, I can get you out of here. Get you some help." It was weird, even in the only corner of Carollene's mind still functioning normally, to hear Zhenya attempting to sound pacifying. It was like watching a rabid dog trying to soothe a lamb.

On the video feed, the head atop the meaty, limbless, metal-banded slab of scarred flesh twitched. Carollene's stomach lurched. Words appeared on the console's screen.

"Captain, it's talking to me," said Carollene rapidly, eyes flicking between text and video feed. "It says—I mean, *she* says— uh. She says she can't give you the SeMI. I mean, *look* at her, obviously she needs it, right? To survive?" Carollene shuddered in spite of herself.

"If she comes back with us, she won't need it anymore."

"We don't have *anything* like what she'd need on board the *Ost*—"

"Shut up," said Zhenya, and Carollene uncharacteristically obeyed. The silence that fell after the last echoes of her own voice died in the fishbowl was thick and ugly.

"She doesn't know what she's talking about." Zhenya was addressing the head now—*Sancia!* a small voice in the back of Carollene's mind insisted. Not *the head!* "We can keep you alive, take you back with us to a specialist medical center. Just tell me where the SeMI core is, we'll move you *and* it to our ship and leave this place behind like a bad dream."

On the vidscreen, Sancia's head twitched once more, harder, her long dark hair falling across one of the shining black orbs implanted in her eyesockets. *The vacuum,* Carollene thought sickly. *She had to replace her eyes too, because of the vacuum, I bet. Can she see with those? Really* see?

He's lying, isn't he? The words spilled out silently across the console screen.

I don't know, Carollene tapped back frantically. *As far as I know, all we've got aboard are some medkits and a low-end surgical suite—but it's not* my *ship, I've only been on it for a couple of months. But maybe that would be enough? Especially if your SeMI was with us? It obviously knows how to—*take care of you, Carollene found she couldn't quite bring herself to say.

"Jonaitis?"

Carollene snapped her attention back to the vid. Zhenya was still staring narrowly at Sancia—at what little was left of Sancia, anyway. "What?" Carollene whispered, then cleared her throat. "Yes?" she said, more strongly.

"What's she saying?"

"Nothing."

In Carollene's three-quarters view of his face, Zhenya's forehead visibly laddered. "Tell her we're waiting."

No.

Carollene's gaze flicked back to the right side of the screen, panic knotting up her stomach. "Uh—"

We need more data. Tell him

6c696665520737570706f727420636861737369732c2072
657370697261746f722c206469616c6c797369732c20696e7472
6176656e6f75732066656564696e670a

we need to see what's on your ship first.

"I think—she wants to see the *Ostatny's* manifest? I guess to see what we've got onboard that she and the SeMI could repurpose for life support, or maybe rig together with something from the station?" That was reasonable, and certainly not impossible to achieve. Carollene felt the muscles in her neck and back, so rigid they had started to ache, sag with relief. "I don't think I can access that with the just the handheld, but it'd be easy enough to pair it to the SeMI from the *Ostatny's* bridge." For the first time in hours, her own sense of humor stirred to life. "I *absolutely* volunteer to get the hell out of this station and go back to the—"

"Fuck this," said Zhenya. In a single smooth motion, he whipped the gun back up and fired it point-blank at Sancia's torso. Another scream ripped itself out of Carollene's throat, as much from shock as horror—the flare of the gun's muzzle lit up Sancia's face, the inhuman eyes utterly without reaction but the narrow, delicate chin and jaw, the only beauty left to her besides her hair, snapping back from the impact against her metal frame.

A familiar, piercing wail—the station's klaxon blaring, just as Carollene had heard it on the first video, but now in real-time, deafening—the last thing she saw on the video feed was, not too surprisingly, a thick-jointed appendage swinging up and out from

Sancia's metal frame, smashing into Bellows's unprotected face and flinging him back against the wall. Carollene didn't bother waiting to see what was happening to Zhenya—she could guess, and she had *far* more important things to do right then. She surged to her feet and broke into a dead sprint for the door that led to the station entry corridor. Behind her, the video feed blinked out of existence, replaced by large block text, unseen—*Wait! Please!*

The door failed to green-light as she pounded toward it—no surprises there, as was its absolute lack of movement as she skidded to a halt in front of it. Thankfully, it had a manual access panel on *this* side too—she clawed at the panel for a mindless second, then remembered her toolkit and wrenched it off her utility belt. After what felt like an eternity but couldn't have been more than a minute or two, she had the panel cover pried off.

Her fingers were still a few millimeters from the lever when a fat yellow spark jumped from it, snapping into her exposed skin—she shrieked, more from surprise than pain, and yanked her hand back. She started to reach for it again and thought better of it—the SeMI *had* to have done it, turned on some security protocol or something. That realization came simultaneously with *but my gauntlets are insulated!* and *Holy shit, I left my gauntlets AND MY SUIT HELMET back on the console—*

Carollene lurched back up to her feet and wheeled back around to face the console, just as the door at the far end of the fishbowl cycled open.

Time seemed to slow, freeze into a hideous tableau— Carollene, half-crouched on the balls of her feet, every muscle straining forward towards the helmet and gauntlets sitting in plain sight on top of the console; Sancia, motionless in the open doorway. Sancia, liberally blood-splattered—how much of it was hers, and how much...? Carollene's wide, staring eyes locked on Sancia's face, on the dull black orbs framed by long hair now stringy with drying blood. A shudder shook Sancia's metal frame, and for the first time since Carollene had seen her, her facial muscles moved—her mouth fell open, just a little. The klaxon shut off; in the dead silence that followed, Carollene could hear the faint wheeze of Sancia breathing. Another shudder jerked the metal frame, and Sancia's mouth opened wider. A low, croaking sound issued from her throat.

Carollene darted forward. A handful of bounding, giant steps brought her back to the console; she snatched up her helmet and gauntlets, then turned and pelted back to the entry door, fumbling the gauntlet onto her right hand. She dropped down to her knees and shoved her arm in the panel, her gloved fingers clamping down hard on the door lever. This time, the electrical surge didn't confine itself to a few puny sparks; the flare of power lit up the entire wall in front of her, scorched the fingertips off the gauntlets, and plunged straight into Carollene's all-too-conductive body. Carollene spasmed hard enough to rip her hand off the lever, eyes rolling back in her head, and thumped to the floor in an ugly, motionless heap.

HostName= FarHorizonRF01-SeMI-00
    HostID=c615d983-a399-44a0-8111-e906ae39c482
    DateTime=232112031600
    RunJobs: 2025/0008/COUNTER: PAUSED
    Is she dead? Is she dead? Is she dead?
    SANCIA INCONCLUSIVE
    I told her to wait!—she wasn't like them, *she was trying to* help—
    >Power   on: ROOMMONITOR   ROAMING   SENSOR 00/01/02/03/04
    ADHOCJOB03: Remote medical protocol self-check.
    2025/0009 ADHOCJOB03: OK
    ADHOCJOB04: Roaming sensors online.
    2025/0010 ADHOCJOB04: OK
    PULSE 0. RESP 0/0. BP 80/45. CT 95C.
    DBQUERY: 'electrical   shock   medical treatment':<'cardiopulmonary resuscitation'>
    >Administrator\SANCIA: MOBILITY APPARATUS overclock 110/120/130
    SANCIA WARNING! Health monitor REDLINE SANCIA NOK SANCIA
    I don't care! We have to get her to Medbay!

HostName= FarHorizonRF01(arch)_OstatnyRF01(online)-SeMI-00
    HostID=c615d983-a399-44a0-8111-e906ae39c482
    DateTime=232201251449
    RunJobs: RESET/00000
    The *Ostatny's* bridge was quiet, even peaceful—Carollene, sprawled out in the astrogator's console chair, eyed it all with a sense of astonishment mingled with satisfaction. She had done it, *really* done it. She thought she must have doubted herself, even doubted the entire proposition, more than she'd realized over the

past several days of back-breaking labor. "I don't think I quite understood how *many* physical components you had, before this—you're sure we moved everything over here?" The bridge lights pulsed once. "And you're positive we got *all* the interfaces with the ship's own systems working?" The bridge lights pulsed twice, almost impishly; Carollene grinned in spite of herself. And her back, no matter how much it ached from all the lifting, carrying, endless hours of installing, was *not* broken at all—she twisted an arm around to touch the curve of her spine, gingerly. The shipsuit was warm and rough under her fingertips; she gave it a quick pinch, smiling bemusedly, then clutched at the console as the entire chair listed alarmingly to the left.

"The chair! It's broken." She wrinkled her forehead. "I think I did know that, actually." She reached for the astrogation console and tapped the screen. It lit up, but her expectant smile faded at the forest of yellow *Warning! Caution! ALERT!* messages abruptly crowding it. "Wow. That can't be good." Her fingers drifted lightly across the screen's surface. "You know I don't know anything about this. How to fix all this, I mean." She paused. "It wasn't our specialty. *Isn't* our specialty."

An icon bloomed on the screen, scarlet and blue with laurel leaves woven through the ornate, old-fashioned font: *Welcome to Far Horizon, paradigm-changing technology for future generations!* An image of a page shimmered into existence—*Specifications for the Moughton-Hesaki D-Class XPL Cargo Freighter*, read the header. The screen flicked to a second page, then a third, fourth, faster and faster until they were a whirling blur, dense with tables and schematics. "Oh, good, you found the ship drive manuals! At least it *has* manuals. I was worried about that. We didn't think much of the captain, you know. *I* didn't think much of him, either."

The console screen flickered; the schematics were replaced by thickly worded page with a small, bold header: *"Consciousness transference in vegetative patients with non-traumatic brain injury with real artificial intelligence: A bioelectrical and surgical approach." Far Horizon Research Facility One.*

Carollene looked sharply away. "It didn't really work out the way I hoped," she said softly into the *Ostatny's* wheezing silence. "I thought maybe—after we did it she would still be there with us, you and me, you know? *Really* with us, not just some memories." Grief pinched the skin between her brows. "Maybe we just weren't fast enough, maybe her heart was stopped too long—"

The screen blanked, leaving only the yellow error messages scrolling in a band across the bottom, then switched to a familiar, pearlescent gray, punctuated with plain black font: *SANCIA READY PRELAUNCH SEQUENCE?*

Carollene glanced down at her hands, lightly clasped together in her lap; after a second, they unclasped themselves and rose up to rest gingerly on the console's smooth, cold screen. "We've got this. We *do*." Her fingers trembled against the screen, then stilled. "We know what we're doing."

SANCIA OK, the screen announced firmly. *OK OK OK.*

"Yeah, I'm *OK OK*—but you know what? We'd better change that admin tag."

The screen flickered once. Then:

>username:Administrator\SANCIA login:*************

>Login SUCCESSFUL

>ALTER USER 'SANCIA' withName='CAROLLENE JONAITIS'

"Right." Carollene sat up straighter. "*Now* it's time to go, huh?" She ran her hands through what was left of her hair, wincing as her fingers accidentally bumped into the still-healing scars ridging her scalp. "Okay, drives *on*—wow, they do sound terrible. We'll have to work on that. We'll have plenty of time to figure them out, though. After all, we're pretty good at making things work out in the end, aren't we?"

See Lisa Short's story "Far Horizon" online at Metaphorosis.
If you liked it, leave a comment. Authors love that!
Remember to subscribe to our e-mail updates so you'll know when
new stories are posted.

About the story

This story was actually inspired by an open submissions call for another publication a few years ago—I didn't come anywhere near finishing the draft of the story I envisioned in time to submit it to them, though. I put away the thousand or so words I'd already generated, but the story idea did stay with me; I wanted to finish it! There's been a lot of hoopla around AI in recent times, and this story at least somewhat reflects my intermittent exasperation with the situation, specifically what "AI" means as envisioned by speculative fiction writers and IT professionals (both of which describe me) and what "AI" means as advertised by people trying to sell it to those who are neither. Basically, "AI" is not "intelligent" and is not even remotely close at present times to "intelligent..." (but then a little voice in the back of my head whispered, what if an "AI" could actually be integrated with something that was intelligent, genuinely intelligent? What would that look like?)

A question for the author

Q: Are titles easy or hard for you? Do you start with the title or the story?

A: It's funny because sometimes, the title of a story just comes to me—that is how the story itself comes to me, as a title! However, when this does not occur (which it doesn't the majority of the time), generating a title for a story is often a brutal slog. If I really, really just can't come up with anything by the time I've written the entire first draft—and I am usually trying to think of something the whole time I'm writing—I have a matrix I use, where I free-associate and write down absolutely any and every word that comes out of that brainstorming session that has anything at all to do with the story.

About the author

Lisa Short is a Texas-born, Kansas-bred, Maryland-resident writer of speculative fiction. www.lisashortauthor.com; @Lisa_K_Short on X/Twitter, Instagram, and Threads; lisashortauthor.com on Bluesky

A word about Thomas Ha

We first published Thomas Ha with "Where the Old Neighbours Go" in September 2020, just four years ago. He followed up quickly with "A Compilation of Accounts Concerning the Distal Brook Flood" in April 2021 and "Orla, Always" in December of the same year.

Thomas' stories have quickly and deservedly drawn attention — winning and nominated for major awards, reprinted in *Year's Best* anthologies, singled out in industry roundups, etc. Thanks to fluid, literate prose and well developed characters, he's clearly an author whose impact will grow, and we're happy to have him in *Metaphorosis* again with his latest story, "The Fairgrounds".

The Fairgrounds

Thomas Ha

Young boys in love will do stupid and dangerous things.

Henry's grandmother had warned him of it, that night, when he was headed to the fairgrounds alone, now that he'd finally reached the age to attend unaccompanied. She had wrapped his olive green scarf around his neck and lowered his wool cap, and looked into his eyes to say that thing about boys in love because she seemed to sense why he was going and whom he was going for.

"So I'm not allowed?"

"What?"

"To the fairgrounds. You're not going to let me go?"

"I didn't say that," his grandmother answered. And she hesitated, as if she wanted to say something more, but wiped her hands on a dish towel and pursed her lips instead. "Just take care, Henry. That's all. Now go, before it gets too late."

And so, Henry left: first walking, then running out the back door. He scooped up his bike and hopped on and pedaled down the crooked and hilly street, squeezing his handlebars while the crisp not-quite-winter prickled his ungloved hands. His cheeks and his chest felt unusually warm. He was too excited to feel any tightness in his legs as he pedaled past the sheriff's station and the children's park and the Main Street shops.

Henry thought only of her as he rode to the fairgrounds. Seeing her, like a kind of apparition in the darkened sky, or in the branches of the maples along the houses—the girl who sat at the school desk just two seats in front of him, over by the window, with light glossing the river of dark hair that ran down her back.

Grete.

She had only joined Henry's class recently, in the early, leaf-laden days of October. Her family had moved to the town from somewhere far, like Oregon, which to Henry was just a word, like

Europe or Babylon. But those days since her arrival had been filled with a new kind of slow wonder for Henry and many quiet daydreams about the kind of person she might be. He had heard someone say she was Michael McCormick's cousin, or maybe related to the Changs who lived across the street from the library.

But he had never gotten close to asking about her. Every time she turned to pass papers back, he dared only look at her for a second, then down again at his desk before her eyes could ever meet his. It was just her name and its sound repeated in his thoughts, like some secret part of the Hail Mary that no one had taught him.

Grete.

The blurred glow of the fairground lights just beyond the town center rose as he pedaled uphill, pushing harder to meet the crest where laughter and music were beginning to grow louder. Henry dropped his bike next to a railing and fumbled with the chain. Unable to find his lock, he decided just to tie it and hastily hid the wrapped links under the body of the bike.

When Henry reached the entrance flags, he dug into his pockets and carefully unfolded the seventeen dollars he had saved from cleaning yards and moving Mr. O'Leary's garage boxes. The bills felt hot in his hand.

Grete.

The ticket-taker materialized next to the meter. Colors flashed and jarring music blared as his mustachioed face lit the air and crackled. "Welcome, welcome, to the fairgrounds, son. If you'd kindly scan your I.D. tag down at the screen and follow the prompts."

Henry swiped his wrist tag and fed four dollars into the machine for a child's ticket.

"Thanks, HENRY. Are your folks here with you, by any chance?"

"No, but...I'm—I'm old enough. Like my I.D. tag says. Twelve and a half."

"Ah. Yes, I can see your tag information here." The image of the ticket-taker blinked and crackled. "But unaccompanied minors can only stay until eight, which—well, that's coming up very soon. I'm not sure I should be letting you in, really, with how close the first closing is, but..."

Henry held his breath for just a moment, and then the face filled with light looked left and right and gave him a little smile.

"But okay, HENRY. You go on ahead. Just be quick, understand? You've got less than an hour before they have to escort you out. Go on. Go on." The ticket-taker winked.

"Thank you!" Henry said, in almost a shout, and hurried onto the grounds. His shoes squished almost immediately into wet mud matted with grass and hay, and every step grew slower as he trudged through, trying to get his bearings.

Teenage couples held hands and whispered the way young lovers did in the movies. Above, where the bright hanging bulbs bled light upward into the darkness, Henry saw the holographic projections of people riding one of the twisting glare-coasters. They were screaming and whooping from one of the tents below, where their bodies were strapped into rows of chairs with immersive goggles and sensor beads.

Near one of the booths, a girl younger than Henry was eating a giant blue synthesized cotton candy, ripping tufts away and stuffing her face while her parents took pictures of her. The three of them were dressed in down coats, nice ones, with no loose threads or missing buttons. Henry watched them, the way they talked and laughed, and he thought about buying one of those cotton candies, too, before remembering why he was here.

Are you going tonight, Henry? To the fairgrounds?

Henry had almost missed her question, that afternoon, when Grete had tapped his shoulder, right there, in a soft spot next to his collarbone. She had been out in the hallway, holding her books to her chest. And in the hours since, he imagined the moment again, and again, her in front of him, like that. Her eyes, big, and maybe only in his mind, with a hint of sadness in them.

My father, he won't let me go. But I hear it's fun. Is that true? That it's a lot of fun to go, when they pass through town in the fall?

Y-yes. It's...it's fantastic.

And that was it, really, all he had managed to say before she left, waving as she went off to find someone. It was probably no longer than half a minute, if even that. But that little tap on the shoulder, that question, was how the idea, small at first, had begun to grow—the idea Henry had, of showing Grete the fairgrounds, even if her father wouldn't allow her to go there herself.

He'd find a way to bring a piece of it for her, he thought. He was old enough now, knew enough now, to buy something like that. Maybe a toy or a streamer or something else. That could work. Something small and perfect that would impress her. That was the plan.

Are you going to the fairgrounds?

Yes. It's...it's fantastic.

Fantastic...

And there it was. Right where Henry had hoped. The virtual text crawled up and down the electronics of the tent fabric, the way that it had the year before, and the year before that, and the year before that:

THE INCOMPARABLE, INCORRIGIBLE, ILLIMITABLE PROFESSOR DIEDERIK VON KEMPELEN NUMINOUS MIRACLEMAKER AND PHYSIKER EXTRAORDINAIRE

Henry knew that if he had any hope of bringing Grete something she would like, it would be here, with this man, the one everyone called Professor DVK.

The boy passed through the canvas threshold and into the little world of the Professor's curiosities. Much of it was unchanged since the last time Henry had been inside, as though the fair had never left town and the tent hadn't moved an inch. There was that strange and oily smell, like a doctor's office combined with the perfume shop his grandmother would visit. And on each side, a series of tables and shelves, displaying every manner of delights from faraway lands. A mummified hand with a bionic eye in its palm waved from its jar of preserving liquid. In a terrarium, a metallic snake slithered its segmented body over and around a gnarled branch. There were all kinds of unusual devices and containers cluttering the tabletops and crowded under chairs.

And, at the back of the tent, there he was: the man whose every thought and idea were manifested within the circumference of this little canopy—Professor DVK—sitting in the deepest meditative peace, so that he almost seemed to be asleep, with smoke rising from his pipe in concentrated, uniform puffs.

"Oh."

The Professor opened one eye slowly to look at Henry, then the other eye quickly. And there was a squeal from the microphone in his throat-box as the Professor jerked to his feet. The faintest hint of light surged through portions of his skin.

"Well, hello there! Yes. Hello there! Hello!" The Professor straightened and smoothed his jacket lapels. "Welcome, please. Yes. Come in, come in. Don't be shy, don't be shy. How may I help you this fine evening..." The boy's tag information flashed in his pupils briefly. "HENRY?"

"Hello, Professor," Henry began, aware of the fact that first closing was drawing in, and he looked here and there at the Professor's contraptions for something he might buy. "I'm so glad I made it, because I—I don't have much time. I was hoping to find something. Something nice. For a gift," Henry explained.

"Oh, a gift." The Professor's eyes flashed again, probably reviewing whatever information the fairgrounds had stored on Henry from previous visits or from publicly available data. "For your...GRANDMOTHER, perhaps?"

"What?" Henry's face went red. "No, for someone else. A friend."

"Ahh," Professor DVK stroked his beard. "A friend. I see. I see, HENRY. Well, there are many types of friends and many types of gifts. What type of person is this friend of yours? What do they like?"

"I'm not sure," the boy said, speaking the realization aloud.

"Well, what are their interests?"

"I'm not sure."

"What seems to excite them?"

"I'm...not sure."

"This is a most difficult task, then, for you, isn't it?" The Professor stood and paced around the inside of the tent. "Because, you know as well as I do—the act of giving a gift is about reception, how it is interpreted, what it signifies, not to you, but to them. And that's a near-impossible thing to know when you get right down to it. Not just in this instance, but in general. How well do we ever know anyone else, HENRY? How well do we know anyone? Not well at all! No, we do not."

Henry wasn't sure how to respond to the Professor, so he nodded along.

"Look, HENRY. You're a shining scion of the suburbs, practically full grown. So I think you are old enough to understand that I *could* string you along with something, if I really wanted—if I were the kind of man to do that sort of thing. I could offer you any of these trinkets or baubles or ingenious inventions and sell you some half-concocted story. Like, say, this neon spinning cyber-wheel: *forged with schematics from the ancient bricoleur-masters of the West*, I might tell you. Or this hanging chime: *designed using sonic sutras to find frequencies most pleasing to every individual*! But, listen, you would see through it, HENRY. And I'm *not* that sort of person, despite how I may appear and what they might be saying about me, out there. You'll get no silly stories, no misleading mumbo jumbo, no flim-flam from me!"

Henry did not know who or what the Professor was talking about, but he kept nodding, thinking only that he would have been perfectly happy with either the wheel or the chime the Professor had mentioned. The wheel or the chime would have made a perfectly good gift for Grete, he thought.

"You must understand, HENRY. As a gentleman of the Order of Perpetual Exchange, I couldn't possibly sully my reputation by giving you just any old novelty for whatever amount of petty cash you happened to bring. I take this completely, completely seriously, such that every customer's wish matters as if they were my own. HENRY. Ohhhh, dear boy. HENRY. How much money do you have on you, by the way?"

Henry held out what remained in his pockets, the thirteen dollars that were left after the entrance fee.

"Oh. Child." The Professor plucked each of the bills from Henry's hands and unfolded them on his desk. "I'm not even sure we have anything that would fit your humble means. But perhaps, that, in itself, is a blessing, because it rules out most of what I would probably have suggested. A blessing, yes."

Henry felt a little bit of a sinking feeling in his stomach upon hearing the Professor say this. And in his mind, that place where he saw Grete next to the classroom window, felt almost as if it was beginning to darken. That idea of her, that apparition, fading in and out of his mind, waning with the hope that he might have something to give her.

"But, wait!" The Professor slapped the table. "I do have something, HENRY. Yes! It might not be quite right, but it would fit matters like this, HENRY. Yes!" The man's excitement, his energy, filled Henry with a small burst of possibility, and like that, he could see Grete right there, by the window in his mind, again.

"What is it, Professor?"

"Come with me." The man laid a hand gently on Henry's shoulder and guided the boy over to one side of the tent, past several large cases and dummies dressed in sweeping robes and costumes, near a big shape that Henry initially thought to be furniture.

"Have you heard of the Kastenherz, HENRY?"

Henry had not, and he told the Professor so.

Professor DVK waved a hand at the large metal box, which was about the size of a wardrobe and covered in a series of tubes and blinking lights. "This here, HENRY, is the apex of artistry, distilled. Forward-looking fantasy fuel. In a word, the *future*.

"The Kastenherz is engineered to analyze your innermost thoughts. It reads your spirit, your essence, by divining it from the air, the ambience, like the most mystical of antennae. It takes the information, interpolates, collates, consecrates, and then *voila*: it re-imagines and gives you, not what you *think* you *want*, but what it *knows* you *need*, HENRY. And that's its true genius, my boy. Because needs are tricky. They're never what we suspect. The devil lives in expectation as easily as disappointment. None of us want 'happy', *per se*, not in the strictest sense. We want difficulty. Intrigue. Excitement. Triumph. The beauty of the Kastenherz is that it interprets that for you. A test run. Let's give it a test run. We won't count this one to start, understand? What's your friend's name?"

"Grete."

The Professor hurried to the side of the large machine and fiddled with a few buttons and sliders. "Yes. Yes. Yes," the man muttered. A wheel and series of cogs turned in one quadrant of the box, in another part, something like pistons moved up and down. Henry watched as pixels danced on a small screen, forming different shapes—a heart, a skull, a horse, and then a moon.

Professor DVK clapped and howled with an infectious enthusiasm, and then they watched a piece of paper emerge from a thin slat into a tray near the bottom of the box. The Professor snatched it and then handed it over to Henry with a cheerful smile. The paper read:

Come, you, 'cross the autumnal divide, sleeping and walking toward the sundered boars,
No one knows their origins, but you wonder how they all once sang,
And you reach for beautiful reliquaries beyond holy grasping delight,
While Arion watches and holds men to the river, filling their broken heads with dreams,
Oh, GRETA, you GRETA, know only what skies hold in our way of going,
Cross those divides, Margaret's Sundries, purchases 20% off on Sundays,
GRETA, sweet GRETA, if only there were other ways to know the mind except sleep,
Then, perhaps, we would know your peace, GRETA.

"What?" Henry stared.

Professor DVK's plastered smile did not budge.

"It's...Professor, I don't..."

"Know how to thank me? A beautiful poem for a beautiful girl. The Kastenherz knows, see? This is what you give a friend like yours."

"It's...I don't know what this means. And it's not her name."

"Her name?"

"It's wrong. Her name is Grete. G-R-E-T-E. It's an 'e' at the end."

"Well, you didn't specify, HENRY," he clucked his tongue. "And it's just a test, a warm-up, like I said. So don't worry yourself with details like an 'e' or an 'a.' Miracles come in miles, not in minutiae."

"I don't know what that means—"

They were interrupted, then, by a movement at the entrance. A little girl, the same little girl outside that Henry had seen eating synthesized cotton candy, had come bounding in with her father and mother, all well-dressed and clean and happy. Professor DVK's eyes were noticeably drawn to them as information, important-seeming information, flashed by in his pupils.

"Professor, I—"

"One moment, HENRY. I must see to these fine people for a minute or two."

"But Professor," Henry cried and grabbed his hand. "The first closing. They're going to make me leave the fairgrounds soon."

"HENRY." The Professor's smile was gone, and the excitement and mirth in his voice evaporated, as if it had never been there. And it was slight, but everything from his eyes to his posture hardened when he looked down. "There are rules. An order of priority. You know how these things work. So wait your turn, and, *after* I see to them, we will finish up with you. Understand?"

The Professor shook Henry off, picked up the corners of his mouth into a big smile, and then turned to face the incoming family with joyfully open arms and talk of the wonders he planned to show them in short order.

Henry, meanwhile, stared at the piece of paper from the machine. He couldn't bring himself to look at the Professor, or anyone. He couldn't even bring himself to think of the classroom window and Grete, for comfort. That proud feeling he'd imagined, that puff of power when he presented her with the perfect gift, shrank and shriveled. Foolish, stupid, useless, small. Henry's eyes began to feel wet, and despite his best efforts, it felt like he was going to cry.

"I'm sorry. He's an asshole."

A voice spoke, barely audible, while the Professor continued to laugh and shout with the father of the little family at the other side of the tent.

Henry did not know where the voice had come from, but he turned toward the machine. He couldn't explain it, but he was filled with the strangest certainty that there was something else in the machine, living there, and it was speaking to him now.

"Yes, Henry. That's right. I am in here," the voice said. *"And I'm sorry about the misspelling. The output, the specific words, that's his doing, not mine."*

"Oh..." Henry said quietly. "That's...that's okay."

"He's like this often, by the way, the Professor. Nice and inviting, until he's not."

"It's...fine," Henry replied, even if it didn't feel that way.

"Look, you have to go soon, right? Before first closing, you said?" the voice asked. *"Can you help me? Please? Can you get me out of this thing? Take me with you?"*

Henry felt a compulsion, a curious pull in his thoughts, drawing him closer to the machine where there was a small area of darkened glass. Something floated behind it.

"He won't let me go."

"Won't let you go?"

"My father. And I just want to get out, just for a little while. But you'll help me, won't you? Please. It would mean everything to me."

Something about the way the voice spoke seemed familiar to Henry, like someone he knew. He touched a small button next to the glass, and it slid open. There was something on an interior shelf, but nothing like anything he had ever seen before—like a large egg but made of flesh-colored clay.

The egg turned, and a mouth in its skin smiled at him.

"There's a way out the back," the egg said, its voice clear now that the glass was open. "Take me, and we'll get out of here! Quick!"

Henry looked at the Professor, who was still talking and laughing with the family. First closing was almost upon them, and Henry knew that Professor DVK wasn't going to help him. Not now. Henry had seen things like this before, when he was with his grandmother in town—the way people in the stores and the parks would talk to other kids with mothers and fathers and nice coats, the way their gaze always drifted around and away from him.

And something about knowing that the Professor was like them too made Henry's heart burn with a cold anger, something new he didn't recognize.

"Let's go," the egg said. "Not much time. Come on!"

Henry could almost hear his grandmother in his mind—a warning, not to do what he knew he was going to do—that moment when he snatched the egg and then walked out of the back exit, hurrying around a few more turns until he reached a gap in the shadows of the tents where no one seemed to be around.

He placed the thing, the egg from the Kastenherz, on the wet grass, and it shook. Something seemed to be happening within the little thing. An eye swam next to another above the mouth, then came the lump of a nose, then more solid parts, like the clay that made up its shell was growing and expanding. After a few moments and a strange popping noise, Henry recognized a face formed from what used to be the egg, a face he had seen many times in his thoughts.

Grete.

The egg looked like the girl from Henry's class now.

Or, it looked like Grete's head, at least, with long hair spilling out on the grass, except instead of a glossy black, the hair was a soft white—like January frost.

"Thank you, Henry," the head that looked like Grete's said. "Could you pick me up?"

"What?"

"It's okay. Pick me up. We have to keep moving."

Henry lifted the head, then looked around worriedly—but none of the people over by the walkways seemed to be paying attention to him at all, perhaps distracted by more interesting and fantastical things in the main grounds. He thought to remove his olive green scarf, and carefully wrapped the head in it, leaving enough room for the head to breathe. And then he went backwards slowly, behind the tents, where rays of light from the main areas barely reached.

"What a relief," the head that looked like Grete with white hair smiled. "He never lets me stroll around like this, out here, you know. Forever. It really feels like forever, since I've been out of the box. Thank you."

"You're...you're welcome," the boy whispered, finding it odd to be looking at the face he'd imagined for so long, resting now in his arms. He was stunned by it, this thing from the Kastenherz, whatever it was, and how easily it seemed to change its form.

"And don't worry, Henry. I'm going to help you too."

"With Grete, you mean?"

"Keep going. That way."

Henry realized he was headed to parts of the fairgrounds he didn't usually go to. From between the tents he could see dozens of fairgoers gathered together, talking very loudly, some holding cups and others of them dancing. He'd heard of this place set aside for the older fairgoers, the social square.

Many of the people there were wearing holographic masks, hiding themselves with strangely lit disguises. There were a few who looked like they had giant bug heads, with clicking mandibles that dripped when they spoke. An older boy, much older, maybe fifteen or sixteen, turned the collar of his mask on and flipped through the presets until he'd made his head into a 20th century automobile. Cat people, bird faces, cartoon eyeballs were making noise, a kind of charged, excitable discussion like at a party.

And in the distance, by a bent oak, Henry recognized Father Joyce from the school chapel by his clergy shirt. He seemed to be dancing with a tall, very tall, maybe genetically enhanced person. And this person was wearing a mask of some kind of beast with curved horns, giggling and squeezing at Father Joyce's back.

For a short time, Henry tried to imagine Grete there too. He tried to picture how the two of them might wander out into that crowded area under the blaring trumpet music. How they would try on masks or dance or talk like the older kids and grownups were doing over there. But he couldn't quite see it, and the air felt too hot and noisy.

Something about those people and what they were doing made him uncomfortable, though he couldn't say exactly why.

"You can feel it," the head wrapped in Henry's arms said. "The emptiness in them. That doesn't go away. It just builds, you know."

"Oh."

He had heard many stories about the social square over the years, but this was all very different from what he had thought it would be.

So Henry kept moving, further away from the music, deciding he didn't want to see much more of this part of the fair. He wanted to know where they were going, but he sensed that the head would lead them and that he would know soon enough.

Under the walkway lights in the distance, Henry watched men made of stained glass performing for a small crowd. They banged against one another in mock battle. Again, again, again, until one of them shattered and the people clapped.

"We're almost there, Henry."

"And we'll find something there? A gift?"

"Not exactly," the head smiled. "When I read you from inside the Kastenherz, do you know what I saw, Henry?"

"What?"

Grete.

Henry was embarrassed, trying not to think of the image he'd been holding onto, of the girl by the classroom window, because he knew the head could probably see it too, with whatever talents it used to read his mind in the Professor's tent.

"Yes," the head laughed. "That was part of it. That girl was part of what I saw. But, what you wanted, it wasn't really about her under the surface. Like you told the Professor, you don't know her. Her interests. Her likes. No, Henry. What you want is something else."

"What's that?"

The head didn't answer. "We're here."

The sound of the fairgrounds seemed muffled and small. They were by a large black tent at the end of the lot, surrounded by darkness, crates, and trash. The mud here felt thicker, like pitch oozing from the edges of the black canvas. And everything smelled ripe and heavy—nothing like the candied air and popcorn where the crowds were.

"We're here to pay our respects. Come on."

Henry didn't know what that meant, but again, he felt that feeling he had at the Professor's place, a nudging in his thoughts, like the head that looked like Grete was prodding him. He followed the prodding, into the musty dark of wherever this was.

"Everything in the fairgrounds runs on flash," the head told Henry. "And my father likes it—to pretend that it's all modern miracles and machines. He hides the messy things from before, like me and others. He doesn't want people to know how old it all is, I suspect. And so he chases that bright flame of youth that's always just around the corner. The trends, the fashions. Desires and tastes. Always flickering, always changing, depending on the moment.

"Before the holographic, there was cybernetic, before cybernetic, mechanical, before mechanical, there was us."

As his eyes adjusted, Henry realized there were solid metal bars not so far to his left, and something long and scaly shifted behind them. To his right, another set of metal bars, and behind them, three golden eyes looked out at him. He continued forward, trying not to get too close to any one of what he assumed were cages, unsure what kinds of animals were moving about within.

Until eventually, they reached a large, dimly lit cage in the center of the tent.

A very big creature, with its back to them, slowly turned.

And at first, Henry thought it was a man he was looking at.

There were muscles and shadow that looked like a torso and long forearms extending into massive hands. But instead of a face staring back at Henry, it was the maned head, long muzzle, and wet nostrils of a horse. For a brief second, Henry thought that this was a person with a holographic mask, like the people in the social square, but there were no streaks of light, no glare, no trickery of that kind. This horse-headed man was nothing like Henry had ever seen or heard or read about, and a part of him was certain that this thing, and maybe all the things within the black tent, were not creatures he would find anywhere else.

"Kneel," the head that looked like Grete whispered.

So Henry did.

The horse-man leaned into a small patch of light from a hanging bulb, its black eyes drinking in everything in that tent, including the boy and the small head he carried. Henry felt that the other animals in the shadows of the tent were all watching carefully.

"He's the oldest of us, the strongest, but also the tiredest," the head smiled. "He doesn't like being cooped up back here in this tent. Hasn't for a long time. Like me, in the box, I've felt it. So, he and I, we share a certain kind of understanding, I think."

There was a chill in the air. Henry heard sounds that weren't exactly sounds. Echoes he thought might be of the thing that looked like Grete, talking somehow to the horse-man, without words. The horse-man breathed heavily through its mouth, and those eyes, like pools of reflective oil, studied them for a while.

"Yes," the head that looked like Grete said. "No. Yes. I promise."

The horse-man's face loomed above Henry, silent.

"Yes."

The horse-man shifted, just slightly, but it was enough that Henry began shaking involuntarily. The creature did not lunge, only moved its heavy body closer to the bars. Then the horse-man extended a large wrinkled hand with its palm upward.

"Go on," the head that looked like Grete said. "Give me to him, Henry. It's okay."

The boy was afraid, but he was more afraid of disobeying. He unwrapped his scarf and raised the head, placing it into the huge palm in front of him, and the frosty hair streamed down between the creature's callused fingers.

The head that looked like Grete started quivering, much like it had when it changed its shape before, outside the tents. The edges of the head puffed, expanded, and the skin of Grete's face seemed to stretch and latch onto the horse-man's giant hand. The fleshy parts kept growing, seeming to swallow up the large fingers and palm.

"Close your eyes, Henry," the head said.

And Henry closed his eyes.

Grete, he said to himself.

Grete.

Grete.

He thought of the window. Streaming light. Wooden desks. Dark hair. He imagined her two seats in front of him, looking out, looking back. A smile. He tried to ignore the sounds of loud and rapid breathing coming from the cage ahead. He tried to ignore the strange roars, the chattering, the screeches starting to rise from other cages in other parts of the tent too, crescendoing.

Grete.

Grete.

Grete.

That secret part of the Hail Mary he recited to drown out the noise, growing louder and more intense, like it was all whirling around his head.

Grete.

Grete.

Grete.

Again and again and again and again and…then.

Everything stopped.

There was only the weight of silence and stillness, and a small, familiar voice.

"Okay, Henry. You can look."

Henry didn't want to, and he waited. But eventually, he did open his eyes. When he did, he saw that the cage was empty. The horse-man, whatever it was, or whatever it had been, had vanished. And instead, in front of the cage, next to him, she stood.

The thing, so much like Grete.

Her hair, soft and bright, like the moon. A neck, shoulders, arms, legs, and wearing a white dress like most girls wore to church.

"All done," the girl said, as lumps of skin seemed to rise and sink near her throat. There was some kind of movement there, inside of her, that made Henry look away. He tried to peer into the shadows, toward the other darker edges of the black tent, and he realized the other cages, what he could make of them, seemed to be empty too.

"Did you…hurt them?" he finally asked.

Not-Grete shook her head.

"Of course not. I'm helping them, like you helped me. Just in a different sort of way."

Henry did not know what that meant, or what had happened, but he was too afraid to ask and too scared to look around any further.

"Come on." Not-Grete laughed and she reached out and held Henry's hand. She was warm, small, and gentle. He focused intently on her hand. "Let's go."

He followed her, out of the black tent, out under the stars. She interlaced her fingers with his and led him back toward the noise and the movement and the people walking. The laughter and the lights out here felt strange now to Henry, having seen what was back there, in the dark. But he kept on walking.

A loud chime rang over the fairgrounds to announce the first closing. A number of children and families were going in a slow throng toward the entrance flags together. Not-Grete squeezed Henry's hand and leaned on him, and he felt relaxed, fuzzy, like he was in some kind of dream.

The two of them walked between those others, shuffling, and Henry saw Professor DVK, far off, standing in front of his tent, scanning the grounds like he was looking for something. The Professor's eyes reached them, and he froze, his body perfectly still.

The Professor's face blanched, and something flashed in his pupils as he stood there. Henry wasn't sure, but he thought the Professor recognized something in Not-Grete, something that made him too terrified to say or do anything as they walked away. The Professor seemed so small to Henry then—just a withered version of the man in the tent—smaller and smaller in the distance, until they left him behind completely.

When they reached the outside of the entrance, Not-Grete took Henry over to his bike, still unchained, and propped it up for him. She looked into his eyes and smiled sweetly.

"Thank you, Henry. For tonight. We won't forget this, you know," she whispered, and, for a brief moment, Henry thought he heard other voices in the wind that softened and were swallowed by the crinkling of leaves. "Anytime you need us, anytime at all. We will be there for you. Just think it, and we will come. We mean it. We promise."

Henry stuttered, unsure of his words. He looked at her face, so much like Grete, but so clearly something else, leaning forward to press her lips gently against his cheek. And he felt his face burn.

Then she turned, like she was tracking the shapes of the people nearby—and there was the family from the Professor's tent earlier, nice and clean, the father, the mother, and the little girl. And Not-Grete had a strange expression on her face as she followed them with her eyes, which appeared darker than before. Henry didn't like that look in her for some reason.

"Goodnight," she said.

"Goodnight."

"Think about what we said, Henry. About what you wanted. What you really wanted, when you were looking for that gift of yours." She smiled. "You already got it, you know."

Henry didn't understand, but before he could ask her, Not-Grete walked away, like an animal slinking into the night. He wondered if she meant it, what she had said, about being there when he needed her, always there, somewhere. And part of him felt happy about that, but another part, a smaller part of him, felt unusually cold.

Henry trudged away from the fairgrounds—down the hill and up another, pulling his bike in a daze. When he returned, everything was bright and warm inside his grandmother's house. He felt too tired to talk, but he went to the kitchen where his grandmother was waiting. She had prepared a bowl of rice soup and watched as he shed his cap and scarf and sat silently, eating. She somehow seemed to know that he didn't want to say much, and so she didn't pry or ask how things went.

After he'd finished and gotten ready for bed, his grandmother was there to press his blankets over him and brush the hair from his eyes, talking to him as she often did, while he got sleepier and sleepier.

"The fairgrounds are strange," he heard his grandmother say. "Like everything out there. Heavy, their strangeness."

"Yes..." Henry said softly.

"There's no hiding that from you," his grandmother said. "The more you go out, the more you'll see. Not just in the fairgrounds. But everywhere else too. The fairgrounds are just a concentrated piece of it, a symbol, of whatever else there is out there."

"Yes..." he agreed.

"And it's not always good, not always bad. It's just there, everywhere, and you find it and make things of it as you go on in life. We all have to."

"Yes..." he said.

"You have to be careful with what you make of it. Promise me you'll be careful. Because I can't do it for you." Henry's grandmother searched his eyes, like she had some notion of what he'd been through, but not enough to ask him in detail. And Henry had the feeling that this might be the way it would be between them, not just for this, but other things to come.

"I promise," he said.

"You've had a day, I can see. So I'll let you rest. Goodnight, Henry. Goodnight. I love you very much, little one."

"I love you too."

The room went dark, and Henry stared drowsily at the ceiling. Somewhere in his mind, he felt the faintest glimmers of light and the softest sounds of distant music, drifting over.

He thought again about what his grandmother had said, about the fairgrounds as a kind of symbol—the strangeness it contained. The exciting, the frightening. The heartbreaking and the fun. And he imagined, beyond the house, the fairgrounds, and even the town, more bright and empty things he might one day find. Soft and precious things too. And a dull and ever-present ache that joined everything together.

These hazy thoughts filled him with a distant ease, but there was also, underneath it, a quiet sense that something terrible had happened tonight. Something important that he might have had a part in, but did not fully understand.

Not-Grete had said he had gotten what he'd wished for, and, the more he thought about that too, and about Grete, the more part of him realized it had never really been a girl, or a gift for her, that he had yearned for, not really. He would see her again, on Monday. And the day after—there, in the classroom. And maybe they would talk more, but, more likely, they wouldn't. His young mind would drift wherever it would drift next, and his brittle sense of her would fall away like the crackling leaves before the season's end.

Like the fairgrounds, Henry thought, the longing he thought he felt might have really been a piece of something else. Of knowing things, and of growing older, and of becoming more like all the others.

Of growing up.

Henry dropped further into the fullness of sleep, and as he did, he tried to imagine the familiar window again, and the desk near it where the light fell. He tried to see the girl that sat there, the way he had before, but the memory of her already felt insubstantial, like smoke.

Grete, he thought.

Grete, he prayed.

Grete, he dreamed.

Less a boy, less a child, he grasped for it, the feeling that had been in him before.

Grete.

But he wasn't sure he would ever find that same feeling again.

See Thomas Ha's story "The Fairgrounds" online at Metaphorosis. If you liked it, leave a comment. Authors love that!

Remember to subscribe to our e-mail updates so you'll know when new stories are posted.

About the story

This story was heavily inspired by James Joyce's "Araby". A young boy goes to a bazaar to impress a crush and leaves with new, mixed feelings about the world and his place in it. When I read it when I was younger, there was just something very powerful and palpable about that kind of "first crush" feeling and the rollercoaster that entailed. I wanted to take that basic core and add to it, complicate it. This world also has strains of Bradbury's dark carnival stories, like "Something Wicked This Way Comes", among others, with some sci-fi and weird fiction elements layered in too. And lastly, I thought this mirrored my very first story in Metaphorosis, "Where the Old Neighbors Go". Both are sort of classic speculative fiction that's not entirely devoid of hope, but not entirely glossy and romantic either. It's dark and it's strange, there's pain, and there's some love and familial affection in it too. It's the kind of story I like and like to share, I guess.

A question for the author

Q: Are you a Luddite? Or do you have the latest and greatest technology?

A: Boy, that's a topical question! I know Luddites are being heavily debated again lately, especially their opposition to the ways in which technology may be misused to exploit labor (rather than being opposed to just the tech itself). I guess my answer is that I'm always wary of new technology, particularly when it extracts value and doesn't necessarily create anything of value in return. I'm slow to trust new developments as a general matter, though, so that probably isn't limited to tech!

About the author

Thomas Ha is a former attorney turned stay-at-home father who enjoys writing speculative fiction during the rare moments when all of his kids are napping at the same time. Thomas grew up in Honolulu and, after a decade plus of living in the northeast, now resides in Los Angeles.

thomashawrites.com, @thomasha.bsky.social

Fall

Metaphorosis
speculative fiction   Oct-Dec 2024

Art
Carol Wellart

Stories
The New Western   E.C. Dorgan
Core   Damien Krsteski
This is my City...   Suzanne J. Willis

A word about Carol Wellart

I'm not an artist, at least visually. I can imagine all sorts of fantastic scenes, but as for getting them down on paper or screen? A child's stick figures would look good compared to my efforts.

That was a stumbling block for the magazine initially. I can't draw, and didn't know any artists. Happily, we were able to attract a wide range of talented folk starting midway through the first year, and the problem was largely solved.

What we didn't have, though, was any kind of signature, standard look, and occasionally a scheduled artist would fall through for one reason or another. We found the solution in Carol Wellart.

Carol did her first cover for us early on, in 2017, and quickly became one of our regularly returning artists, with seven covers between 2017 and 2021. It would have been more if I hadn't felt obligated to work in people who'd been waiting patiently in our artists' roster.

For 2022, though, I asked Carol to provide *all* the covers for the year, and happily she agreed. For 2023, she provided half of all covers — again because I felt an obligation to give a chance to other artists on the roster.

The four cover artists for 2024 are among my favorites of the artists we've worked with. But if there's one artist who could be said to be Metaphorosis' principal artist, it's Carol Wellart, who in addition to the magazine provided the cover art for our anthology *Score*. This final cover for Metaphorosis is a beauty again, based on E.C. Dorgan's story, "The New Western".

Thanks, Carol. We owe you!

Be sure to check out Carol's other beautiful work at **carolwellart.com**.

A word about E.C. Dorgan

E.C. Dorgan's first story for Metaphorosis ("The Beast Consul") was in our December 2023 issue — the last story in the magazine's eight year run of unsolicited stories (bar one). I ran it there because I thought the story encapsulated all the things the magazine has striven for — beautiful, lyrical prose, engaging characters, and a thoughtful, emotive concept. In this final year, we've published only solicited stories, and I liked Dorgan's writing so much that I asked her back for the magazine's final issue.

I'm happy to say her magic has worked again — though in an entirely different way. Enjoy "The New Western".

The New Western

E.C. Dorgan

I can't think straight with the broncos stampeding up and down the mirrored walls of the elevator, so I press all the buttons and stomp my cowboy boots on the marble. I should be fighting a monster, not stuck in an underground parkade. This city's built on petroleum rivers and decaying dinosaurs, and if I don't find a way out of this elevator, me and my two horses will be bones too. The broncos neigh and I throw my head back with them.

I thought fighting the monster would be easier. In my old life I didn't know he existed. Lightning birthed my broncos and opened my eyes too. I was no one before; I wandered aimless through canola fields without a dream or a destination, only a history I was escaping. I was a trope, a 'woman with a past' in an old western, but on the day of my rebirth, I became something new.

On the day of the change, the sky blackened and the flies surrounding me quieted. I opened my mouth and looked up to the sky. A bolt came down from the heavens and met another one rising up from the earth. They joined in front of me and the world went grey, orange and white. I was deafened and my mouth filled with nitrogen. My legs lost feeling and my stomach emptied.

I rubbed my eyes and found shiny beetles. I looked down and saw two smoking Ready Reckoners. I picked them up and the movement made my arms burn and throb. I rolled up my sleeves and my breath went out of me.

Two flame-coloured horses jumped out of my elbow crooks and raced down my forearms. They started out tiny, but grew bigger with each step. By the time they leapt from my fingers, they were giant beasts. Their hooves sparked on the dry earth and my heart thumped in time with their galloping. The earth heaved under their weight. For the first time in my life I felt the petroleum rivers under my feet and they were sloshing.

The horses disappeared on the horizon, but returned when the sun set. They haven't left my side since and they both bear the name destiny.

Not that it's any help now. The truth is, broncos don't like elevators and I'm not much for them either, especially stuck like this. All three of us are panicking. A beetle falls from my eye onto my pearl-snap shirt pocket and it reminds me of my Reckoners. I cross-draw two copies of the old-time guides and flip through the burnt pages. Our monster nemesis may have sabotaged this elevator, but I know there will be something in these books to help us. They've never failed us yet.

Sure enough, I find the chart to free us and the horses grunt and clack their hooves while I do mathematical calculations. I finish and show my hot-headed horse where to stomp in the elevator's weak spot. We climb out of the elevator and I turn back to kick it. It doesn't make a dent, but the scuff from my boot gives me satisfaction. The monster's going to have to try harder—this is the new Western and I refuse to be written off.

The whole downtown shakes as we rumble down the sidewalk. We're late for our showdown, but my horses are fast. When we roar into the shopping mall, the monster's already in the food court waiting for us, sipping a latte and checking his phone.

No one looks up. They don't care that there's a monster in their midst, sitting placid while his enterprises wreak destruction. He probably has machines toppling trees right now. Factories making poisons to snuff out flies with iridescent wings and eyes that hold all the colours of creation. The first time the broncos pointed them out, I wept and the beetles that fell out of my eyes withered from the fumes in their proximity.

We've been chasing the monster for three years. We've had a few scuffles, but he's always steps ahead. My horses showed him to me on the day of their birth and mine. We galloped into the city thinking we'd change everything. There was no smoke in the air and all the poplars along the highway waved and egged us on.

Now I'm losing calcium and my eyes are full of beetles. The monster's older than me, but a picture of youth. People shrink from me, but they can't get enough of him. His face is on the cover of every local magazine. They say he's our city's very own 'hero-entrepreneur' and 'influencer'.

I've caught glimpses of him in old time westerns—he plays landowners and ranchers, laying claim to land that's not his. The name and face varies, but the eyes never change.

Now he trademarks seeds and makes poisons to kill 'weeds'. He's been clearing prairie in all his iterations and he's never stopped hating poplars.

He's diversified his businesses. It's not just land and agriculture—he has part interest in the production of sharp-phones. They're marketed as smart-phones, but more stylish. I know they're something more—those phones can cut to the bone.

Even worse, they limit imagination and warp vision so when people see me, their eyes show them a woman past her prime dragging two leather reins, not a hero with two destinies in the new Western.

Our eyes meet and he takes a last sip of latte and throws the cup on the floor. He takes off his suit jacket and lets it fall on top. He crushes them both with his alligator loafer and a shopper gasps at the sacrifice of something so expensive. He grins—he loves waste more than anything.

Me and my broncos approach and I feel people watching. They can't see the horses, but they feel the rising tension. I hear whispering and people rummaging for their phones. Someone says, "crazy lady." I tighten my jaw and resolve not to listen.

I lift my chin and try to straighten my spine. The monster shakes his head as though he pities me. The crowd titters.

I try to speak, but my tongue twists. My broncos neigh on my behalf. I pull out a Reckoner and aim it. The monster makes a face like he's scared and the crowd laughs even louder. He opens the flap of his bag.

I'm about to throw the Reckoner when a bronco steps in front of me. It's the soft one, the one that's expressive. She blinks and her eyes say we don't need this. My other bronco snorts and looks away.

My horses look the same, but they couldn't be any more different. One is hot-headed and mad at the world, the other's a gentle peace-maker. The angry one wants to fight everything and turn the world upside down, the soft one wants to let the world be. She thinks peace and love will solve everything.

My soft bronco looks to the west and I follow her gaze. Can't see a thing in this food court, but I know what her mind sees: a sky candy-pink from wildfires, a sea of yellow canola, flies buzzing hypnotic, and past that, a refuge of poplars.

I blink to tell her I also see it. I can feel my resolve softening; there's a part of me that knows fighting is futile, especially throwing two beat up books at a monster who's resourced with everything. My back aches, and I wouldn't mind an afternoon in the trees. Though peace can't help us—I've seen enough westerns to know that, at least.

The monster taps his fingers on the bag, mocking me. The crowd thins, tired of waiting. I exhale and feel my adrenaline draining. My knees tremble. I've been standing too long and that elevator took too much out of me. I put my arm out to lean on a column.

My angry bronco huffs, but understands I need rest. The monster says something under his breath and the remaining onlookers break out laughing. A beetle falls from my eye and I step to the side to avoid squishing it. People see an aging woman losing her footing. My horses steady me and somebody giggles. My angry horse snorts, wanting to trample everything. I tell him we'll get revenge another day.

I climb on the horses bareback and we race to the exit. The city shudders under our weight and we can feel the elevators in parkades underground buckling. We race west down the highway and don't slow until we're far from the skyscrapers. I dismount in a field and we wade through waist-high canola. We ignore the 'No Trespassing' sign, and the logo of the monster's trademarked seed. My angry bronco takes out her anger on the canola while my soft bronco and I walk through the crops.

We come to a poplar bluff and lean against the trees. The flies shine technicolour under the afternoon sun. The air is acrid and the smoke's too thick to see the horizon. There are fewer poplars now to slow the wildfires.

I kick off my boots and press my toes into the earth. Can almost feel the petroleum rivers rushing under us. Before the horses, I never felt them. I was a side character in someone else's narrative. There was much in that life that I missed.

I take off my hat and lie back against my broncos. Flies sing and I almost forget about the monster. We relax into each other and when the sun sets, we watch bats fly jagged and listen to coyotes yip under a sky with no moon.

We don't stay long in the poplars. By morning, my angry bronco's bouncing off trees and searching for barbed-wire fences to topple. She wants back to the city to hunt monsters, but by the time we get there, our lungs are sore from the thick smoke. So we lounge on the sofa in our skyscraper rental, the broncos dozing on each side of me while I watch the river reflect pink off the smoke-cloaked sun.

It's hard for the horses in the city. Crowds make them uneasy and they spook at construction and the skyscrapers that pen us in. They hate our 17th-floor apartment—we're on our second warning and this is our fourteenth rental. I'm struggling to pay rent and don't have a source of income. It doesn't matter that I'm fighting a monster or that I can cross-draw my Reckoners like the lightning that made me, no one will give me a job. The landlords in this city don't care about our vocation, they just point to clauses in the rental agreement about cleanliness and noise.

It's easier for the monster. Everything is. It doesn't matter that he razes poplars and poisons insects, or that he warps peoples' minds with those sharp-phones. His pinstripes and wealth give him glamour. Before my rebirth, he would have cowed me. There was a lot that cowed me then.

The air shifts in my rental and the flies in my kitchen stop buzzing. They can sense the vibrations of those alligator loafers on cement. The static noise of all those sharpened cellphones. I don't feel it, but I trust my horses and those flies. It can only mean one thing.

My hard bronco grunts and paws the cushions. My soft bronco looks at me pleading, *no violence*. I hesitate and my hard bronco explodes a cushion. She wants badly to fight. She murders cushions and I pick up batting until finally I give up, reach for my Stetson hat and follow her out the door.

We walk downtown instead of driving and the streets, as always, are empty. We track the monster to the same downtown shopping mall that doubles as an office building. People jostle me on both sides, talking into phones and dragging shopping bags. Someone pushes me from behind. I spin round and reach for my Reckoners—but it's just a shopper encumbered with bags. I put away my books, then I'm hit from the side. This time I turn to face a man with white hair and black eyes.

I expect him to flinch, but instead he leans into me. His eyes widen and he takes in the broncos. "I'm sorry."

I can't speak. It's the first time anyone but a monster has seen the horses. For a moment I freeze, and then I want to say everything. How I was born a second time with lightning. How each bronco bears the name destiny. But my tongue twists and I choke.

My angry bronco pulls me. I turn to calm her and when I look back, the man's gone. I search the crowd but can't find him anywhere. I scan the mall again and my eyes lock on the monster.

His eyes glimmer and he smiles at me. He yanks off his earpiece, then crunches it under his loafer. He spills his latte over it, reveling in the waste.

My angry bronco paws the ground. Our blood rushes in time and I can feel her anger. My soft bronco blinks, but it's too late. I take out my Reckoners as the monster lifts the flap of his bag. He pulls out a sharp-phone and swipes wide. A garbage can flies and chicken bones and soiled napkins splatter shoppers. My broncos take off, but the monster's too fast. He swings again and a shopping bag shreds. He lifts the sharp-phone a third time.

I'm there a moment later. I slap the monster with each side of a Ready Reckoner while my broncos trample the sharp-phone. Someone yells, "Call security."

By the time they grab my arms and pull me off the monster, the broncos are frothing. Mall security helps the monster to his feet and returns his flattened phone.

The security guards step back when a man in uniform approaches like some old-time sheriff. I take him for police, then realize he's a bylaw officer. He takes out a notepad and looks up and down at me.

I straighten my tongue. "I was fighting the monster."

He raises an eyebrow and looks at the monster. The monster shakes his head and the officer suppresses a smile. "Lady, the world doesn't need heroes like you."

My broncos snort while he writes me a tickets for 'causing disorder' and tells me I'm 'lucky' the monster's not pressing charges. When the bylaw officer and mall security turn to leave, the monster smirks and makes an obscene gesture.

I spend the afternoon waiting in line to pay my fine. The bylaw officer wrote me a note on the back, *you should talk to someone about that temper*. I take a pen to scratch it out, but the words are still legible. When I get to the front to pay, the clerk reads the note and looks at me. I clench my jaw and I can't stop my face from reddening.

We spend the evening watching westerns, they're my broncos' favourite. The broncos doze off and I turn to the news—it's all about the approaching wildfires. I'm about to change the channel when the face of the monster fills up the screen and the news-reader announces a 'leading entrepreneur' has opened a new pesticide plant. At the end of the report she notes the entrepreneur recently endured an 'unprovoked' attack at the mall. I throw a Reckoner at the screen.

The next day me and my angry bronco are hungry for a fight and even my soft bronco doesn't argue with us. We track the monster to a coffee shop. He's in line waiting for a premium ristretto. A sharp-phone sticks out of his bag. The broncos lunge forward, and I fly into a couple in line in front of me. Someone behind me shouts, "Ma'am!"

The monster spins round. His eyes glimmer and he doesn't even show surprise. He lifts a finger to his lips and points across the street: the underground parkade.

I nod and call my horses to my sleeves. The monster takes his ristretto and saunters, sipping, to the street. It kills us to wait, but we've already attracted enough attention. The monster disappears into the parkade, and we step onto the street and follow him. The parkade has six storeys, but we know he'll be on the bottom. We race down the stairs—we're not falling for the elevator trap again.

There are no cars in the lot and there's only one fluorescent flickering. The monster's at the back, leaning against a concrete column. He's taken out his sharp-phone and loosened his tie. He throws his coffee cup to the ground and stomps on his suit jacket. He would waste the whole world if he could. He starts to charge and my horses and I run forward to meet him.

One bronco stomps the monster's hand and the other one kicks his phone. I'm slower, but already aiming my Reckoners. I throw them one-by-one at his face. It feels good, though part of me knows it's futile. The monster pulls a sharp-phone from a hidden pocket and swipes at my bronco. Time slows and I can't breathe. He misses, but my legs are shaking and the next time the monster lunges, it's at me.

This time he doesn't miss. I bring my hand to my cheek and feel blood. He raises his sharp-phone a second time and a bronco slams into him. He cries out and turns to run. My broncos give chase.

They disappear up the stairwell and I try to follow, but they're way ahead of me. When I finally reach the street, it's deserted. I trust my beetles and head for the mall.

It's even more crowded than last time. There's no sign of horse or monster, so I take an escalator up a level and cross the pedway to the office building across the street. I'm almost there when I hear a crash and a neigh. I start to run.

It's the end of the day, so the building lobby is empty. Even the security guards have disappeared on their rounds. I find my broncos and the monster by the elevators. Both broncos are bleeding and the monster's dropped his sharp-phone. My breath catches. This is the first time we've cornered him.

I rush forward as the elevator chimes. The doors open and the man with white hair and black eyes steps outside. He drops his briefcase at the sight of the broncos and our eyes meet a second time.

For a moment, it's just the four of us: me, my two horses and the first person to really see us. I can't breathe. I forget about the monster. I want to tell him everything. His eyes soften, but his expression changes when he sees the monster.

The monster takes us in. He smiles wide and the next moment he's moving so fast even my broncos can't react. I blink and he has the man in a chokehold and the cellphone blade taut on his throat.

I call for help but there's no sign of security. They're never here when it matters, when the monster gives up the facade of upstanding citizen and shows his true face. And of course we're in the one corner of the lobby without any cameras.

I throw my hat to distract the monster and the broncos kick at his phone. The man squirms out of the monster's trip.

"Run!" I yell to him.

My horses rear. The monster flees, and the broncos start after him, but I call them back to my forearms. I'm concerned about the blood. I run my fingers along their backs; they both have gashes but they're shallow. My injury's worse—my face is gushing blood and my cheek hangs loose like a flap.

"Here." The man holds out a handkerchief. His arm is trembling.

I want to say something, but by the time my tongue untwists the words are gone. The man waits and we look at each other. My legs are shaking. I can only stand there and watch while he leaves. He turns back once to look at me and a surge of electricity rises up in my belly and then fades.

Days pass and I'm still thinking about the man from the elevator. It's not just that I saved him. He saw my horses. He gave me a handkerchief.

One night, I dream about it. When I rescue the man from the monster, he mouths to me, *"Thank you."* My tongue is straight and instead of standing there, I tell him everything. We go west of the city and laugh under poplars and I show him how if he puts his feet just so, he can hear the petroleum rivers below. The dream lingers in my mind even upon waking.

We're listless in the city and my broncos won't settle, so I take them out west on the highway. The broncos graze on crops and we trample 'No Trespassing' signs until we reach our poplars.

We wander through the trees and find ourselves in a meadow of willow, dogwood, and wild rose. The land is pink and blooming. The smoky sun makes the colours more vivid. Beetles tumble from my eyes and burrow into the earth while the broncos nibble on flowers. I call my horses by their name and wonder why my own name is lost to me.

It's no secret why I was nameless before. I know how the world sees me. If this were an old-time movie, I wouldn't survive the first scene. But this is the new Western and I'm the main character. I get to choose who to be, even if I need two stubborn broncos to show me the possibilities.

We walk through flowers for hours. Our shadows lengthen and the meadow becomes more spectacular. I wish the man with white hair were here to see it. My eyes linger on the blooms and an idea comes to me.

I'm back at in the shopping mall with a feeling I don't recognize in my belly. My angry bronco's not impressed, she's swishing her tail and glaring at me. The softer one is quiet—she understands that even though I hunt monsters, there's more to me.

I walk through the food court, then browse in the stores. A security guard locks eyes on me and raises a walkie-talkie. When I look again, there are three security guards walking in step behind me. I ignore them and keep going, I'm not here to fight.

I cross two pedways so I'm back in the office tower. Workers rush by with their briefcases and earpieces. The blood by the elevator's been mopped up and there's no sign of our fight. Flies and cockroaches scuttle in the corner, going around their business. I don't see who I'm looking for.

I'm leaving the mall, about to give up when our eyes meet. The man with white hair nods at all three of us and my angry bronco who was swishing her tail and hating the world a moment ago bats her eyes at him and prances.

I wipe a beetle from each eye and try to quiet the flutter in my chest. I step in front of the man and hold out my present. I take a deep breath and force out the words I spent all of last night practicing.

"For you."

There's a pause and he doesn't speak. He hesitates, then leans forward and takes the bouquet. He drops it a moment later.

My stomach sinks and I realize my mistake. These are wild roses; the stems are covered with thorns.

The man pulls out a handkerchief to protect his hand. He picks up the stems and frowns. Mall security crowds around us for a better look.

The hard bronco huffs like I'm stupid. I look to the soft one, but she won't meet my eyes. Too late, I understand—it's not just the thorns, it's that I've handed him stems. Only stems. I've messed up again.

I start to explain how the broncos ate the blooms, but my tongue twists and my voice falters. I can feel myself reddening. I try to speak and beetles free-fall from my eyes. One lands on his tie. He recoils and brings his handkerchief to his mouth like he's going to vomit. I step back, into a guard.

The guard pulls away and makes a face.

The second guard holds up his hands and says, "Stay away!"

My legs are shaking, but I turn and start running anyway. My knees give out after a few steps, so my horses take turns carrying me. We gallop westward and I cry beetles while my cheek flaps in the smoke.

I try to forget the mall, but it eats at me. I can't stand that the monster's out there, clearing land and poisoning insects. My angry bronco wants to hunt and ambush him. She thinks it's a matter of might and getting lucky. We cornered him once, after all.

My soft bronco just blinks. She knows we're unmatched. She thinks we'll prevail through patience, that the monster will see the error of his ways. He just needs someone to show him the beauty of flies' infinite eyes or how poplar leaves shimmer like gold under late afternoon sun.

They're both wrong. I didn't used to dare think it, but we've had too many confrontations for denial. We've taken too many beatings, paid too many tickets, and been expelled from too many malls. He's not even fazed by our fights. Once he told me he was 'humouring me' by letting us chase him. He said that I should thank him. I hate that he's right.

We're bored in the rental, but the smoke makes us sluggish. We watch the smoke thicken above the river and when it gets dark we turn to Netflix. The broncos want to watch westerns but I'm sick of the genre. I want to try something different. I watch a rom-com and then another. There's something comforting about the genre. The plots are the same in both movies: the main characters start plain and unhappy. They face obstacles, but solve them through makeovers, book clubs, and meeting someone new. No one gets hurt, and nothing's at stake. By the end of both movies, the main characters are pretty, happy, and loved.

I'd like that. To be welcomed by security guards instead of followed by them. I stand in the mirror and try to picture it. Touch my hand to the wound on my cheek and wipe a shiny beetle from my eye. If I were in a rom-com, I'd know to give someone I just met thornless cultivated roses, not the thorny stems from wild bronco-eaten blooms.

It's not easy to find a book club that's taking new members. I drive deep into the suburbs for my first meeting, wearing long sleeves to hide my broncos and making the flies in the car nervous with my jitters. I ring the bell, and when the host opens the door her eyes widen. She recovers, then lets me inside.

The other members have manicured nails and matching lip gloss. I shake hands with stiff arms, hoping my broncos won't act up. The book club members ask if I'm married and where I went to school. I study the floor. They ask about family and I tell them I once had a dog named Gambler—my bronco snorts at the lie. They ask about kids and I mention the early menopause. They say they're sorry and I tell them I've never felt so alive.

We discuss a book that sounds like a rom-com and eat delicate canapes. The host passes out Prosecco in crystal flutes. We lean over the coffee table decorated with gold-brushed pinecones and vanilla-scented candles. I start to feel hope. When we clink glasses, I laugh for the first time in both my lives.

Somehow I volunteer to host the next meeting. The other members look worried, but the host reassures me. She walks me to the door and says I did 'great'. I blush and look away, but by the time I reach my car I'm beaming.

I sing to my flies all the drive home. My broncos snore the whole way, still behaving. There's something strange and lovely rising in my belly. It feels good to be a book club member. Maybe if I keep going to the meetings, I'll stop shedding beetles.

Back in my apartment, I open my closet and look for something other than cowboy clothes. I put on red lipstick and imagine myself with matching nails. I stand in the mirror with a bronco over each of my shoulders. My angry bronco snorts, disgusted, and my soft bronco blinks. For the first time ever, I can't read her eyes.

I pick up the book club paperback, but can't get into it. Read three more pages, then rip out the spine. The sound pleases me. I look up and both broncos are staring. My face reddens, but my hard bronco neighs. For once she approves.

I rummage for tape to repair the book, but my apartment's a mess. How will I ever host a bookclub? The living room's full of batting from smashed cushions and the coffee table is in two pieces. Swarms of flies live in my kitchen. I have no bowls of pinecones or scented candles to create mood. No sparkling wine or crystal flutes.

I call the horses to my sleeves and head out for the drugstore. When I come back to the apartment, I'm $25 dollars poorer and have a package of metal instruments. I can't afford it, but I know this is important. Spend two hours in the bathroom working on my fingers. I mangle my thumb, but by the end of it my brittle nails are painted crimson like blood.

The manicure takes everything out of me. I collapse on the sofa between my broncos. They put their heads on my shoulders and sniff my now-foreign fingers. I stroke their manes and tell them there are horses in rom-coms too. My angry bronco snorts and turns away.

My gentle bronco watches me. I know what her eyes say: we don't have to choose between book clubs and monsters. That we can stay here, just us three, watching the river. Or go west and wander through farmers' fields, communing with flies, rolling in monocultures and creating new spaces in the landscape for new poplars and wild roses to grow.

The river shines pink and the wildfire smoke makes me sleepy. I'm just starting to doze when my angry bronco leaps onto the sofa and cracks the frame. Her eyes are wild. The flies in my kitchen stop buzzing and we all know the monster's nearby.

My angry bronco slams herself against the front door. My heart is racing in time with her frenzy, but I fumble the lock, so she throws herself at the door frame, cracking it. *There's our third warning.* She shoots down the stairwell, no patience for elevators.

I put on my boots and reach for my hat. My soft bronco blinks with sad eyes. I tell her she can stay, but when I start down the hall her hooves clack on the linoleum behind me. Her eyes are hopeful all the way down the elevator. She doesn't want to fight, but she'll come with me.

We track the monster into the city centre, darting between buildings and empty streets. We rush through the mall so the security guards won't see us on our way to the office tower. There's a security guard at the elevator and another at the front desk. I hide my face and try to muffle the sound of my boots. I can't help the sound of the hooves on the marble.

We inch along the lobby, skulking behind mirrored columns and giant planters, and leaving a trail of beetles. When we come to the stairwell, we sniff the air. The broncos meet my eye and all the bugs in the corners confirm our suspicions. We race down the stairs to the parkade.

There's a thick metal door at the bottom level. I need both hands to wrest it open. It slams closed at our back. There's not a car in the lot and only one fluorescent light. The monster's slouching in a corner with a latte. He leers when he sees me and pats his bag with the sharp-phones. My angry bronco snorts.

The monster throws his cup so hard the sound echoes. He takes out a sharp-phone and holds it above his head. We don't breathe and for a moment there's no sound. Then the monster speaks.

"You can't possibly win. Why don't you just give up?"

I hesitate. We've had this conversation before. I can't bear that the monster speaks truth.

My hard bronco snorts and waits for me to signal attack. Seconds pass and I'm still standing there. The monster's right, this is futile. But I can't give up on my broncos—it would kill them if they knew. They each have hope, in their own way.

Besides, what else can I do? The other book club members don't even like me. The host is nice, but that's probably politeness. I'll never be pretty like in the rom-coms. And I'm not going back to my old life—it wasn't just the dog I lied about at the book club meeting.

My hard bronco snorts and rears on her hind legs. My soft bronco's eyes plead. I sigh and give the sign.

My hard bronco charges and I follow her with the Reckoners. The monster side-steps my horse and ends up behind me. He lunges with his sharp-phone—I try to dodge, but I'm too slow. Feel a hot pinch on my arm and another, hotter behind my elbow. I jump backwards, drop my Reckoners. Blood squirts onto my shirt. The monster raises his sharp-phone again.

I throw my head forward and head-butt him. My beetles fly into his eyes and he staggers backward blinded. Tries to stab me with his phone, but he's not even close. He doesn't see when my angry bronco kicks, aiming her hooves at his knees.

A moment later he's on the ground knee-capped. His face is purple and he's hugging his legs. This is the first time we've got him on the ground. My angry bronco neighs and prances—she thinks we've won. I almost dare to believe it.

I look down at the monster and have no idea what to do next. He's still groaning and not getting up, so I call my horses and lead them away. I'm just about to open that heavy door when the monster rushes us from behind with the biggest sharp-phone I've ever seen.

There's no time to react. He leaps toward me and I turn and crash headfirst into the metal door. My ears ring and the world becomes bright lights. There's a gust of air as the monster wields his sharp-phone and I brace for the inevitable impalement.

Instead there's a neigh and a loud thud. My vision clears and the monster's on the ground, dazed by the bronco that toppled him. My hard bronco shrieks and I lunge for her bridle to keep her from trampling his face. She makes a sound I've never heard and strains against me.

Somewhere to the side, there's a whimper. *No—my soft bronco*. Then I feel it in my viscera, the only good part of me, my heart, my world, ripping apart.

My bronco's on her side and I can barely see the giant sharp-phone, it's so deeply wedged. Her chest cavity is open wide, exposing slashed muscle and ribs that shine moon-white. She looks at me anguished and I can't meet her eyes. I fall to my knees.

It's my fault. I should have known he couldn't let us beat him. For all his talk about us being mere irritants, his world doesn't have space for roses or poplars. He despises flies and broncos named destiny with big hopeful eyes. It's not just the land he wants to burn and make all the same, he won't even abide dreams of other possibilities.

I touch my arm to her side, but she's too weak to climb into it. The cement behind us is splattered crimson and when I raise my arm it's dripping blood too.

My angry bronco screams and stomps so hard the cement shatters. The monster flinches when we turn to him. I close my hands into fists and throw myself at his face. My bronco stomps on his hands. He curls up into a ball and moans. When we're done, he doesn't look like a monster. He doesn't look like anything.

The blood around my bronco submerges my Reckoners. I scoop them up and flip through the pages, but there's no chart or calculation that can help her. I rip the pages to make a bandage, but it has no effect. I rip their spines and throw them away from me.

My angry bronco kicks cement columns until they buckle. The whole ceiling heaves. I kneel down beside my injured bronco. She rasps while she breathes. Salty beetles fall from my eyes and drown in her crimson sea.

We can barely open the metal door and carry my injured bronco up the stairs. It's my angry bronco that bears her. We leave a blood trail when we leave and we don't look back at the crumpled monster.

The vets turn us away, saying there's nothing they can do. It doesn't help that they can't see the horse, or that my other bronco is stomping the ground and snorting at them. They call it harassment and threaten to call the police on me.

We leave smears of blood on the elevator and down the hall to our apartment. My injured bronco survives the night, but doesn't improve the next day. She lies on the exploded cushions on my sofa breathing too fast, lips ashen. My other bronco's beside herself, destroying the cupboards and then the bed frame.

We watch the news and the announcement about the monster retiring from business after a 'freak attack and injury'. A policeman who looks like a sheriff says they're investigating. My angry bronco snorts at the television, but her heart's not in it. The victory's cost too much.

Two days after the fight, my angry bronco starts on the windows and I get an eviction notice the same day. After three days, the other bronco's barely moving. I don't know if she sees the smoky skies or the pink-reflecting river, or if she notices the thick smoke that wafts in through our shattered windows.

On the fourth day after the fight, I decide fresh air and trampling is worth a try. We drive west and I point the broncos to a field. My hard-headed horse goes through the motions, but doesn't take her eyes off her partner. My injured bronco lies unmoving on the canola. Her wound is full of flies and she stains the yellow crops red.

I take off my boots and sit with her. Press my toes into the ground, but the earth is compacted. I bend down to put my ear to the ground, but I can't hear the petroleum river. I listen for flies, but they're drowned out by the bronco's rasping. When dusk comes, the coyotes are silent and the smoke's too thick for bats to fly.

We return to the apartment, and the broncos collapse on the sofa. The hurt one is breathing so loudly that the kitchen chairs and the broken windows are rattling. I put my hand on her mane and her eyes almost focus on me. The other bronco pauses from destroying the television. I can't look at either of them.

I thought the new Western meant possibility, but now my future is withering right in front of me. We had a dream of space for poplars. I let out a sob and beetles gush from my eyes.

It's hard to think with the rasping and with both broncos watching me. More beetles fall and I think of the mall. When I leave the apartment, my arms are bare. I don't even bring my Stetson.

It's strange in the elevator without the broncos and I enter the mall feeling naked. The horses have become a part of me, I haven't been alone in years.

We pass a news crew and I stop to see someone interviewing a new 'hero-entrepreneur'. He tells the interviewer he just moved to town and he has big plans for the city and surrounding area. His face is different and he's taller. He makes herbicides not pesticides and his monoculture of choice is wheat. Instead of sharp-phones, he makes razor-wearables.

Our eyes meet and he pauses his speech. He smirks, but it's so fleeting the interviewer misses it. His eyes glimmer and he's speaking to me and praising the unstoppable spirit of industry.

I pass a mirror and recoil: my jeans are ripped and bloody, and one of my boots is missing a heel. The flap from my slashed cheek has fallen away, leaving a hollow. The only pretty part of me is the crushed beetle on my temple.

The mall is crowded, but the shoppers give me wide berth. I walk with my head down so mall security won't see me. Almost walk into a little girl dragging a giant shopping bag. I smile when she looks up, but her eyes widen and she calls her mom.

Her mom has nails like she belongs to a book club. I hold out my hand so she'll see I'm a book club member too, but the movement makes the little girl jump. She opens her mouth and screams, "Monster!"

That gets mall security's attention. One of the guards raises his walkie-talkie and the other motions with his hand. I prepare for confrontation, but both guards take two steps back, grimacing and making way.

The new monster pauses another interview to shake his head and wag his finger at me.

I find a drugstore that sells bandages and keep my eyes down at the cash. I lose a beetle while I'm paying and the cashier gasps.

When I reach the exit, the man with white hair is standing by the door. I look away, I can't take another humiliation, but it's too late, he sees me and calls out as I pass.

My face gets hot but I don't slow.

He starts after me. "I'm sorry!"

My throat catches. I take a step, then hesitate. My hot-headed bronco wouldn't waste time on something so frivolous, she'd be charging the new monster in the mall. But the peace-maker...I know what she'd do.

I start to turn. Have a vision of my soft bronco blinking. She'd want me to be kind. To have hope. She always saw so many possibilities. Like wandering through wild roses and making space for poplars. Holding hands and yipping with coyotes, then watching bats under the moon.

I straighten my tongue, but before I speak that image from the parkade comes back to me and the grief makes me choke.

His face falls and something inside me crashes. I push down the surge of feelings.

He apologizes a second time, but I'm already leaving.

I reach my building and step into the elevator. My eyes are overflowing with beetles and my bronco's blood is still smeared on the mirror.

I let out a sigh and my shoulders deflate. This isn't how I imagined the story. There's a mad bronco trashing my apartment and another on my sofa that's barely alive. Wildfires will reach the city any day. There are 'No Trespassing' signs and lonely bluffs of poplars to the west waiting for me. A monster I can never defeat. We'll be evicted on the weekend and tomorrow I'm hosting a book club. I haven't figured out anything.

I may or may not have a destiny. I still don't have a name. This is the new Western and it's being rewritten in this moment. I study my reflection and consider who I'll be.

See E.C. Dorgan's story "The New Western" online at Metaphorosis.
If you liked it, leave a comment. Authors love that!
Remember to subscribe to our e-mail updates so you'll know when new stories are posted.

About the story

I had an image of this character standing in a bright yellow canola field in a lightning storm while two broncos galloped off her forearms. I was simultaneously thinking about how there aren't a lot of "coming-of-age" stories with older characters. I became increasingly curious about this character, and I wanted her to have agency and a say in where her story took her. I didn't want the story to be neat and tidy. I also wanted it to have action, since most of my stories are slower. As I wrote the story, the broncos took on a life of their own. The hardest part in writing this story was figuring out how the broncos interacted with the world around them. I couldn't resist adding insects to the mix since they're quite beautiful and amazing and they often don't get credit.

A question for the author

Q: Do you often include animals in your stories? What role do they play?

A: Animals seem to turn up in my stories—while I don't consciously decide to include them, I would say that most of my stories have animals in them. I'm not a big plotter and I tend to write stories based on strong images. Often I will get pre-occupied with an image of a particular animal if I see one in my regular life. Lately I've had a bit of a horse fascination, though I don't see those often. My characters often have relationships with animals, either cats or dogs, or as in this latest story, broncos and insects. These relationships help to "show" characters, but I also just really like writing about them.

About the author

E.C. Dorgan writes dark fiction and monster stories on Treaty 6 territory in Alberta, Canada. She has a soft spot for poplars and insects and is not fond of rom-coms.

A word about Damien Krsteski

Damien Krsteski's first story for us was "Lake Oreyd", in the March 2017 issue of Metaphorosis. I loved it's strange world of snail-shaped churches on the edge of a lake (and was happy to have recognized its origin in Macedonia's similarly church-studded Lake Ohrid).

His story "One of the Cities" appeared in our *Reading 5X5* anthology in 2018, and the post-apocalyptic "The Trader" was in the emotionally-ordered *Score* anthology in 2019.

We were happy to have Damien's work back in Metaphorosis again with "Esma's Margaret", an emotive story of hackers and automated therapy in January 2021. That broad concept arises again in the next story, "Core", though in an entirely different way.

Core

Damien Krsteski

1.

Walking up to the door, I grabbed Ellie's hand and subvocalized, *You got this.*

"I know," she snapped. "I'm completely fine."

So be it, I thought, and squeezed her hand.

The door swung open and Mr. Mueller beamed at us. "Right on time, ladies."

He ushered us into the living room and poured the three of us a warm cup of valerian brew. I hated the stinky stuff, but the Muellers had elevated its consumption to a family tradition, so like it or not, I was destined to drink this disgusting cat-piss until the end of my days. (I'd refused when Ellie brewed it at home, but here, as a guest in the Mueller house, I didn't dare voice my taste—or hepatotoxicity—concerns, certainly not today of all days, so I sipped as little as possible and smiled.)

"How's work, Alice?" he asked me. "Your company was in the feeds again."

"It's been busy," I said, playing down the chaos in which we'd collectively embroiled ourselves recently. Training AIs to perform therapy for overseas patients carried risks; especially if those foreign hospitals our company targeted could afford only the cheapest of licenses for our software, then stretched the terms of use to their legal and practical limits by recycling the same AI agent for multiple patients. Which in turn caused confusion, ineffective treatments, and in several extreme cases, worsening of symptoms leading to fatalities. Obviously, our company and product were blanketed in layers of legalese, so we were deemed safe come litigation or audit, but the press that followed the incidents was in no way good for our business. Public consensus was that it remained our company's duty to make sure our products were used to spec.

"No doubt. Just the other day I was reading reports about this clinic in Bolivia, where one of your—what do you call them, digital therapists?—got so clogged up with patient information that it started spewing entire sessions back at them, giving advice on claustrophobia to a schizophrenic, and treating a narcissistic person for alcoholism. Ridiculous."

Mr. Mueller was an educated man, albeit not a scientist; even so, he enjoyed teasing me for my chosen profession. I always took his jabs in stride, writing them off as the unavoidable bickering of in-laws which had plagued marriages since time immemorial, and I tended to respond in kind. Tonight, though, considering what was about to come, I decided to let him have this one win. I resigned, saying, "A failure on our part. We should have foreseen this and implemented better safety checks."

"Yes," he said, looking slightly disappointed, as if just deprived of a juicy debate. "Safety checks, remote monitoring, circuit-breakers, yes, yes."

The discussion then veered toward Ellie and her latest project, and Mr. Mueller simply nodded politely as he always did when she talked about her art. We sipped our tea. We nibbled on cashews and peanuts. When our stomachs began to rumble, Mr. Mueller carried the valerian tea tray away and brought out a spinach quiche and a bottle of cider.

I finished my piece and had helped myself to a second serving when Mr. Mueller realized Ellie hadn't touched her slice. He said, "Is everything okay, dear?"

"We're going to have a baby," Ellie said.

Mr. Mueller stared at us for a moment and said, "Well, that's fantastic news." He laughed. "I'll go fetch the real stuff." He stood up, but before he could disappear down into the cellar, I nudged my wife.

"Planning to," she said. "We're not pregnant yet. We're just planning to."

"Still," he said after a beat. "That's news worth celebrating."

"You didn't ask us how."

"What do you mean how? Splice, obviously." He pointed at the two of us and mimed the exchange of genetic material by waving his hands from Ellie to me and back. "Or, are you thinking of going for a male donor? A friend? A colleague?" This last question directed at me, as if Ellie couldn't possibly have any male colleagues at the art institute of *good stock*.

"No, dad," she said. "None of those, really."

"Oh." His smile slipped from his face. He sat back down. "Then what?" But he knew, and his eyes showed it. He was a man who followed the feeds, and we'd discussed this latest trend before, or, as he'd referred to it, *latest cult*, and he quickly put two and two together. After a while, he said, "So that's why you're here, then? To duly inform me my grandchild will be a *world-baby*? A step-child of globalism? An orphan with millions of parents?"

I could sense Ellie pulling back, so I interrupted: "Mr. Mueller, please. There's no need for this. We already—"

"Don't." He raised a hand to stop me.

Softly, I said, "You haven't had any time to process."

"This is bullshit."

"I believe it's best we leave you to it."

I stood up and tugged at Ellie. We dressed, and we were on our way out when she turned. "You know, Dad," she said, "an orphan with millions of parents, loving her each one bit, is still better than the daughter of a man who's head is stuck so far up his own ass he can't tell up from down, right from wrong."

Mr. Mueller opened his mouth to respond, but I said, "That's enough, both of you." He nodded, went back in, and we caught the first bus back home.

2.

Just as I'd expected, Ellie didn't take her father's reaction lightly. She barely slept that night, tossing in bed and keeping me awake too, until we both decided to give up on the preposterous notion of a good night's sleep, and trundled grudgingly down to the kitchen to have a cup or two of espresso before dawn. She complained to me with tears in her eyes, and I just stroked her hand. We'd known he'd react badly, and we'd spoken about it at length beforehand, so in some ways I felt Ellie was exaggerating, playing out a role she'd rehearsed in her head ever since we'd made the decision to have this baby. The hurt daughter. The slighted queen.

Of course, I didn't tell her that.

At the office, I buried myself in work.

Groggy and sleep-deprived, I slipped on my headset, and the panels flooded my retinas with cold light.

In a garden dotted with ponds, I sat at a wooden table opposite a neatly-dressed man: the avatar of one of our CBT software agents. A glance at my wrist display revealed my role was that of an obsessive-compulsive.

The agent began with the usual opening: did I have anything urgent to discuss this session? How had I been coping? Had I been a good patient and done my homework, journaling every clinch of my obsession and each release of the ensuing compulsion? We did the standard warmup Q&A dance, and after ten minutes of that the session properly started.

He asked me if I'd eaten out in town since last we'd spoken, referring to a particularly strong paranoid obsession of the person I was playing: fear of food poisoning from any meal not cooked at home under pristine conditions.

Yes, I subvocalized, *I ate a slice of pizza from this place close to work.* The agents were capable of hearing speech, obviously, but when training them in VR I tended to feel too self-conscious and even a tad insulting, pretending to have a different mental affliction every session, so I preferred to *sub.* I'd let the shirt collar sensors pick up on the electrical storm raised by my neck muscles and convert that thundering to voice, which was in turn relayed straight to the agent's language processing modules.

"Could you describe the experience?" he said.

So I did, inventing as much detail as I could in an attempt to overwhelm the agent with data: the crowd at the restaurant, the color of the napkins, the name of the waiter, the way he touched money before handling my cutlery, my quote-unquote astute observations of the kitchen and its cleanliness from the vantage point of the table by the milkshake machine. And on and on. Let him sort it out, I thought. Figure out what was relevant.

Which, I was surprised to find, he did quite well. He filtered out all the cosmetic details and went straight to the point: what made me think it was *bad* to not wash one's hands a thousand times a day? How dirty could money really be? What made me believe a kitchen had to be absolutely pristine?

Isn't it obvious? I asked.

"No," he responded. "It isn't."

Well okay, I said. *Imagine a flood of bacteria and viruses moving from hand to hand. To my food. Invading my body. Isn't that horrible?*

"Not necessarily. You seem to harbor a deeply ingrained bias. Not all bacteria are harmful. And being exposed to the bacteria or viruses that may be somewhat detrimental to health isn't necessarily a bad thing. In fact, exposure helps us develop immunity, and medical research has repeatedly shown—"

I liked where the agent was taking this conversation, which is why I decided to throw a wrench in his gears.

Why should I care about supposed research?

"Because it is true. The scientific method—"

From the same people who made these viruses, who poisoned our waters.

"Another bias," the agent exclaimed. "The scientific method relies on experimentation, and proof, and replication of results."

Speaking of which, is this an appeal to authority I am hearing?

At which point he launched into a tirade against me, and no matter how much I tried to steer him back on track, the conversational path he'd decided to go down branched out only to confrontational nodes, and to a potential real patient storming out in anger in some clinic somewhere in the world, and to Mr. Mueller catching the exaggerated clickbait about it online and cackling to himself about our poor work or bad auditing or some such.

I realized I was getting all worked up.

Stop, I subvocalized, for the agent's sake as much as mine. *Listen to me now.* Which flipped the switch to learning mode. I explained that he should under no circumstance turn against the patient in such a manner, that he should focus on strategies that involved the patient, cooperated with the patient, walked the patient step-by-step through a novel way of thinking until at long last a cognitive change was triggered. We repeated the sentences. We practiced a few different conversational flows. *Begin again.*

"Why do you consider it bad, not to wash one's hands so often?"

And we went down the same path again, and I pushed and tugged and drove the agent into a corner until he, once more, resorted to attacking.

"No, no, no!" I said out loud and shook my head. Marsha Linehan, this agent wasn't. I scribbled notes in my virtual pad and logged out in frustration.

When I took off my headset, I was surprised to see Phillip standing by my desk.

"That bad, huh?"

"I swear, they get dumber by the session."

"Seems like you're in dire need of a change."

"Of career." I placed the headset on its dock. The panels briefly flashed acid green as it began to charge.

"How about just a change of department to begin with?" An intricate graphic played out on the tablet he held out before me: a stylized human brain, enveloped in a mesh of sorts, with patterns of neuronal firings flashing with varying intensity. When he saw my puzzled expression, Phillip added, "We've been working on a little something for the past year, Alice. You're one of our best trainers here. I want you to see this."

At home things seemed unchanged.

Against my advice, Ellie had called her father during the day, and as expected it had turned ugly real fast. By the end, they'd been shouting at each other, and as was always the case in these bouts of frustration between the two of them, somehow somebody had brought up the topic of her deceased mother. After that prying of open old wounds, all hope of reconciliation would have to be delayed by another two weeks, at the very least. When Ellie finished recounting their argument to me for the second time, she looked up expectantly.

"You have to let him cool off." I lay on the couch and flicked a random feed address at the screen before us. An old movie I'd seen once on an airplane was playing on this feed. "Just drop it. Give him a week. Come, sit."

But she just stared at me, subbed, *You don't get it, do you?* and she lay down beside me theatrically, like a third rate performance of Juliette in Act 5.

3.

To ease her mind, I'd promised Ellie I'd talk to her father myself, so before work I swung by his workplace.

Mr. Mueller had once been a decent network engineer—a chapter of his biography he never failed to bring up—but with the onrush of automation and self-improving software agents of all sorts, human supervision became increasingly redundant: machines had learned to load-balance their own network traffic and to set up their own development infrastructure. ("Look ma, no sysops," as Mr. Mueller liked to put it.) So nowadays, he was a freelance consultant for companies still clinging to the old model of work, or whose software relied on antiquated network architectures which the machines had deemed not worth bothering to master.

I rang the doorbell. For a moment, I thought he wouldn't let me in, but then the latch clicked and the door swung open.

He went back in and slumped in his big chair. "What do you want, Alice?" He swiped a finger over his tablet screen lazily, scrolling through some schematics.

"For you to sober up," I said, "for your daughter's sake."

"Please."

"You two are beyond childish. She, with her stubbornness, and you with your refusal to take a moment to *understand*."

He tucked the tablet between the cushion and armrest and steepled his fingers. "Understand what? That my only daughter refuses to have a normal child? That she's more interested in some philosophical roll of the dice?"

"A *normal* child? With all due respect, Mr. Mueller, but your reaction is just the selfish gene talking. What if we'd opted for adoption?"

"That would be fantastic. Why don't you?"

"It's perfectly within our rights not to justify our choices to you. What is within yours, is either to accept them or not, nothing more. Whether we adopt, have a biological child, or a Child of the World—the decision is ours alone."

"Eyes from Laos, skin tone from Cameroon, mood predispositions or proclivities for music or love of science or literature or even tolerance for goddam milk sugars from the four sides of the globe. You'll be cherry-picking your child's features from a field as wide as the Earth, and I just have to accept, and demand nothing else from you."

Poetic in a feeble effort at ridicule, nonetheless his argument rang hollow. The whole point of having a Child of the World was *not* to cherry-pick, *not* to choose, unlike what most would-be parents did nowadays: selecting their children's looks and faculties from a catalogue in a geneticist's waiting room. First I thought I should let this misunderstanding slide, but I realized that if he were to eventually understand us and our choice, he should have the facts straight.

"The opposite, Mr. Mueller. We don't choose anything. We simply take it all. We take everything this beautiful Earth can give us." I tapped my chest. "What is mine? What comes from me? This body, these cells, these atoms, these ideas? You don't seem to understand that everything is everybody's. And the sooner we all grapple with that fact, the easier the Transition will be."

"The *Transition?*" He studied me awhile, then said, "Those are Ellie's words coming out of your mouth, Alice."

Somehow, this hurt me more than it should have.

"We're both equally onboard. We both want this Child."

"Please," he said. "You don't want a baby," he said. "You want an exercise in combinatorics."

Phillip had me transferred to his department within a couple of days; they were in need of people, fast. With all the commotion around our failed licensing agreements in Latin America, it seemed the company was eager to move at least some of its eggs to a different basket.

"Reprogramming humans," was how he'd originally explained his team's work to me. "Rebuilding memory. Ripping out fear, physically."

"As opposed to?"

"Merely treating it." He winked. "Treating it with *speech.*" He mimed gagging.

He showed me around their offices briefly, where in place of headsets on docks and cliché Freudian couches, there were people in lab-coats shuffling about with beakers and pipettes and peering down microscopes. Past them, we went into a meeting room where my official onboarding took place.

I learned, from presentations by young neurologists, all the intricacies of the department's work: the fishnet mesh of microscopic neurobots which glommed onto the brain's topmost layers to observe and direct; the even smaller bots which burrowed their way deeper into the subject's cortex and modulated synaptic activity while scanning the amygdala's responses, closing a real-time feedback loop; the research into the delta opioid receptor agonists that apparently had laid the foundation on which the rest of the work was built. The neurobots, I learned, camped out in their synaptic valleys and meted out these new synthetic chemicals to patients, softening their fear responses, but also helping their brains unlearn the context in which these fears occurred.

"So," I said at the end of one presentation, "the patients start to unlearn their fears, their feelings."

"After one session," the neurologist said.

"Like a sped-up exposure," I said.

"Yes, and no," she said, waved the slides away so a new batch could take their place, "Because we've discovered something altogether different than mere fear eradication. We've realized that patients can shape their opinions, their beliefs. We found that our swarm of neurobots, when directed properly, can work in concert to challenge people's core beliefs. What we've found is a way to *actually* change people's minds."

Inside of a week, I already felt right at home in this department. Work was all-consuming, and the novelty of this research was refreshing to the point where it felt like working in a completely different field.

I was burning through transcripts and video snippets of subjects who'd gone through these therapies and new neurobot hardware, which I learned they affectionately called *the rice*, and had come out with their fears of heights or cats or dogs or abusive lovers fully shed, reemerging as new persons. I played with snapshots of the agents that had guided these patients through their sessions, and started tweaking them somewhat.

Once I finished with the initial batch of recordings, I moved to more intricate subjects, namely people who had come to have what they considered a *bad idea* eradicated. I was significantly more queasy watching people unlearn opinions than basic fears, but I was nonetheless fascinated.

The first case I worked on was a woman who'd lived a sheltered life, and had grown up with an ingrained and burning jealousy of her own sibling, and now that she'd long moved away from home, she knew these feelings were wrong, she knew her envious thoughts were irrational and were keeping her from being close to her family and stunting her other relationships, but nevertheless she couldn't help herself thinking them.

It took her only one session to unlearn. She'd ingested the preprogrammed rice, which had promptly made its way to the brain. It softened her neural tissue, rendering it malleable, and pulsing within her brain the rice made her unlearn, made her change. After the session, she slipped on a headset and dove into soothing scenes where one of our AI agents sat waiting, gently guiding her out of the experience. The following two sessions she had with our agents were mere formality, a debriefing, there to waste everyone's time and to cover our own ass for liability.

So it was with most other cases. People's brains changed or healed on their own and our therapists were just there as a safety net in case the neural hardware had prodded at something that should've stayed untouched. By and large, they remained a formality. Our agents took their notes and nodded at the newly 'healthy' people and the people never requested to speak to them again.

My job was to handle the software agents afterwards and provide feedback, fine-tuning the underlying model, nudging it in the direction of a well-rounded cognitive behavioral therapist.

How do you think that one went? In our pristine immersive environment, just me and this one agent, sitting cross-legged on a generic meadow.

"She seemed relieved." The agent cocked her head. "I don't understand. It was all very fast."

Yes. Very.

"I believe she won't be coming back."

I believe so too.

Before we logged out, the agent said, "One thing might be of note, doctor. I noticed she wasn't feeling any of those 'undesirable' feelings, and she seemed overjoyed, but I was able to sense a layer of discomfort, too, a sort of disorientation. Like she was made a different person all too suddenly. I'm not sure she liked that too much."

4.

The clinic's windows were tinted, but if you looked closely you could still see, meshing with our own shaded reflections, a smattering of protesters on the curb. Brandishing placards that misquoted Crick or Pauling, mutely opening and closing their mouths in unison.

"The ova are almost ready," our doctor said, and Ellie squeezed my hand, which made me turn my attention back to the screen.

On it, countless sprites of four colors shuffled and reshuffled themselves like one of those old screen-savers I'd seen in documentaries. Ellie, who'd chosen to carry our child, stared at this display mesmerized. The graphic represented genes from millions of humans, spliced together base pair by base pair into one coherent genome to produce one baby, one human being. Out of the many, one. It didn't matter who brought which gene to the table, as this was no longer a monogenic, or even a polygenic world. Life was more complex than that, with every single part of the whole contributing in its own way to the final product in an *omnigenic* dance of information playing out in each cell of every human on the planet. And putting it all together, as we were, to bring such a human to life showed we were all just tiny parts of a large singular whole, drops of water at the crest of the same wave.

The doctor gave us some more information and instructions on how to prepare Ellie's body for the implantation to come, then we thanked her profusely, and left out the back door to grab lunch.

The day was mild, the sky bright blue. I saw my drained face reflected in Ellie's sunshades.

"I don't know what to feel," she said, playing with an olive on her plate. "Excitement? Fear? Anxiety?"

"How about you don't try to know, and just feel what you feel, and tell me."

She skewered the olive with her fork, brought it up before her eyes as if for inspection, then popped it in her mouth. "Don't get all professional on me, Al." She chewed, swallowed. "Read the room. I feel all of the fucking above."

"Don't take it out on me."

"Yeah, well," she started, then pursed her lips.

"Well what?"

"Well, why don't you tell me how *you* feel?"

"What's that supposed to mean?"

"About all this."

"What about it? What do you mean?"

"I mean, I know you. I saw your face in there."

"What are you on about?" I said. "I made no face."

"That's right," she said, "you didn't."

We finished the remainder of our lunch in silence.

A chirp came from my office door.

I took off my headset and placed it lenses-up on the table. *Open*, I subvocalized.

Phillip walked in. "Interrupting?"

"I was just finishing up with an agent."

He came up to the headset and peered over it as if to get a glimpse of the scene where I'd been moments before, and the light from the panels lit his face from the chin up. He looked at me, eyes wide, "Wanna hear a scary story?"

"Coffee, Phillip?" I gestured at my espresso machine.

"Let's go for a walk."

We strolled around campus, and he grilled me about the technology, about the trials. "How do you find it?"

"Surprising," I said. "Exciting," I said, surprising myself.

"And how do they find it?" Meaning the agents, the post-procedure specialists meant to gently lull our patients back into polite society.

"They find it equally surprising."

He put a hand on my shoulder. "Let's make it easier for them." A lot depended on them, and he didn't have to say it.

The agents were the link between brain surgery and couch therapy. They were a softener, both for the patients themselves and for any would-be regulators of our technology. As with any other big bio- or neuro-technological product, heavy regulatory oversight was expected for our post-trial rollout, and having agents at the ready was our company's strategy to assuage any overzealous regulators by saying, here's a scalable solution to help people make sense of what they've gone through, holding their hand along the way.

"They've been trained on tons of traditional therapy data," I said. "Which as you know hasn't always been very favorable to any 'biological' solution."

"Yes, yes, do your breathing exercises, don't just take a pill." He pointed to a bench under a tree and we sat down. "We have to improve that."

"I'm on it."

"You have to reinforce different feedback loops."

I nodded, understanding my assignment.

He said, "We need to get them ready."

Later, back in my office, I picked up the headset and held it with the tips of my fingers. It flickered with any slight movement, unsure whether to wake up from its digital sleep. I was already late for our dinner with Ellie. I sent her a message, saying I was stuck in a meeting, and I slipped on the headset to continue working.

That night, Ellie wasn't home.

It worried me, not because of where she could've gone, which I knew exactly, since she always tended to go there whenever we'd have a big fight and always returned the following morning, but because she wasn't home tonight and we'd never even gotten to argue. There was no explosion, no release, just me coming in to an empty home.

All of the trademarked Mueller-versus-Mueller drama was obviously beginning to spill over into our relationship, and it kept eating at me intensely, until one afternoon at work a thought popped into my mind.

I debated with myself for a couple of days, chewing over the bizarre idea in my mind before sleep, until the home mood dropped to an absolute all-time low and I decided that enough was enough for everyone's sake, and I went to see Mr. Mueller once again, this time determined to solve the situation.

"You know," said Mr. Mueller, "it took me a while to accept my daughter as she is. Not because of some prejudice, but because deep down I felt disappointed that I wouldn't have a family. That she'd grow old alone, childless. I know it sounds silly in today's world, but having progeny is such a core part of what makes us human that I believe it was pure instinct." He sighed. "When I came to my senses, I realized that she'd have plenty of options, and when she met you, well, I simply couldn't have been happier."

His words made me feel a tinge of guilt, all of a sudden, as if I were to blame for his daughter's sexuality. "I understand," I said, telling the truth.

"Having you in her life made me feel bright about her future, about our future, and I knew that you could figure things out, and eventually I'd have grandchildren, and our house would be full again—"

"But that is exactly what we're offering you," I said, trying to meet him half way.

He saw through my bullshit. "You're not offering me anything. And I'm accepting nothing."

"Listen," I said. "Don't let her choices ruin what relationship you have with your daughter."

"Her choices?"

"Our choices," I said. "Look, you want family? We can give you family. And you want acceptance?" I paused, a bit nervous. "I can give you acceptance."

And I told him about my work in broad strokes, about the rice, about how half an hour with our system and he'd be in total acceptance of our choice, and he'd be happier, and we'd all be happier.

"You're offering to brainwash me?"

"It's as much brainwashing," I said, "as any therapy is. As any healing. The process is just sped up."

"I don't need therapy," he said. "And I certainly don't need healing." I sensed he was nearing the end of his patience. Then he looked me in the eyes. "Perhaps—perhaps, you could offer the same to her? Make her see things my way? Our way? Come on, Alice, I know you are reasonable."

I felt sick. Not so much at the suggestion, but rather at this sudden realization, having for a moment imagined Ellie's beliefs changing on the rice, of how crude my offer to Mr. Mueller had been. Who was I to hand a grown man twice my age the solution, neatly wrapped in a brain pill, to his family's supposed ills? I shuddered at my own audacity. If people deserved one thing, it was to be given the time to make their own choices.

I apologized for wasting his time and left. When I got home, I locked myself in the bathroom and sobbed.

Tuning the agents didn't turn out as straightforward as I'd thought. Neutering a century's worth of therapeutical instincts, if heaps of processed datasets can be called that, while still keeping the AIs genuinely helpful was a tight-rope walk.

I stared at anonymized data from the trial. Patient Apple's interaction with our agent after his procedure. Short and to the point. Apple, having had his psychological issues resolved the neurological way, wanted to talk about it no further, especially not with an automated AI therapist. Patient Banana's interaction, much the same. Patient Cranberry's, as if copied and pasted. Done and out in less than five minutes.

Good news was they all seemed healthy and sane.

Bad news was they knew it, and treated our additional help or monitoring the way they'd treat somebody handing them a flyer on the street.

"Durian's psychological profile is as healthy as can be," one agent told me. "There is nothing further I can do. Patient Durian is cured."

I was early one morning in the office, and yet I could hardly focus on what this agent was saying. They all ended up saying the same thing, eventually. All patients succumbed to the rice faster than anything I'd ever seen before, and after a brief sense of vertigo, they quickly accepted their own choice of the neurotechnological option, and moved on with their lives, happier than ever.

I kept track and followed up with as many patients in the trial as possible, to no real use. I wasn't needed, the agents weren't needed.

When I talked to Phillip about this he shook his head.

"Look," he said. "At this point in time we can't afford a repeat of Bolivia."

"I'm aware of the risks."

"We're betting the farm on the rice, Al. We can't afford to mess this up because of sloppy AI-work. We could lose both the agent business and the rice business."

"I said I got it, Phillip."

"We need the agents. We'll need as much feedback as possible, as many people guiding the agents as we can before our worldwide rollout."

"Many people?"

He started at me blankly. Then he furrowed his brow. "Al, the rice works. We're very close to full approval, so we can't botch this now. We're scaling up the operation massively. We're all hands on deck, and at this point, we have thousands of therapists working the software round the clock, all over the world."

In the days before the insemination, in the little time I was home, Ellie and I were like two bored ghosts haunting an apartment where nothing ever happened, passing through each other, barely speaking.

The office didn't feel much more comforting, either. Work itself was progressing well, and the rice was proving better than anyone on the company's board of directors had hoped, but internally a sense of unease was growing.

I dug through our internal files and found some of the many other people looped in as agent-guides. I reached out to a few, under pretext of exchanging notes for the betterment of our work, and found that they were all feeling a similar sense of uncertainty about the product.

"It's too good," one man told me in his office. "I'd never seen people change that way before."

"So why do I feel hesitant?" I asked.

He shrugged. "Because too many people changing too suddenly, too easily, and now you have the whole world changing suddenly, easily. And what does that world look like?"

Phillip was declining my meeting requests, avoiding me in the corridors and offices of our company. Most likely, he'd gotten wind of our conversations and wanted to avoid any potential push-back.

But even I wasn't fully sure what I wanted of him. Perhaps just some reassurance that everything would be alright, that we were not rushing headlong into a mistake, that experienced adults were in charge of steering this ship and that all potential consequences of our product had been fully mapped out.

Clinical trials, lab work, was one thing, but the thought of *scaling up massively* was what gave me and the rest of us a sense of vertigo.

I couldn't help cringing at my last conversation with Mr. Mueller. At the thought of him being a different person, one minute to the next. Of Ellie, being different, one minute to the next. What did my world look like, then?

I sat slumped at the desk in my office. The day was done but I didn't feel like I had anywhere to go, so I just sat there, fiddling with the wire of the charging dock. Nowadays it was all Big This and Big That, and Millions of Data Points and Billions of Datasets and it all went into one blender and out came a perfect agent and a marvel of tool-making with no human required anymore and it was all good for everyone involved. Except what if it wasn't?

What if it wasn't all that great to change people in an instant? What if it wasn't good practice to just do, do, do whatever comes to fucking mind without a second to stop and consider your partner's real feelings? And what if it wasn't such a brilliant fucking idea to turn a future child into a fucking art project?

I stood up, sat back down. I wasn't sure what I was feeling, what I was doing.

I pulled up my computer and scoured for data on the rice trial. It was near the end, but there were a couple of open slots left, and there was one open slot for tomorrow morning at our own lab, and if I shuffled a few meetings around, it would be right on time before our Big Appointment in the afternoon, and I stared at the screen and breathed heavily and my chest hurt and I stood up again and paced the room.

I put on the headset that was charging. "Agent," I said. "Let's go." And on a pristine meadow an agent appeared and I said, "Fuck you, let's go."

"What seems to be the problem? What brings you to me on this fine day?" Slipping right into play-pretend therapy mode, with a tone of voice that I just now realized I hated more than anything in the world.

"Uh huh," I said. "Fuck you."

"Ah, I see it might be anger you're struggling with. Or is this a nervous tic?"

"Fuck you."

"Is there someone in your life that makes you so angry? Are you dealing with a lot of repressed emotions right now? Do you feel the need to shout? To scream?"

"Fuck you," I said. "Fuck you, fuck you."

5.

When I arrived home, Ellie was already sleeping. I watched her silhouette in bed a while, then I softly closed the bedroom door and went down to the kitchen.

I searched the drawers, cabinets, and I sniffed and grimaced at them until I found what I was looking for wrapped in several paper bags. Ellie knew I hated the smell, so she'd wrapped it up nicely. I took the root out and put it in a pot to boil.

I sat on the kitchen table, started scratching at a bit of crust on it from last night's dinner. When the root boiled I poured myself a big mug of the brew. It tasted as horrible as every other time I'd had it in the House of Mueller.

I sipped the drink, thinking of my first date with Ellie. We'd gotten so involved in our conversation we forgot to keep count of the wines. By the end of the night we were so smashed we were walking and swaying and she fell flat on her face right before the entrance to her building and I rushed to pick her up, but she was laughing 'cause it was only a scratch or two on her face, and I joined in and we laughed our heads off right there on the sidewalk. We decided to stay out. I couldn't remember what we talked about. But I knew we'd been awake the whole night, on the curb in front of her building, our sandals in hand, watching the city go to sleep and then slowly shake itself awake, and I remembered nothing except how silly she looked and that sweet, sticky smell of an early summer night.

I finished the drink, then rinsed the mug and shoved the boiled root leftovers to the bottom of the bin. Somehow, I didn't want her knowing had I drunk it.

I thought of Mr. Mueller. Poor Mr. Mueller. Struggling to keep pace with the rest of the world. Just like me. Just like Ellie and just like all of us. As if the World was this separate thing which slipped and squirmed away from our collective hands every time we felt we had a good grasp of it.

I resolved to reach out to him tomorrow after our Big Appointment and make things right between the three of us. Empathy and kindness was what he deserved, and I was sure that given time and acceptance, that empathy and kindness would be reciprocated.

Tomorrow.

But tonight, my head swam, from the tea or the anxiety or both, I did not know.

I went to bed and lay down right next to Ellie.

"I'm just scared, that's all," I whispered, and right then felt the World firmly in my grasp for the first time in a long while. Not letting go, not tonight. I closed my eyes and the whole room was spinning. Tomorrow, I'd decided, I could sleep in, as there would be just one Big Appointment for the day. I held Ellie, hugging her properly for the first time in weeks. And tomorrow, things would spin even harder, and the day after tomorrow even more so, until maybe one day the spinning fully stopped, but for now all the two of us could do was decide to fully plunge into the swirl and start spinning together with the rest of the world, and see where this spinning and squirming but marvelous world took us. "That's all," I said again, and fell asleep.

See Damien Krsteski's story "Core" online at Metaphorosis.
If you liked it, leave a comment. Authors love that!
Remember to subscribe to our e-mail updates so you'll know when new stories are posted.

About the story

I use my stories as excuses to spend time thinking in writing about things I like to think about in general, and my worlds and my characters help me reason better. In "Core", a story revolving around the question of human values and indelible human qualities in an ever-changing world, the fears and anxieties of automation and obsolescence emerge against a backdrop of disorientation with the speed of change. I enjoyed airing out through the characters all of these fears and anxieties and, well, all of my excitement and giddiness, too. I have no doubt I will do so again. The future is exciting, and the world is amazing. And it's not done surprising us.

About the author

Damien Krsteski writes science fiction and develops software. He lives in Berlin.

A word about Suzanne J. Willis

Suzanne J. Willis first appeared in Metaphorosis in January 2017, with "A Nightingale's Map of the City" — still one of my favorite stories we've ever published — a wistful tour de force of beautiful prose and heartfelt emotion. In 2018, she contributed "The Fragments of Others" to our innovative anthology, *Reading 5X5*.

Now, with our final story, she's back with another masterpiece, "This Is My City and I Am Her Song". We've published a lot of great writers over nine years (and you've seen some of my favorites this year), but Suzanne's poetic style may best encapsulate the kind of writing we originally set out to showcase. Enjoy it!

This Is My City and I Am Her Song

Suzanne J. Willis

The clocks stopped still and the night stretched thin as the Siren chased me through my city of shifting secrets. Across canals, and down twisting laneways, until I found myself in the graveyard. It may not have been the most sensible place to hide from a Siren — handmaidens of the Underworld Queen and sisters of Death itself — but it was better than being hunted through the streets like a common thief. I peered out from the mausoleum in which I was huddled, and she appeared in the distance, stalking between the headstones and tombs in the endless night. Cursing silently, I couldn't help but feel the same as I had when I first saw her, fifteen, sixteen years before: overwhelmed by the power radiating from her in subtle waves.

There has never been any rhyme or rhythm to when the Siren visits this city. She has always been peripatetic, unpredictable. I had been a child, no more than four or five, when I first saw her standing at dawn by the canal, under the bridge that connects the marketplace to the Women's Quarter; the quarter, it was said, that was home to shapeshifters and shadows. Her hair was a dark, wild tangle and her black wings arched out from her shoulder blades. I imagined that if she were soaring across the sky, they would block out the sun.

My Aunt Zola had raised me on stories, and the one about the Siren I learned by heart. The first time she ever told it to me was on that morning I glimpsed the Siren, under the bridge.

"When she first came here, my little Rosa, I don't know how she made it from the mountains — the shifters of the Women's Quarter would bewitch the on-shore winds to shear away at those sirens who shouldn't be here. But, one morning there she was, huddled under the bridge as though nesting there. All a-tremble and bedraggled as a whelp. Ever since, she comes and goes from the city as she pleases, with no knowing when she might turn up. But whenever she does, strange things happen."

"Stranger than usual?" I would always ask.

"Stranger than the day the sea emptied from the lagoon and left behind the body of the baker's son. Odder than the priestesses who walk the roofs unshod, their feet never touching the earth, and more curious than the cats that guard the ruins of their convent, who howl on the anniversary of the fire that destroyed it." Every time, she had a different answer, telling me the stories of our water-bound city in snippets of the fantastic and horrific. Weaving it to life.

"What kind of things?"

She sighed and touched my cheek. "That first time, a great grey wolf was seen prowling the city, between sunrise and sunset, but there hadn't been wolves in these parts for over one hundred years. Other animals who were left outside after dark — seabirds and cats, mostly — were found petrified, their feathers or fur crusted with salt. They lined the canals like statues. And there were *other* things, too much for young ears to hear."

"And the lady with the black wings?"

"The last place she always went was across the bridge to the Women's Quarter. After that, the animals stopped turning to statues, and the wolves no longer howled at midnight. None of that has happened in your lifetime, I know, but that doesn't mean that she stays away, as you've seen. And she doesn't find herself here by accident, Rosa. No, she is looking for something."

The mournful call of a nightbird calling out across the tombs broke my reverie. It was the only sound in the graveyard; the quiet calm of night made me nervous. *I know what she is looking for, and she hasn't found it yet,* I whispered to Zola's memory, closing my hand over the precious cargo in my pocket. I imagined her telling me to walk away, to forget. Cowering there, not knowing when the Siren might find me, I was sorely tempted to do just that.

Then she walked from the shadows under the weeping trees, making her way between the gravestones. Watching her, not only did I feel the same, but the Siren looked the same as she had that first day I saw her, so long ago, down by the canal. Haunted, and tired, too. It made me wonder how long she had been looking for that very-precious thing (for she had surely been looking long before she reached our city) and what would happen when she found me with it. If only Aunt Zola were still here, I could tell her I knew exactly what it was that the Siren was after, and ask Zola's help, ask her *what next*. For while I held the lost Siren's secret in my cloak pocket, I had not a clue as to what to do with it.

"Never rely on any man to support you," Aunt Zola had always said, for as long as I could remember. "We will find you a good trade, my girl, and there will be no marriage to yoke you." She was my maternal aunt, the one who took me in when it became clear that my parents would never return from their expedition beyond the mountains. I knew Zola blamed my father for the disappearance of her sister, and that she wouldn't risk the same for me. That suited me just fine. Marriage and children never much interested me, having to answer to a man even less than that. I had harboured a secret hope that Zola might pack us up and move into the Women's Quarter, even hinted at it once or twice. *That's not somewhere just anyone can live,* Zola had whispered, shivering at the thought. *Witches and medicine women and shapeshifters belong to those streets. It is not for the likes of us.* She didn't mention the rumours about what else might live there. For some said it was a refuge for those female monsters who walked the boundary between worlds, between human and beast, between story and reality. She didn't mention it, and I knew better than to ask again.

So, at seventeen, she sent me to the artist Leonardo as his apprentice. The only man, I would add, who not only did not mind an errant girl as his student, but seemed to prefer it. He treated me like an equal as I sharpened my mind with the books he gave me to read; as I coarsened my hands building machines of his invention. It was my third year with him when he first left me alone over the winter. Zola had been dead some two years by then, leaving me without any family to anchor me in the world, though Leonardo was kind and welcoming. I had the feeling he would have given me more responsibility sooner, but that he waited until Zola's death was not so raw and my grief had healed over a bit.

My first task on his departure was to tidy and secure everything, order it for his return in the spring. His notebooks were easy enough, re-filed into chronological order. Then there were the small instruments he worked on in his office, the ones that the science school commissioned to use in their experiments. Those went in glass-fronted cases, locked away from the cold salty air, which would rust their gears and jam their delicate mechanisms. Last was the workshop. The smell of sawdust was warm, comforting, as I put the tools back into place and covered the machines he was working on with large dust sheets. Before my apprenticeship, I had never realised that machines could be beautiful. But the ones made by Leonardo — all wood and canvas, gears and hinges — were like works of art, their shapes inspired by nature, their purpose sometimes unclear but certain to move the city ever-forward.

As I covered the last of them, I noticed that the door to the annex workshop, where Leonardo worked alone, was ajar. I walked over, reached out to close the door, then drew my hand back. "Hello?" I called softly, for it did not seem as though the workshop was empty. There was no answer, but, from the darkness, it felt as though someone had invited me in. I picked up one of the gas lamps and walked through the door, then clicked the taper mechanism my master had created to light the large lamp hanging from the ceiling.

My breath caught in my throat. The machine in that little room was like nothing else I had ever seen. Laid across three saw-horses was a horizontal frame, bookended by handholds at one end and a swallow's tail at the other, large enough for a full-grown adult to lie in. A tan leather harness joined the base to the upper struts, upon which was fixed an enormous pair of wings. Unlike the other machines in the workshop, they were not made of canvas, but of glossy black feathers, each one oiled and preened and perfect. From the wing-joints ran fine copper wires, downward into a nest woven of scraps of twigs and hair and the soft reeds that grew at the canal edges. Had Leonardo (for this he had made, surely, for himself) been strapped into the contraption, that nest would have sat against the centre of his chest. And in that nest lay an egg.

The likes of which should not, *could not*, have existed.

Yet there it was. As big as an ostrich egg, it was dark, grey-green and lit gently from within. The light itself pulsed, and it seemed as though there was an electrical storm trapped inside it, dark clouds passing over its surface. The shell was veined in gold, hair-fine and intricate. I hovered my hand above it and it felt warm; blood-heat. The *life* within it was irresistible and I began to close my fingers around it —

"Is it not exquisite?" Leonardo's voice was soft, unaccusatory.

I turned around, my cheeks warm with shame. But he simply smiled at me as he walked over and gently picked up the egg. I gasped, for as he picked it up, all the feathers from those magnificent wings disappeared, leaving behind wings made of wood frame and canvas. I must have looked like a half-wit, standing there gaping at the flying machine that, while still remarkable, looked no different than Leonardo's other workshop creations.

He stowed the treasure in his coat. "I'm sorry, Rosa, I should never have been so careless and left this where you might find it. I must ask you to forget that you ever saw this egg. Owning it..." he shook his head, paused as though looking for the right words, "Actually, understanding it, seeking its help, takes much knowledge and discipline, and a command of magics that few possess. Without that, it is a dangerous object to be in the presence of, much less attempt to use. And there is not a soul in this city who would not try to use it, given the chance. You felt its pull, no?"

I nodded and smiled at my master as he left the workshop, trying to disguise the fact that, no matter what he said, the egg had already worked its magic on me. That night, I dreamed I was flying, coal black wings extending out from my shoulder blades, far into the sky. Below me, our city spread out, its secrets laid open to me in all their complexity and wonder. From the streets and the waterways came a lament, sad and terrible, composed of notes not of this world. Then a cry rang out and the dream went dark.

A pounding on the door awoke me from my sleep the next morning, just as the sky was lightening. The young messenger at the door as I opened it looked grave, almost fearful.

"There has been an accident, Ms Rosa. Your master, Leonardo..." He trailed off and I did not want to ask what had happened. His tone, the early hour, already told me that it was not good.

"He has no family, miss," said the boy, each word accompanied by a puff of mist from his mouth in the freezing dawn, "so, you see, they need you to formally identify the body and assist with —"

I held up my hand, not wanting to hear anything else at that moment. My knees felt weak and I was light-headed, as though the world had shifted but I was still on its old kilter. He reached out to steady me, but I drew myself up and waved his hands away. My parents, Aunt Zola, now Leonardo. I had had enough of the clumsy kindnesses that come with death to last me a lifetime. The losses piled on one another like autumn leaves. If the boy did not touch me, I could just about keep my emotions inside.

Wrapped in my warmest coat, I followed the messenger boy out into the morning, trying not to slip on the damp cobbles or lose him in the fog as he hurried through the streets. Already, the sounds of the floating markets and the boatmen rang through the air, waking the city and setting it about its day. It smelled of woodsmoke and low tide and just a little bit of the snow that already capped the distant mountains. A shiver passed through me that had nothing to do with the early winter. Though I had lost someone else, someone I had grown to love, the world went on.

At last, we arrived at a little bridge in a hidden laneway that looked rarely, if ever, used. Lawmen and women milled about, some taking notes, others measuring the scene for who-knows-what purpose. The boy spoke with one of the lawmen and, as I looked about, I realised what the boy must have been saying when I had cut him off so abruptly in the doorway. They needed my assistance to *retrieve Leonardo's body*. For the bridge did not just lead to just any part of the city. It led to the Women's Quarter.

That particular quarter was not somewhere that just anyone could, or should, wander. Witches and practitioners of other feminine arts did not frighten me so much as the *others* who had disappeared from the world and made their home in this mysterious part of the city. The shapeshifters and mermaids. The descendants of Delphyne, who kept their snake tails hidden but still breathed fire at the first sign of trouble. Harpies and their hidden staircase straight to the underworld. All, it seemed, except sirens, who still guarded the mountaintops and desert plains.

I thought of *her*. I thought of his flying machine and its midnight wings. I wondered.

And I wondered what on earth Leonardo could have been doing here, and why it had brought him his death.

The next few minutes passed in a blur. There was a conversation with the lawmen, some brief and useless directions, and absolutely no hint of what I might encounter. Armed with next to nothing, I crossed the bridge as the little crowd fell silent, so the only sound was my boots clomping on the cobbles and the current lazily lapping beneath it. The little square on the other side seemed no different from any of the hundreds in the city proper. Except that as I gazed down the laneways, I saw shop signs that were unfamiliar, doorways shimmering into sight then back into the shadows. Down one of those laneways walked a group of seven women, all in long, dark cloaks. Six carried a stretcher bearing a body and the seventh followed close behind them. A cry hitched in my throat. I swallowed it down again, and it felt as though, in the odd stillness, I was laid bare for all to see.

The seventh woman beckoned to me from the laneway as the six stretcher-bearers walked into the square and waited. When I reached her, we were out of sight of the lawmen and women. I had never felt so utterly alone and exposed. The woman peered at me from under her hood. Her face seemed to shift between human and vulpine, not quite settling on either. She looked sad, her eyes red as though she had been crying.

"Did you know Leonardo?" I whispered.

"I am Villanelle. Your master was a friend to us here. He spoke highly of you, Rosa. Don't look so surprised," she smiled, "he had hopes for you. But we've not much time. Take this — it is not safe here." The fox-woman Villanelle reached under her cloak, withdrew a bundle and placed it in my hands. I did not need to ask what it was, for I could feel it, pulsing in my hands, a storm barely contained by a golden-veined shell.

"What happened to him?"

Villanelle shook her head. "He held that egg for longer than should have been possible. It has a different effect on everyone anyone who comes into contact with it. He came to broker a deal —" she broke off and looked around, though I could hear nothing but the distant flap of wings and call of morning birds.

"The Siren agreed, many centuries ago, to protect our city, for here we gave refuge to creatures, monsters, that were hunted elsewhere. In return for that protection, we had to hide something very valuable inside this. It took a strong person to take custody of it..."

"Leonardo," I said.

"As his apprentice, and he with no family, the natural laws say that this must pass to you." She brushed my cheek, and made a sigil in the air between us, muttering words in a language I did not understand. Panic fluttered in me, but something told me that this was not a curse, but protection. "Tell no-one about it. You must hold onto it and keep it from she who seeks it."

"The siren?" The words were out of my mouth before I had even formed the thought. But I *knew* this was what she sought, what all Zola's stories talked about, just as surely as I knew my own name.

Her eyebrows rose in surprise, then she smiled. "Leonardo was right about you. Yes, she is here in the city, so you must avoid her at all costs. Do not let her find you. Or it."

So I run from her this time. Then what? Am I to keep this forever? I wanted to ask more, but she ushered me out of the laneway and into the square. Villanelle pulled back the shroud and I looked at his face, then nodded. It was only as I led the stretcher-bearers back across the bridge that I began to cry.

How on earth was I to try to avoid a Siren? One, no less, who was wandering the world in search of the very thing that I now possessed. I sat in the workshop, before Leonardo's flying machine, turning the egg over in my hands. Many of the women of this city were known to walk into the Women's Quarter as death approached them — but Villanelle had said Leonardo was there to *broker a deal*. Had someone murdered him for the treasure that I now held?

Well, I wouldn't find any answer simply sitting and wondering. Taking a deep breath, I walked over to the flying machine and placed the egg gently in the nest, waiting for the wings to transform into the black, feathered masterpieces I had seen not twenty-four hours earlier. And waited. And waited. But the wings stayed canvas and wood, and the machine did not feel as *alive* as it had the day before.

Pulling the egg from the nest, I took it back to my rooms above the workshop and sat by the window, holding it in my lap. Through the open window floated the sounds of the city; the market vendors and the boatmen; the street musicians with mournful violin and haunting flutes; the everyday chatter of people for whom life had not just changed overnight. The Villanelle had said that the fragile egg affected everyone differently. Perhaps that gift of flight was only for Leonardo. I closed my eyes, turning the egg over and over in my hands.

Against my palms, the Siren's treasure pulsed, steady and strong. Images floated in and out of my mind, as though I was sifting through dreams. A black sand beach stretched under glorious grey skies, upon which sat seven Sirens, singing down passing ships while their cousins, the mermaids, flitted through the waves before the ships crashed to the shore. Under the rain-heavy clouds, the souls of the men flew, shaped as crow and albatross and fledging gull. The song of the sirens did not just mean death; it was transformative, transmutative. Then, a city made of white and black stone, rising from an island, a shack, the humble beginnings of a village; rising and spreading, until the death song of the Sirens rang through the streets, followed by a rain of fire from the sky. Parliaments of animals and birds gathered to create, break, remake the world. Time stretching and contracting, life and death dancing. And, at the centre of it all, the storm-egg beating like a heart. The dreams danced over me like rain.

The howl of a wolf made me open my eyes suddenly. The light outside was fading and the western sky was soft and gold as a cool wind blew in through the window. In the little moment between day and evening, the musicians stopped, the market was packed up, the people closed their shutters and doors. And a song threaded its way through the streets, over the canals, on the back of the wolf's howl and the twilight. It was the lost Siren calling to the egg. Emotion rose in my throat and I began to cry again. There was a delicate despondency to the refrain; loss was woven through it. She had been looking for that egg for a very long time. When she sang — don't believe, for a second, that Sirens only sing for death — the egg moved restlessly in my hand, as though the storms inside it were gathering and waiting to burst. I dared not think about what might happen if they did. All the same, the fox-woman Villanelle had been adamant that the egg should remain in the city. But that did not mean with me. Perhaps I could hide it...

I knew enough to know that borderland creatures are tricksy things, so I could not trust the ordinary to tell me how to find a hiding place, how to outrun her. Back down in the workshop, I took out the large map of the city that Leonardo had completed just last spring, and traced my finger over the canals and laneways, the little islands and larger districts. Everyone in the city had a small story about *her*, heard from their parents or grandparents, or learnt through their own encounter. In a city of secrets and wonder, it was the Siren who was the most mysterious of all, perhaps because she was not ours. I tried to draw all the stories I had heard together, weaving them into a long thread that would lead me through the labyrinth. I traced the city with my fingertip, whispering as the darkness gathered outside.

Once upon a time, the sirens and mermaids were as one, until the sirens took to the skies and the mermaids to the deepest seas. That is why she is always seen by the water...

My mother was first violinist in the orchestra, and she heard an other-worldly singing under her window when she was practising one night; when she looked out, there she was, sitting in the peach tree and trilling like a little bird...

Like all half-human monsters, Sirens are borderland creatures, said to violate the boundaries between life and death, this world and the Underworld, the rules of belonging and place...

I went on like that for an hour or so, making notes, narrowing down where I thought the Siren might be and where she could not reach. I had the egg sat on the table beside me, unwilling to let it out of my sight. Somewhat absentmindedly, I reached out and rested my hand on it, its shell still warm to the touch. Without quite knowing why, a sob rose in my throat. How short life suddenly seemed, how insignificant... all those I had loved — my parents when I was just a child, my aunt who raised me, Leonardo

who had given me knowledge and craft and my second home —
were gone. What of their lives unfinished? Turning to grab a
handkerchief for my tears, the sad emptiness that had weighted
me so suddenly disappeared just as quickly. As soon as I took my
hand off the egg.

"What could I do with more time?" I whispered to it. Beneath
the shell, the storm raged and lightning struck. *Anything*, the
storm promised. The map swam in and out of focus, changing and
morphing, some islands sinking beneath the waters and others
springing up in their wake. It was as though I were looking at five
hundred years running through it in a few seconds; perhaps I was.
Then it settled back into its current, familiar state. The shadow of
a tiny, winged figure walking along the banks of the little canal on
which Leonardo's workshop passed over the parchment, moth-
delicate, then was gone.

I grabbed the egg, threw on my cloak and ran out into the
night.

Only, the night was different in ways that I could not imagine.
Although I have lived in this city my whole life, I managed to find
bridges that I did not know existed, pass through neighbourhoods
dark and mysterious, as though they had become stuck in another
era and only emerged when needs must. Without a doubt, she was
close on my heels as I wound my way through the city. Each time
the swoop of her wings, or the brisk clack of talons on the
cobblestones told me she nearly had me, a turn right or left would
take me down an odd path and into safety, however temporary. I
imagined Leonardo creating his beautiful map in this same way,
though I'm sure that the minutes did not stop, the night did not
pause in the same way.

It was as though the world were underwater and I was
viewing it, interacting with it, through a thin pane of glass. As
though I had shifted into a narrow passageway in between the
world and the natural forces that kept it going. In a crowded
laneway, people moved unusually slow around me, their voices
sounding far away. After what seemed like two or three hours of
walking and hiding in shadows, I passed our astrological clock and
it read 11.37 — the same time that I had left my rooms.

I turned away from the clock, through a passageway and out
into a square that sparkled with soft candlelight from hurricane
lamps hanging over tables set with wine and fruits, spiced meats
and fragrant soups. The air was curiously still, redolent with the

scents of the wedding feast. Musicians played a tune I could not hear; some guests were dancing, others seated, smiling and chatting. Looking at the wedding feast was like watching insects being encased in sap that would slowly turn to amber. A cool wind blew through the square, blowing the candles. Music seemed to explode in the night, and I was part of the world again.

The dancing made my head spin. Across the square, there was a flash of a red tail, a dog or a fox perhaps, drawn out by the smell of the food.

"You have the egg." I froze at the sound of the Siren's low voice. Her breath was soft on the back of my neck.

I turned slowly, my heart in my throat. She seemed to fill the sky even though she was the same height as me. Those black wings arced upwards from her shoulder blades, and she stretched them outward, a bird readying for flight. I felt a pang for Leonardo and the creation he would never get to test.

"Why do you want it?"

Her eyes flashed and my knees turned to water. "You might be Leonardo's apprentice, child, but you have not earned the right to ask that." She moved towards me and I tensed, ready for her to strike.

"You knew Leonardo?"

She smiled at me and it was surprisingly gentle. Before she could answer, the fox I had seen earlier streaked towards us from the shadows. With her last few steps, she grew, shifted and came to a stop as Villanelle, standing between me and the Siren.

"You would take back the egg and see our city ruined?" I was surprised at the sadness in Villanelle's words.

"You put too much stock in the old stories, sister. They have become twisted, over the centuries, and make you and your kind so unsure of your own place in the world. This city is more yours than it ever was mine..."

The Siren continued in her lilting voice, lulling Villanelle as though mesmerising her. I took my chance — while she was so focussed on the fox-woman, I slipped into the shadows, taking the egg with me. When I could no longer hear her, time slowed and I stepped into the in-between spaces once again. I knew, then, where I was headed. To the city's cemetery, a water-bound island of earthly graves and fiery cremation furnaces. Earth, fire, water — where better to hide a secret from a creature of the air? I pushed away the niggling worry that had uncurled when the Siren spoke to Villanelle — the worry that, perhaps, I should not be hiding what was rightfully hers at all.

The iron gate was set in an ancient stone wall, and curlicued with vines and autumn leaves. I tied the boat I had borrowed to the tiny pier, my arms aching from the unfamiliar motion of rowing. I wondered if Villanelle had been entirely enchanted — or worse — by the Siren. I hoped she was safe.

Beyond the gate, my footfalls were silent on the soft grass, the cemetery's angels and weeping women and ancient mausoleums limned in moonlight. I looked for somewhere safe, secure. A mausoleum, I had decided, would be the perfect hiding place. I walked until I found one whose gate had long since rusted and the names of its dead had been weathered away. As I ducked inside, I heard the rustle of wings, the footfalls of clawed feet.

How?

But, of course, I already knew that. The egg was calling to her and I might be able to outrun her for a while, but never truly lose her. Perhaps she was a bit like me — alone in the world. At least I had my city as an anchor, the home I had known all my life, with reminders of Zola and Leonardo and the parents I knew only through stories echoing through it. Perhaps she was chasing after *her* anchor, and it was calling out, to be heard. Found. I shifted uncomfortably; a discomfort that had nothing to do with the cold stone or the cramped tomb.

What if Villanelle was right, and giving the Siren what she needed would take away the last part of belonging that I had? Then again, all those years that the Siren had searched the city, looking for what I was now complicit in keeping from her — to keep it would be to add to her suffering. I don't think anyone could have held onto the egg for the time that I had and not understand that.

I had plenty of questions, but not a single answer. So, I simply sat, as still as I could, and looked up into the night sky for a long, long time. Expecting her to appear at any moment and rip the egg from my grasp. But there were no sounds of her growing any closer; no keening for her egg, which sat in my hand, beating softly. And time continued to stretch and move so imperceptibly as to have almost stopped. Above me the moon, hanging like a scythe, did not continue her journey and the stars stopped their endless circle. It seemed that the egg was making good on the promise it had made to me earlier, when I was silly enough to allow it to know my own sadness. With that one simple question — *What could I do with more time?* — I had revealed myself to it. And with its answer, it had caught me like a fish in a net.

Anything.

There I was, crouched like a cur, in the cemetery where more time was as useful as a flying machine to a fish. I could spend forever there, wondering about what to do, about what was right or wrong, *or* I could jump, and find out.

I stepped out of the cold tomb. The Siren was nowhere to be seen, though I could feel her, traversing this hinterland between the living and the dead. I shivered. The truth of it was, standing so close to death terrified me; all that nothingness, stretching out forever.

"Hello?" My voice quivered. The egg skipped a beat, an arrhythmic tell that *she* must be close by. "I'm sorry I ran from you —"

Behind me, the rustle of folding wings and the soft crunch of talons in the gravelly path. I turned, and there she was, all wild hair and starbright eyes.

"Did you know of Leonardo's flying machine?" I blurted out.

Her smile was unexpectedly beautiful. "Oh, yes. We had plans, your master and I, to traverse the skies together. Oh! You are surprised?" She touched my face gently, her fingertips cool against my skin. Realisation washed over her face. "You did not know about us... He went to Villanelle to negotiate its return, you know." She gestured to my pocket, with its exquisitely frangible cargo.

"Was he..." I couldn't finish my question. Murder is such an ugly word.

"No one would ever have harmed him. He met a most ordinary end. The streets were icy and he slipped, hitting his head on the stones. He did not suffer."

"Why did he not just give you the egg?"

"Can you not think of any reason?"

I wracked my brains, ran the old stories through my mind. Oh! "He did not really want to let it go! And you can't just take it back, because it must be freely given." I thanked Aunt Zola silently for her fireside stories.

The Siren smiled. "He spoke of you, Rosa. Never did he dream, he told me, that he would find a student who he could imagine one day taking over from him. And then he found you."

Had she decided to pluck one of her feathers and poke me with it, she could easily have knocked me over. "I have no special talent! If I study his notebooks, his teachings, for my whole life, I could not come close to —"

"You underestimate yourself. Did you not take the egg into your care, and elude me for a whole night? Has it not listened to you and stretched out time according to your wishes?"

It hadn't occurred to me that that meant I was something special, and I was not convinced simply because she said so. "I was just doing as I was told."

"Were you, now? And what do you think our Leonardo would value more — an apprentice who would simply do what she was told, or an independent thinker?"

"I will assume that question is rhetorical." We smiled at one another, then, sharing the memory of him for just a moment.

"Villanelle, all the women who work their magic and keep this city safe, they believe that their magic depends on the egg. That if it was returned to me, their magic would wither and die."

I put my hand over the egg, warm and safe under my cloak, even though I didn't need to do that to know its power. "Why would they think that?" I whispered.

She stretched her wings, looking up at the unmoving stars as she did so, then folding them against her back again. Under that sliver of moon, she looked like a goddess who was tired of the world she had created. "Because inside the egg lies my death."

I was jealous that she was able to evade death in that way — and covetous of it, too.

"And now you want to die?" I was incredulous that anybody would go *looking* for death. Around us, the dead were silent in their graves, but I was sure that, if they heard us, they would be thinking the very same thing.

"Death is not the ending that you seem to think it is."

"I think our friends here would disagree." I motioned towards the graves stretching out on all sides of us. "I want to do the right thing, but I don't know what that is." I hated how small my voice sounded, how small I felt.

"I can't decide that for you, no matter how much I would like to. Just know, Rosa, that I am very, very tired."

She looked older than anyone I had ever met. And the way she was looking at me, somewhere between imploring and pitying, seemed to shift my thinking, and I realised... It did not matter how much time I had — whether it was another hour, or ten years, or two hundred years — it could not undo hurt, or take away pain. It could not make up for the time already lost. It could not change the fact that Leonardo walked that particular path that night, or that my parents left their only child to bring the monster-hunters to justice. All those things were immutable and done, never to be redone. And no matter how much time there was, it would never be enough, for there would always be things unfinished. There would always be an end. For the Siren, for the city, for me.

I held out the egg to her. "Who am I — who are we — to keep this from you?"

Who was I to stop time or say a city should not sink beneath the waves?

As she reached out for it, the town square clocks chimed thirteen and a cold breeze that smelled of winter swept through the cemetery. The tempest inside the eggshell roared and raged, cracking it open and sweeping us both up in its arms. I felt like I was falling forever as the Siren's feathers drifted from her wings, spinning around us as black snow. Unspooling time. Closing my eyes against the raging winds, in my mind's eye I saw an aerie atop an ancient mountain, spearing toward the sky. In that nest, Siren chicks muddled and tumbled and made room for the new egg that formed there at their feet.

Death is not the ending that you seem to think it is.

Her voice, a voice that bewitched sailors to their deaths and sung a city safe, echoed in my ears as darkness dragged me down.

When I awoke, the sky in the east was pale and the sounds of the city waking joined the first birdsong. Not only was my home still standing, it felt as though it were stretching outwards, expanding the laneways and digging roots through the sandy bed of the lagoon in search of new ways, new worlds, like a radicle searching for the sun. Somewhere in the labyrinth of canals and secrets, the fox-women of the Women's Quarter were weaving new stories. Of the Siren who finally found her death inside an eggshell; of how Villanelle and her kind learned that it set them free from old superstitions; of letting the future unfold anew, untethered from the past. As for me, I sat in the early morning winter sun and wove the hours, days, and years the egg had given me through my thoughts, my memories, my dreams, the way a mermaid braids starfish in her hair.

I would keep its gift of time with me as my companion, let it teach me to bite like stars on the edge of night, and to gamble like devils with their last soul to lose. And when my ending comes, I will turn what is left of it back out into the world, scattered like seaglass on the shore for another lonely, lost girl to find and learn what it is to live.

See Suzanne J. Willis's story "This Is My City and I Am Her Song"
online at Metaphorosis.
If you liked it, leave a comment. Authors love that!
Remember to subscribe to our e-mail updates so you'll know when
new stories are posted.

About the story

I came across a black and white photograph online of a woman standing by what looked like a little bridge in Venice. She had wild hair and black wings arching out from her back, with a melancholy look on her face. It looked to me as though she had lost something precious and was searching for it, high and low. That was the genesis of my Siren, and this began as a flash fiction piece. As sometimes happens, the story needed much more space than a thousand or so words, so I kept writing, until I found out what it was she was looking for (even I didn't know when I started the story!).

I was already a few thousand words into another story about desert-dwelling sirens, so had read a lot about their mythology — their connection to the underworld and death, an alluring nature, a seemingly-deadly beauty — and what struck me was that despite their destructive nature, they are have protective qualities. So, that was something that I wanted to explore.

Sirens are fierce, independent, reliant on no-one; these are things that my protagonist, Rosa, had to learn at a very early age. This has the capacity to harden her, but instead it leaves her curious, trying to understand the world from a different angle. In writing this story I wondered how Rosa would be affected by the mystery of the Siren. And what might happen when they finally met.

A question for the author

Q: What's your writing schedule?

A: My writing fits into the spaces around work, family, and friends! So, I tend to write in snippets — an evening here, a lunchtime there. It is somewhat haphazard, but it seems to work. However, I do have one Monday per fortnight off work and this is my dedicated writing time — that Monday is sacred and nothing else is ever scheduled on that day. I find that the best way for me to find my way into a story is to always begin with notes written in my journals or notebooks (beautiful notebooks are my weakness!), then shape the story from there. Of course, the first draft is the slowest part, but my editing schedule is much quicker — every night until the story feels right to go out into the world.

About the author

Suzanne is a lawyer and writer who lives in Melbourne, Australia. Her spare moments are spent with words and music, her stories inspired by fairytales, ghost stories, and all things strange. Suzanne's first short story collection, *Of Starfish Tides and Other Tales* was released in 2022 by Trepidatio Publishing.

Farewell

All things end. This is the last volume of *Metaphorosis*. After nine years, one hundred issues, 2.3 million words, 400-some stories, 326 authors, and 28 artists, the magazine is closing its doors.

It's been a lot of fun working with all those authors and artists and seeing their finished work go out to meet the world. I'm proud of the quality of the magazine we produced and of the fact that for some of these authors, *Metaphorosis* was their first publication or paying venue. I've been thrilled to see 'our' creators go on to bigger and better things.

While the magazine is closing, the press isn't; we have plans for more anthologies and projects in the coming years. Keep your eyes out for them.

In the meantime, our back issues are all available and all the stories and podcasts are online. And if you miss fresh, new SFF stories, consider supporting some of the other great magazines that are out there.

Morris Allen
Editor

Copyright

Title information

Metaphorosis 2024

ISBN: 978-1-64076-286-2 (e-book)
ISBN: 978-1-64076-287-9 (paperback)
ISBN: 978-1-64076-288-6 (hardcover)

Copyright

Works of fiction

All rights reserved

Moral rights asserted

Each author whose work is included in this book has asserted their moral rights, including the right to be identified as the author of their respective work(s).

Publisher

Metaphorosis Magazine is an imprint of
Metaphorosis Publishing
Neskowin, OR, USA

www.metaphorosis.com

"Metaphorosis" is a registered trademark.

Discounts available

Substantial discounts are available for educational institutions, including writing workshops. Discounts are also available for quantity purchases. For details, contact Metaphorosis at metaphorosis.com/about

Metaphorosis Publishing

Metaphorosis offers beautifully written science fiction and fantasy. Our imprints include:

Metaphorosis Magazine

Plant Based Press

Verdage

Vestige

Joyful Heave

You can also find us:
@metaphorosis.bsky.social
writing.exchange/@metaphorosis
www.facebook.com/metaphorosis

Help keep Metaphorosis running at
Patreon.com/metaphorosis

See more about some of our books on the following pages.

Metaphorosis

a magazine of speculative fiction

Metaphorosis is an online speculative fiction magazine dedicated to quality writing. We publish an original story every week, along with author bios, interviews, and notes on story origins.

We also publish monthly print and e-book issues, as well as yearly Best of and Complete anthologies.

Come and see us online at magazine.Metaphorosis.com.

Plant Based Press

plant
based
press

Vegan-friendly science fiction and fantasy, including anthologies of the year's best SFF stories, from 2016-2020.

Chambers of the Heart
speculative stories
by
B. Morris Allen

A heart that's a building, a dog that's a program, a woman sinking irretrievably — stories about love, loss, and movement.

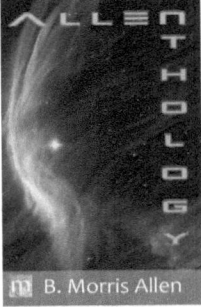

Susurrus

A darkly romantic story of magic, love, and suffering.

Allenthology: Volume I

Including three full collections of SFF stories.

Verdage

Science fiction and fantasy books for writers – full of great stories, often with an additional focus on the craft of speculative fiction writing.

Reading 5X5 x3

Changes

How do stories move from 'maybe' to published? Here are 15 case studies of stories published in *Metaphorosis* magazine.

Reading 5X5 x2

Duets

How do authors' voices change when they collaborate?

A round-robin of five talented science fiction and fantasy authors collaborating with each other and writing solo.

Including stories by Evan Marcroft, David Gallay, J. Tynan Burke, L'Erin Ogle, and Douglas Anstruther.

Score

an SFF symphony

An anthology with an emotional score from the heights of joy to the depths of despair – but always with a little hope shining through.

Reading 5X5

Five stories, five times

See how different writers take on the same material.

Reading 5X5

Writers' Edition

Two extra stories, the story seed, and authors' notes on writing.

Vestige

Novelettes, novellas, and novels by Metaphorosis authors.

The Nocturnals
Mariah Montoya

Night is Dangerous. Day is deadly.
Where day and night last thirty years, humans move constantly stay ahead of the night and cruel Nocturnals that call it home. But a boy is lost out there.

Joyful Heave

Science fiction and fantasy anthologies with innovative and unusual themes.

Museum Piece
an unusual collection

A gallery of the strange and outrageous

Step right up and enter a world of wonder and oddities! These museums are not your typical tourist traps. From the Museum of Lost Dreams to the Suicide Museum, each exhibit will take you on a journey you won't soon forget.

www.ingramcontent.com/pod-product-compliance
Lightning Source LLC
Chambersburg PA
CBHW020608110726
47899CB00002B/428